Brothers by Betrayal

by

Rita M. Reali

Little Elm Press

Copyright 2024, Rita M. Reali
Cover art by Al Esper Graphic Design
Author photo by Dee Lynk

Scripture quotes from *The Holy Bible, Douay-Rheims Version*, 1899

For information regarding permission, contact Little Elm Press: permissions@LittleElmPress.com.

Contact the author via email: Rita@LittleElmPress.com.

Reali, Rita M.
Brothers by Betrayal

Print ISBN: 978-1-7368236-2-0
Ebook ISBN: 978-1-7368236-3-7

Printed in the U.S.A.
First American edition, January 2024

Acknowledgments

Major thanks and gratitude to my physician and friend, Kimberly Peaslee, for invaluable assistance (yet again) as my medical adviser. Without her information and expertise (and supplementary input from Nurse Paige), medical aspects of this novel would have been sorely lacking.

Equal thanks and gratitude to my cousin Lisa R. Humble, RA, NCARB, retired State of Connecticut Chief Building Inspector, for her vital information regarding the architect-licensure process.

Huge thanks to my thought-provoking, compassionate and eagle-eyed editor, Elisa Krochmalnyckyj, for her expertise and insights during the editing process (and allowances for my literary quirks).

Thanks to Father Mark Schuster, pastor of St. Alphonsus Parish in Crossville, Tennessee, who took valuable time from planning the dedication ceremony for our new worship space to offer insightful answers to my questions regarding the Church's position on divorce and remarriage of the same spouse.

Copious thanks to:

— My husband, Frank, who after thirty-plus years still has not made good on this threat to put me out in the garage to fuss over my fictional characters.

— My ace team of beta readers: Joe Clarizio, Kim Dwelley, Dee Lynk, Patti Pensanti, Marian Sullivan and Cynthia Ward. I honestly don't know what I'd do without your phenomenal insights and feedback!

— The Write Away! and Write On writers groups at the Art Circle Public Library in Crossville, for their invaluable support and encouragement along the way.

And endless thanks to you, my dear reader, for being the reason I wrote this in the first place.

Dedications

For Kimberly D. Dwelley, my college buddy (and probably greatest fan of the Sheldon Family Saga books)

Her enthusiastic reception of my writing and her ever-welcome, valued feedback as a beta reader have made this longtime (is it *really* almost forty years since Curry?!) friend and partner in silly and often outlandish adventures a treasured part of the Sheldon Family Saga production team.

For Peggy Sugden, president and founding member of the Marc Lindsay Fan Club

This sweet church friend's fondness for Marc – and her periodic inquiries about the status of the next manuscript – have helped to keep me focused throughout this writing process. Sorry I've had to put him through the wringer in this book…

Brothers

by

Betrayal

Chapter 1

(September 21, 1999 – Tuesday)

"Good morning."

As the door to the radio station opened, the resonant voice Brenda knew so well caught her ear. Except, it seemed somehow different – formal. Almost hesitant.

She looked up, wondering why he stopped at her desk instead of continuing on toward his office.

"Hi, Gary…" As her voice trailed away, her ready smile eroded. Her cheeks flushed pink. "I'm sorry! I mistook you for someone who works here. You look – and *sound* – so much like him. It's uncanny!"

The visitor, clearly not Gary, met the receptionist's surprise with a smile.

"How can I help you?" Brenda asked, at last recovering her professional demeanor.

"I was told I might find Gary Sheldon here."

"Uh… y-yes," she stammered. "He's here – I-I mean, he *works* here… but I'm not sure if he's in at the moment. Let me ring his office. May I tell him who you are? Is he expecting you?"

The man handed over a business card. "Name's Jim Griffin – but that won't mean anything to him. And no, he's not expecting me." He sounded apologetic.

She reached for her phone. In the moments she waited for the music director to answer, she tried not to be obvious about studying this stranger who could pass as Gary's twin.

"Oh, hi – you *are* in. Good," she murmured, turning discreetly away from the other man.

Gary let out an uncertain half laugh. "Well, I work here, Bren. Where else would I be on a Tuesday morning?"

"Good point. Umm… could you come out here a moment, please?"

"Kinda busy right now. Can it wait?"

She sucked in her breath through her teeth. "I'm… afraid not." Her tone sounded evasive.

Gary didn't have time for elusiveness. He let out a soft sigh. "Fine. I'll be right out."

Replacing the receiver, Brenda gave the man in the lobby a hopeful smile. "He'll be with you in just a moment, Mr. Griffin." She motioned toward the seating area off to the right. "Why don't you have a seat. Can I get you some coffee?"

As he settled onto a brown leather couch, he waved off the offer. "No, thank you. I'm fine."

In the music-department office, Gary glanced at the pile of work on his desk. Tuesday was always his busiest day. Brenda knew that. He had new music to add to the playlist, a report to submit to Pete and Charlie before he went on the air at three, and — as if he didn't already have enough on his plate — a looming deadline for an article he'd promised to write for *Radio & Records*. Whatever Bren wanted, it had better be important. *And what's with the phone? Why didn't she just use the intercom?* He shoved away his keyboard and assumed she must have a valid reason.

Getting to his feet, Gary winced. He'd misstepped during his run on the beach this morning and twisted his ankle. Trying to ignore the pain, he left his office and ventured out toward the lobby, a slight limp impeding his gait.

"I sure hope this is important," he called out, hobbling a little dramatically toward the reception area a moment later. "You know Tuesda—" The word died on his lips as he caught sight of the man in the lobby, who stood as he approached.

Gary suddenly felt as if he'd entered an episode of *The Twilight Zone*. Casting a questioning glance at Brenda, he approached the other man. "Hello," he said cautiously, extending his hand. It was like looking in a mirror. "I'm Gary Sheldon. How can I help you?"

The other man had a light, firm grip. "Pleased to meet you, Mr. Sheldon. I'm James Griffin. Is there somewhere we can talk?"

Gary hesitated a fraction of a second too long.

"I came at a bad time," the other man inferred. "I'm sorry. I don't want to infringe on your day if you're busy. I probably should have called first, but…"

"Where would be the surprise in that?" Gary asked with a shrug as he studied the other man. A vague smile played about Gary's lips, setting the other man at ease. "I'm sure I can spare a few minutes for you, Mr. Griffin. Come on back."

As they headed toward his office, Gary turned back to the receptionist. "Could you hold my calls, please, Bren?"

Gary motioned toward the break room, from which the aroma of recently brewed coffee wafted. "Would you like a cup of coffee or tea? Water?"

The other man shook his head. "Thanks, but no."

In his office, Gary invited the visitor to sit, then returned to his desk. He leaned his forearms against the desk and gestured with one hand toward the other man. "What can I do for you?"

The man looked more than a little uncomfortable. "I uh… well, I suppose by now, Mr. Sheldon, you've probably guessed why I came."

Gary's lips pressed together into a thin line; he gave a slow nod. "If I were a betting man, Mr. Griffin, I would say this is likely some sort of awkward family reunion."

"That's one way to put it. And please, call me James."

Another nod. The tight line of his lips eased into a slight smile. "Fair enough. As long as you cut out the 'Mr. Sheldon' crap. It's just Gary. And given our physical similarities, I'll assume you're Jeremy Sheldon's"– he tilted his head and squinted one eye – "*eldest* son?"

James nodded, gave an unsteady half smile. "I guess my kid brother's a pretty smart cookie."

Now Gary shook his head. "Don't," he said, raising a hand in caution. "I don't want to seem off-putting or offensive, but please don't assume any familiarity here. I don't know you, James. And you clearly don't know me. At the moment, as far as I can tell, all we've got in common is Dad's nose. And that doesn't carry with it some inherent sense of entitlement."

Evidently stung by the other man's unexpectedly harsh words, James gave a perfunctory nod and stood. "Well, Gary, I guess you told me. I presume that also means I'm not welcome here. So I'd better jus—"

"I did *not* say that, James," Gary clarified softly, motioning for him to sit. "And I don't want you to go; certainly not like this. What I meant was while you and I clearly have a parent in common, we don't have a relationship… *yet*. I'm open to building one, but it's not going to happen in twenty-seven seconds. Or even half an hour."

James sat back down. "So, what are you saying?"

Gary ran a hand through his hair. "I'm saying I'm sorry I started us off on the wrong foot. I'm glad you came to see me, James – I honestly am. And I'm looking forward to getting to know you. But the surprise and the timing made things a little awkward. Tuesdays are super busy days for me. And while I'd love to spend the rest of this morning talking with you, and getting to know you, I simply can't" – he shook his head – "not today. But if you can come back late tomorrow morning, or Thursday, I can spare about an hour."

Now James nodded. "I totally get that. And I shouldn't have just dropped in and expected you to welcome me like – well, like your long-lost brother." He grinned. "Thursday would work for me. How's eleven sound?"

Gary flipped a page, consulted his desk calendar. Jotted a note. "That sounds perfect. I'll see you then."

"Great. I'll bring pictures."

Getting to his feet, he came around from behind his desk. "Looking forward to it," he told his half-brother with a smile.

James extended his hand.

Gary took it, then drew the startled man in for a hug. "What the hell," he said, thumping James on the back, "you might as well get used to it. We Sheldons are a huggy bunch."

(10:55 a.m., September 23 – Thursday)
This time when James entered the radio station, Brenda greeted him with a smile that did not decay in confusion. "Good morning, Mr. Griffin. It's nice to see you again. Gary's expecting you. Please have a seat and I'll let him know you're here."

Before she could reach for the intercom to buzz into Gary's office, the phone rang.

"Brenda, it's Michaela." The caller sounded frantic. "I've got to speak with Gary. It's urgent."

"I'll put you right through."

After connecting the call, Brenda turned back toward the visitor. "I'm sorry, Mr. Griffin, it'll just be another minute. I had to put a call through to him."

As soon as the light on the switchboard went out, indicating Gary had ended the call, Brenda buzzed in to the music department. "Gary?"

He didn't respond.

A moment later, the music director raced toward the foyer, keys in hand. "Bren, I've got—" He stopped cold as he noticed James sitting in an upholstered chair, waiting for him. "Oh crap. I'm sorry, James. I can't see you today. My wife's on her way to the ER with our baby girl. She—" He shook his head. "Can't explain now. I gotta go. I'll call you," he promised over his shoulder.

Brenda gave the other man an apologetic look. "I'm so sorry, Mr. Griffin. I hope you didn't have to travel a long way."

James waved off her apology. "No problem, miss. I just hope his little girl's okay."

Gary tore out of the parking lot in a cloud of gravel and sped toward St. Mary's Hospital. Frantic, he darted in to the emergency room and approached the matronly woman at the main desk.

"My baby was just brought in here – a little girl. Nine months old. I need to see her – *please*!"

Doing her best to still the panicked father's anxiety, she replied that no one under seven was currently being treated. In a soothing tone, she asked him to take a seat and be patient.

Gary left the intake area and paced the lobby. Less than three minutes later, he returned. "Have they arrived yet?"

"No, sir. Not yet," the woman replied serenely, watching his knuckles whiten as he gripped the edge of the countertop. She kept her tone tranquil, to ease the man's obvious anxiety. "It's only been a couple of minutes."

"Could you check, please?"

She offered a reassuring smile. "Of course." Getting up from her seat, the woman disappeared into the triage area.

A moment later, an ambulance arrived, sirens wailing.

Within a few seconds, the woman bustled back out to the entry area. "They've just pulled up." She held the interior door open as she motioned Gary forward. "They're bringing her in now. Come on back."

Two and a half hours later, Gary returned to the radio station, visibly drained.

"Is Josie okay?" Brenda asked, her pretty blue eyes filled with concern.

"She's gonna be alright," he replied woodenly, nodding.

"What happened?"

"She had a seizure. They called it a 'simple febrile seizure.' She woke up this morning with a high fever. Nothing seemed to help. When it hit a hundred and two, Michaela called the doctor. While she waited for him to call back, Josie's arms and legs went all stiff and she started twitching. That's when Micki called 911. By the time the EMTs got there, Josie's temp was up to a hundred and three and she was still jerking."

Brenda's eyes widened as Gary spoke. "Oh, Gary… how frightening!"

"Yeah. Micki was really freaked out. Fortunately, the seizure passed before they got to the ER. The doctor checked Josie out and said these seizures aren't necessarily normal, but they're not unheard of. Apparently the fever triggered it."

"Has Christopher exhibited any signs of seizures?"

Gary shook his head. "No. None of our kids did. They even said they're more common in boys than girls – and they tend to run in families. Then again, they said it could have been an isolated incident. So just to be on the safe side, they did an EEG. That came back normal."

"That had to be a relief. So what happens now?"

"Micki's taking her to the pediatrician to be checked out."

***

The next afternoon, Gary phoned James. "Sorry I had to bail on you yesterday."

"Don't apologize. Family comes first. How's your little girl doing?"

Gary let out a trembly sigh. "She'll be okay."

"Thank God," James said, sounding relieved.

The brothers made plans to meet for lunch one day the next week. Friday worked out best for both of them.

"You like Chinese? There's a great little place in town. Wong Lee's," Gary suggested. "Ever been there?"

"Can't say I have. But yeah, I love it."

"Best Chinese this side of New York City. Been going there the better part of two decades. I even proposed to my wife there. Never had a bad meal, either – and we go there plenty. Excellent service, too." Gary gave James directions, adding, "I'll make reservations. Twelve thirty okay?"

***

That evening after work, as he finished an email to one of his record-company contacts, Gary called Marie.

"Hey, sis," he greeted her. "You sound frazzled. Bad time?"

She gave a weary moan. "Gary, you've got twins, too. You know it's never a good time. What's up?"

He grinned. That was true, and he knew his niece and nephew could be a real handful. He heard a commotion in the background and wondered how parents of triplets and more managed. "We haven't talked in a while and I just wanted to catch up."

"You see Marc all the time. I'm sure your best bud keeps you up to date on everything that goes on over here."

"Yeah, but you're my sister. I miss talking to you. Besides, he really only tells me about the fights and the wild sex."

Marie grinned. "Yeah, I suppose that's kind of a guy thing to do, huh? Just curious: Did he mention the whips and the handcuffs?"

"He didn't elaborate on specific restraints, but there was general talk of bondage," he joked.

Marie gave a throaty chuckle, one that left her brother wondering. "You crack me up."

"You started it."

Now she let out a groan. "If I never had to hear 'you started it' one more time, I'd be a happy woman."

Gary laughed. "Spoken like a true parent of young children. Speaking of which, how are the young'uns?"

"They're loving kindergarten. At least, Edward is. Isa— I mean, *Fern*. She flat-out refuses to answer to Isabella. Fern doesn't understand why she has to keep going back there, day after day. She figures she's ready for grownup stuff. After all, she already knows her colors and shapes, cutting and pasting, simple addition and how to read."

"Izzy's reading already?"

"Has been for a year. And don't *ever* let her hear you call her that. You may be her favorite uncle, but she'll cut you to ribbons. And to answer your question, yes, she reads to her brother all the time. At bedtime she insists on reading me stories. And when Marc's doing homework, she'll climb up in his lap and make him read his calculus and engineering textbooks to her."

"Sounds like you've got a regular little tyrant on your hands."

Marie gave what sounded like a sigh of resignation. "We're working on preventing that."

Gary understood he had touched a sore spot and changed the subject. "Nice to have another word nerd in the family."

"Who's yours?"

"Erin. That kid's always got her nose in a book. Actually, it's kind of refreshing to have kids you don't have to worry so much about. When she's not out doing sisters stuff with Mandy, she's in her room reading all the time. We know she's not out getting into trouble."

"Like you were?" Marie baited her brother.

"I was never a problem child," he retorted. "I was a total radio geek. If I wasn't working at the station, I was—"

"Out getting into mischief with Ellen," she finished.

"Well… yeah," he admitted. "There was that."

"But you're right – it's nice having kids who are interested in reading at such a young age. Edward and Fern both love books. I think they've got more books than toys in their rooms."

"Yep. Same with ours. Although Michael does love his cars."

"Little gearhead," Marie said. "I'd be willing to bet he gets that trait from his dad."

Gary could hear the smile in his sister's voice.

"You know what they say: The only difference between men and boys is the price tag on their toys. Michael's all about new and flashy."

"I wish some of that would rub off on Marc – he's had that stupid Saab of his forever."

"Are you kidding? That 900's a classic, Marie."

"Call it what you want. It's an ugly heap."

"Actually, it's in pristine condition. Not a bit of rust. And it still runs well."

"Not all that well – especially lately. I'm just glad it hasn't left him stranded there at midnight."

"Only 'cause you don't want to have to drive all the way here to retrieve him," Gary teased, but he suspected it wasn't far from the truth.

When Marie grumbled in response, he laughed. "Busted!"

"Oh, hush."

Gary wanted to tell her about the sudden appearance of their half-brother, but an inner voice – *Is it Grandpa?* – made him feel it was wiser not to mention James… at least not yet.

"I better let you go. I've got some emails to finish up before I head home. You want me to put you through to that husband of yours?"

"Yeah, if he's available. I can always think of something to nag him about."

"I'll get him. Nice talkin' with you, sis. See you at the house next Sunday."

"What for?"

"Erin's birthday party," he prompted.

"Oh, that's right. I've got it written on the calendar, but I totally forgot. After two kids the brain goes to mush," Marie replied. "See you then."

Gary pressed the hold button and went to the broadcast studio. "Marie's on line one."

Marc's smile was automatic at the mention of his wife. "Great. You sticking around for a while?"

Gary shook his head. "Just finishing up some work. Be outta here in about ten minutes."

"Okay." Marc nodded as he reached for the phone. "See you tomorrow."

Chapter 2

(8:27 p.m., October 7 – Thursday)

While she was finishing her math homework, Erin called to her dad from the door of her room.

On his way to bed – he had to be up at three because he was covering the morning-drive show all week – Gary stopped and stuck his head in the open doorway. "What's up, punkin?"

"Daddy, all the kids are going to a party at Sue's tomorrow night."

He already knew where this conversation was headed. And he wasn't going to get roped into it. "That's nice," he replied noncommittally. "I hope they have a good time."

"Can I please, please, *please* go?" Erin wheedled.

Gary shook his head. "No. You're grounded – this weekend and next. You know that."

"But Daddy," she began. "It's my birthday…"

"I know. Happy birthday. But I'm sorry, sweetheart. The answer is still no. You should have thought about that before you swore at Mom. And if you want me to extend it another week, keep arguing."

"But Daddy… grounding me for two weeks just for swearing isn't fair!"

Gary leaned against the doorjamb, his arms folded. "Look, Erin, you keep saying you want me to treat you like an adult. Then act like one. Children whine. Grownups accept the consequences of their actions without complaining."

"But it's not fair."

He shook his head. "I'm done discussing this, Erin. I told you no and that's final."

"But Daddy…" she whined.

"Punkin, I gotta be up early. I'm going to bed. Talk to me again on Monday."

"But the party's tomorrow night."

"I'm aware of that. And we've already established you're not going."

Erin thrust her lower lip out in a pout. She kicked at the leg of her desk. "Then what's the point of talking on Monday?"

Gary gave a weary sigh and shoved away from the doorjamb. "I'm not having this discussion with you now, Erin. Goodnight."

After he got off the air at 10, Gary got through his production assignments as quickly as he could so he'd make it on time for his twelve-thirty lunch. After filing the commercials in their proper spots, he returned to his office, grabbed his keys and tucked the small envelope on his desk into his jacket pocket.

When he entered Wong Lee's at 12:28, he greeted his favorite waitress cheerily.

"Gary!" she exclaimed, a look of perplexity on her face. Her hand flew to her mouth as she stared at him, then turned to look at the nearly identical man she'd seated not three minutes earlier at the table Gary had reserved.

He smiled. "No, Ming, you're not seeing double. We really do look that much alike."

Her cheeks colored slightly. "That explains why he acted like he didn't know me when I greeted him – and had no idea where your usual table was."

Partway into their lunch, Gary picked up his chopsticks. "I'm at a distinct disadvantage here, James. You've made me do all the talking, and now not only is my mu shu cold, but you know pretty much all there is to know about me." He gestured toward his brother. "Tell me about you."

James set down his chopsticks and dabbed at his mouth with his napkin. "Fair enough. What do you want to know?"

Gary leaned forward in interest. "Everything. Are you married? Do you have kids? Other siblings? What do you do? I want to know everything."

James smiled at his brother's enthusiasm. "My adoptive parents already had two toddlers before they adopted me when I was six –

so I've got a little brother and a sister. No wife, no kids." He paused. "My job doesn't allow that."

Gary gave him a fierce look. "Excuse me? What business is it of theirs whether you have a family? That's just… wrong."

"I'm sorry. I deliberately phrased that badly," James confessed, his grin broadening, "just to get a reaction out of you. Truth is, I'm a priest. And the pope kind of frowns on that whole wife-and-kids thing."

"Ah," Gary said, chuckling. "That explains it. And I hope my reaction satisfied your obvious need for amusement."

James nodded. "It was strangely gratifying."

"I'm not sure why that surprises me," Gary admitted, trying not to sound stunned. "I mean, your being a priest. That's great – and from what little interaction we've had thus far, you seem like you'd be a wonderful shepherd. Your parish must be lucky to have you."

James shook his head. "I'm not the pastor. I'm what they call a parochial vicar. Just your average, ordinary underling priest."

Gary grinned. "I'm a lifelong Catholic and I've never heard it put quite that way. Never heard that designation. But I've heard the term 'associate pastor.' Is that kind of the same thing?"

"Pretty much. But what's in a title? My role is bringing my flock closer to Christ."

"So how did you come to contact me?" Gary asked at last. "This was kind of out of the blue… at least for me."

"It's been in the works for a while," James admitted. "See, when I was assigned to the parish in Litchfield a while back, one of my parishioners told me about a billboard along the highway with a guy on it who looked like me. I didn't believe him, so he took a picture and showed it to me. And there you were – larger than life – looking exactly like me. And then, when I saw the wording, 'Gary Sheldon, weekdays, three to seven on Z97-3,' I knew there was no way we weren't brothers."

Gary's brow wrinkled. "When was this? It had to be ages ago. That billboard's been gone for" – he paused. They'd taken it down a week after Thanksgiving in '97, just after he was arrested – "for a couple years."

James thought. "Middle of ninety-seven."

"So you waited two years to get in touch? I've heard of procrastinating, but that's taking it to extremes."

He gave a diffident shrug. "I was trying to work up the courage to approach you – I didn't know what I was going to say. I mean, what do you say to someone you don't know who's obviously your brother?"

Gary grinned. "Oh, I dunno… maybe you show up at his place of business and say hi?"

James returned the grin. "That… wasn't my finest hour," he admitted sheepishly, reaching for his teacup. "But just when I *was* about to reach out to you, all your legal troubles started… and I figured you didn't need the distraction of a new brother amid all that upheaval. So I decided to keep my distance and just pray for you."

In late November of 1997, Gary was arrested and charged with raping a teenage intern at the radio station. He'd spent much of the following year working to clear his name – and restore his life to normal.

Sudden recognition crossed his face. "That was you! You sent me that Saint Gerard medal – right? The patron saint of the unjustly accused."

James' smile overtook his whole face. He nodded. "Yes! I'm really surprised you remember that."

Gary's fingers automatically went to the oval talisman on the gold chain around his neck. "Remember it? I still wear it."

"And I kept that lovely handwritten thank-you note you sent."

Ming glided by and unobtrusively replaced the empty teapot. She cleared away their dishes and discreetly laid the check nearer to Gary's side of the table.

"We're probably pretty close in age," Gary observed, changing the subject, as the waitress retreated again.

James nodded. "Looks that way. When were you born?" He reached across the table for the check.

Shaking his head, Gary moved it out of his brother's reach. "Not a chance, pal. I invited you, remember?"

"Fair enough," he replied amiably, withdrawing his hand. "Thank you."

"My pleasure. Anyway, don't you priests take a vow of poverty or something?"

"Nah, that's just a myth to make you feel sorry for us." James grinned. "I'm kidding. Some priests in different orders do. Fortunately, I'm not one of them."

Gary's left eyebrow arched. "You don't take orders?"

"Different kind of orders. And yes, actually, pretty much all I do is take orders. From my pastor, from our parishioners, from the archbishop. The pope. But no vow of poverty."

"In that case, lunch is on you next time."

James laughed. "Sounds fair. So you never answered, Gary: When were you born?"

"January of sixty-four. You?"

"Huh, I was wrong. I'm *not* your older brother. Same year. March nineteenth."

Gary's eyebrows rose. "Wow… two surprises there."

James tilted his head. "Oh?"

"I'm kind of surprised to find out my dad was that much of a dirtbag. Screwing around on Mom while she was pregnant? That's a new low – even for him."

"I kind of suspected he was a less-than-honorable fellow." James nodded. "What's the other surprise?"

"That you were born on St. Joseph's Day and they didn't name you Joseph."

"They did. Joseph Brian Sheldon."

"So then how did you end up being James?"

James set down his tea. "Just lucky, I guess. Not a lot of kids get to pick their own names."

"I can't imagine they do."

"When I was four – a few months before my fifth birthday – I was put into foster care when my mom was sent to prison on drug charges."

Gary's expression sobered; he nodded slowly, absorbing this news. "That had to be rough."

He shrugged. "I was lucky. I ended up with a good foster family. I stayed with them a little over a year, and after my mom's rights were terminated, they decided to adopt me. Thing is, they already had a son named Joseph. So to avoid confusion, they asked me if I'd mind if they changed my name once they finalized the adoption."

James took another sip of his tea, then set his cup down. "I figured, new family, new name. Why not? They asked whether I had a name I'd prefer to be called. I chose James because it was the name of my best friend in preschool – before I got placed in the foster-care system. And they kept Sheldon as my middle name. I never bothered to let them know I didn't care one way or the other, because I didn't know my dad. Never met him. I had no emotional attachment to that name." He offered a sad smile. "But now that I've met you, I feel differently about that, and I'm glad they kept it as my middle name. I kind of wish I'd known you when we were kids. It would've given me a sense of connectedness, kind of a sense of family."

"You never knew the Sheldons at all?"

James shook his head. "It was just my last name. Just a name. I never felt a sense of identity as a Sheldon. I was in my second year of seminary when I got word my grandfather had died."

Gary gave a sober nod. "He died just over a week before your twenty-first birthday."

James' brow furrowed at the pain evident in his brother's face. "You two must have been close, huh?"

Gary cradled his teacup in his hands, enjoying its warmth. "Yeah. I spent a week or two at the beach with him every summer when I was a kid; and after my dad threw me out, I lived with him for a few months, 'til I got my own place. Truthfully, he was more than just my grandfather. In a lot of ways he was my best friend. My protector. And my dad. He was my role model for what it meant to be a man… and a father. He was the wisest man I ever knew." He pulled the small envelope from his shirt pocket. "I brought some pictures."

Gary showed his brother photos of him and Marie as kids, then photos of their younger brother, Joey, and their father, Jeremy, and his mother, Diane. He even shared photos of Grandpa Sheldon. And plenty of fond stories about Grandpa.

"Sounds like a heck of a guy. I never knew him. Never would have known he existed, either, if it hadn't been for that inheritance. It was like one of those impossible-sounding stories at the end of the news, where someone finds out their long-lost uncle left them a crazy fortune," James said, "except, in my case, it was a grandfather I never knew about who left me a ton of money. His attorney contacted me and sent word my grandfather had left me almost seven million dollars, to be held in trust 'til I turned twenty-five."

Gary nodded. "That's pretty much what Derek told the rest of us, too. I'm guessing it came as kind of a shock." He took a sip of his tea. "So what does a priest do with that kind of money? I know you said you didn't take a vow of poverty, but… aren't there general rules about priests and money?"

"You'd think so, but no. Some orders do – like Franciscans and Dominicans. But, like I said, I'm just a regular, garden-variety parish priest. I earmarked a chunk of money to set up a foundation to help families adopt kids from the foster-care system."

"That's interesting. How's it work?"

James gave a dismissive wave. "I don't want to bore you with details."

"No, I want to hear about this."

"The bulk of it funds legal representation for families experiencing difficulty with birth parents refusing to sign TPRs – termination of parental rights – once the adoption process is underway."

"Do you run it yourself?"

He laughed. "Are you kidding? I couldn't run a two-man fishing derby. I've hired a team to manage the foundation's day-to-day operations. I just fund it."

Gary nodded, thinking about the PATCHES of Hope Foundation he and Michaela started a few years back – and the five local houses associated with it – to care for pregnant and abused teens; and the rape-crisis center she'd worked to establish at St. Mary's Hospital years earlier. The crisis center still received regular financial allocations from the archdiocese, as well as donations from some of the local parishes. Gary inconspicuously funded a portion of its annual operating expenses. And he was glad to do that. "Sometimes that's the best way to do it," he acknowledged with a knowing smile. Upon suddenly realizing all the other tables around them were vacant, Gary glanced at his watch. "Oh my goodness!"

"What?"

"It's quarter to three. I had no idea we'd been here this long."

James grew worried. "Don't you have to be on the air soon?"

He shook his head. "I covered the morning show all week. But I do have to get back – I've got work to finish before I head home – and I *can't* be late tonight. It's my oldest daughter's birthday."

"Oh yeah? How old?"

"Seventeen."

James looked surprised. "You're not old enough to have a seventeen-year-old daughter."

Gary gave a reticent shrug. "I'm old enough to have made bad decisions. Still, I wouldn't trade Erin for anything. She's a great kid. High-school senior, good grades, editor of the school newspaper – and for some reason she wants to follow in her old man's footsteps by studying radio broadcasting in college."

"Can't ask for more than that. What've you got planned for tonight?"

"Just a small family celebration. She's actually grounded this weekend… speaking of bad decisions." He gave a wry smirk. "It's only immediate family tonight; dinner and cake, plenty of off-key singing. And a few presents. The extended family celebration – with aunts, uncles, cousins and grandparents – will be Sunday."

"How many kids do you have?"

"Five."

"Wow! So even a small family dinner is a full house."

"Pretty much, yeah."

"How old are they?"

"Erin's the eldest. Then Amanda – she's eight. Michael's gonna be five in December. And the twins are not quite a year."

"Sounds like you've got your hands full."

"It's not bad, but I'd be lying if I didn't say Micki's got her hands full. But Erin's terrific with the little ones, so that helps. And Amanda idolizes her big sister."

"That's terrific."

"Yeah, and I'm glad Erin's so accepting of my little one's hero worship. She's not just accepting; she goes out of her way to include Mandy. Takes her to the library or on errands. Every so often Erin announces a 'Sisters Adventure Day' and Amanda runs to the car, eager for whatever surprise she's got planned."

"That sounds like fun for her."

"For both of them, really. They'll go out for breakfast, or clothes shopping… or to a movie. Or they get their hair and nails done. It's so cute! Sometimes they just go out for ice cream and talk about girl stuff. They tell each other everything! They share all kinds of secrets. Amanda absolutely adores Erin – that kid would crawl to the ends of the earth for her big sister. And vice versa."

***

The phone's ringing shattered Marc's concentration. He'd just returned home from class – he was in his second-to-last semester at the Yale College School of Architecture – and was studying for midterms. He answered distractedly, really not wanting to talk to anyone.

"Uncle Marc, can I ask a favor?"

He smiled at the sound of his eldest niece's voice. "Hey, birthday girl! Of course."

"Can I borrow your car tonight? My friends and I wanted to go to a movie, but Mom's car's in the shop and she and Dad are going out. He said as long as you don't mind, it's okay with him."

"Sure. I'll pick you up around six. Only thing is, I need to leave work early tonight – so you have to bring it back before ten thirty. Your aunt's covering a midnight shift at the hospital, so I gotta be home by eleven."

"No problem. I'll have it back. I promise. Thanks, Uncle Marc. You're the best!"

Chapter 3

During dinner, Erin stole anxious glances at the clock on the dining-room wall every few minutes and only picked at her chicken and asparagus with pasta.

Finally, she lay down her fork and looked at Mom. "May I be excused? I don't feel very well. I wanna go lie down."

"Sure, honey." Michaela reached over and laid the back of her hand against Erin's forehead and cheek. "You do feel a little warm. Go on. I hope you feel better. I'll be up later with some tea for you."

"N-no, you don't need to do that, Mom. I think I'm just gonna go to sleep."

Just before 9, after Amanda and Michael had finished their baths, brushed their teeth, said their prayers and been bundled off to bed with kisses and bedtime stories, Gary and Micki settled onto the couch to watch TV. Before long, they heard crying, so Michaela ran upstairs to check on Christopher. She changed the little boy's diaper and settled him back to sleep. Just as she was about to head back downstairs, Josephine began squalling, so Micki changed her and rocked her back to sleep.

By the time she returned, she'd missed too much of the program and had lost interest in it. Besides, she had other interests to pursue. Returning to the couch, Micki straddled Gary's lap, facing him, and kissed him. "Nice to have a Friday night to ourselves, huh?" she murmured against his throat between kisses, raking her hands upward through his hair.

Nearly a decade of marriage hadn't dimmed the electricity between them.

"Mmm," he replied, kissing back. His arms encircled her middle and he gave her behind a squeeze and a fond pat. "What do you say we shut off the TV and take this upstairs?"

"Why?" A playful glint lit her eyes as her fingers deftly undid his belt. "I could do with some old-school messin' around on the couch."

Gary offered her a smoldering kiss. "It'll be more comfortable in bed. After all, we're not as young as we used to be."

"Speak for yourself," she said, giving his earlobe a playful nip. Nevertheless, she climbed off him and scampered upstairs.

Gary followed, right at her heels. After checking on the babies and peeking into Amanda and Michael's rooms to be sure they were asleep, he and Michaela retreated to their bedroom to continue where they'd left off.

Chapter 4

When the phone rang, Marie leapt to answer it so it wouldn't wake the twins. "Hello?"

"Honey, it's me. Erin hasn't come back with my car yet."

Marie glanced at her watch. 10:17. "She knows you have to leave by ten thirty, right?"

"I reminded her of that just before she took off."

She could tell Marc was already antsy. He hated to be late for anything, and really despised it when other people were late, or made him late. "Give it a few more minutes. I don't absolutely have to be out the door 'til eleven fifteen."

Thirty-five minutes later, the phone rang again.

"Still no sign of her. I'm sorry, *querida*. Even if she were pulling up right now, I still wouldn't make it home in time."

Marie's brow furrowed. "It's not your fault, honey. Don't worry. I'll just ask Val and Tim to keep an eye on the kids."

"I hate to impose on them."

"What choice do we have? And anyway, the kids are sleeping, so all they'd have to do is keep an ear out if they wake up for some reason," Marie reassured him. "Just get home safely."

"I hope nothing's happened. The car's been acting kind of cranky lately. I've been meaning to have Jerry take a look at it. I'd hate for it to have broken down and left her stranded."

Jerry, one of Marc's engineering classmates, was a whiz with repairing vintage Saabs. He had no fewer than a dozen of them in his garages in Woodbridge – and he'd often remark that his wife was no particular fan of all those cars.

***

Just after 10:45, Middlebury police responded to a call about a vehicle off the road. Officer Terry Bigelow parked behind the car – an old brown Saab 900 – and engaged his flashing blue lights.

Getting out of the cruiser, he noticed a teenage girl at the side of the road, seemingly in distress.

"Are you okay, miss?" he asked, approaching her.

She was crying.

The teenager looked startled to see him. Backing away, she nodded.

The officer assessed the situation. The vehicle had run off the road and struck a stone bridge abutment. Its right front end was crumpled, probably beyond repair. The roadway was dry, with no skid marks. And being such an old model, the car had no airbags to deploy.

The teen wandered perilously close to the road.

"Get back inside the car, miss," the officer directed.

The girl obeyed, still crying.

Officer Bigelow shone the beam of his flashlight around the vehicle's spotless interior. "Are you injured?"

She shook her head. "I… I don't think so."

"May I see your license, registration and insurance, please?"

Erin dug the wallet from her purse and handed it over.

"Please take the license out of the wallet, miss."

She did so and handed it to the officer.

"Wait right here," he directed, then retreated to his cruiser.

When he returned, he said, "Erin Sheldon. Are you any relation to Gary?"

She was no longer crying, but she sniffled loudly as she nodded. "He's my dad."

"I see. Erin, may I see your registration and proof of insurance, please?"

The girl looked worried, like she might begin to cry again. "Um… it – it's not my car."

"They should be in the glove compartment," he told her, his voice gentle. "I'll need to see them both, please."

The teen reached into the glove box; aside from the owner's manual, the registration and Uncle Marc's insurance card were the only items in it. She handed them to the officer.

"It says the vehicle's registered to a Marc Lindemeyr."

"He – he's my uncle."

"Does your uncle know you have his car?"

Her voice wavered. "Of course he does."

"Erin, have you been drinking tonight?"

"No, officer," the girl replied, her eyes wide.

He bent down to eye level. She squinted as he turned the beam of his flashlight toward her face. Her eyes appeared red and she smelled strongly of alcohol. "Now, Erin, I'm going to ask you one more time: Have you had anything to drink tonight? Anything at all? Even earlier this evening?"

"N-no, officer. Honest," she said, her voice unsteady.

"Would you step outside the car again, please?"

"Is there a problem, officer?"

His lips formed a tight line. "I think you know what the problem is, miss."

Erin got out of the vehicle. "Please don't tell my dad," she begged the policeman, her voice shaky. "Everyone thinks he's so nice 'cause he seems so friendly on the radio. But he's really not like that at all. If he finds out about this, he's going to beat me." When Officer Bigelow cast a dubious glance at her, the girl shrilled, "He *will* – he's not as wonderful as everyone thinks he is. He's a *monster*!"

When the teen finished her blustery tirade, Officer Bigelow calmly asked her to submit to a breathalyzer test. It returned a 0.05. Then he asked Erin to perform a series of field-sobriety tests. She was unable to count backward from fifty by four or balance on one foot for fifteen seconds; she couldn't close her eyes and touch both index fingers to her nose; nor could she walk heel to toe for nine steps along the fog line, turn around and return to her starting point.

By the time she failed the final test, Erin was in tears again.

A few minutes later – by law, the officer had to administer the breathalyzer tests at least ten minutes apart – he asked her to submit to another test. When she blew a 0.05 for a second time, Officer Bigelow asked her to put her hands behind her back. As he fastened the steel handcuffs around her wrists, he informed Erin she was under arrest for driving under the influence and read the girl her rights. He also confiscated her driver's license.

She begged the officer not to arrest her, repeating her desperate plea not to tell her dad, whom she insisted would beat her.

"I'm sorry, miss," the police officer replied kindly as he walked Erin to his cruiser and placed her inside. "I wish I didn't have to do this, but you broke the law."

***

At ten past eleven, the studio line rang.

"Hey, Marie," Randy said. "Yeah, he's still here. Hang on a sec."

He pressed the hold button. "It's your wife."

"I'll take it in prep."

A minute later, Marc picked up the line in the DJ prep room.

"Hi, honey," she greeted him. "I'm about to leave. I'm guessing she hasn't shown up yet?"

Marc ran a hand through his hair. "No sign of her. I'm beginning to worry. She's usually so responsible."

"I'm sure she's fine. She probably just lost track of the time. You know how teenagers are."

"I guess. Drive safely, *querida*. I'll see you tomorrow. I love you."

"Love you too." And she was gone.

Meanwhile, ten miles away, in Southbury, the phone was ringing at the Sheldon home.

"Don't you dare reach for that phone," Michaela warned.

"What if it's impo—"

She clamped a hand over Gary's mouth. "Then they'll leave a message. It's probably some oaf who doesn't know enough not to call late at night while decent people are busy making babies."

The ringing persisted.

He cast an anxious glance at the nightstand. The phone was almost within reach.

"I swear to God, Gary, if you touch that receiver, I'll beat you to death with it," Michaela told him, panting as she approached climax. She shifted slightly beneath him, tilting her hips upward and grinding her pelvis against his. Within moments, she shuddered with a pulsating orgasm. A minute afterward, Gary let out a throaty groan as he came.

As her husband collapsed against her, Micki grinned. "There… wasn't that worth not answering some stupid phone call?" Reaching up, she ruffled his hair.

Three minutes later, as they snuggled together, the phone rang again.

"You gotta be kidding me," Michaela muttered. She gave Gary a look of death but knew he wouldn't let it continue to ring.

Scowling, he reached for the receiver. His "Hello" sounded clipped, impatient. It conveyed *This better be good!*

"Mr. Sheldon?"

"This is he," he said distractedly. "Who's calling, please?"

"It's Officer Terry Bigelow from the Middlebury Police."

"Yes, officer." Instantly panicked, Gary scrambled to a sitting position. Officer Bigelow was one of the night-shift cops who'd guarded him Thanksgiving weekend two years ago, while he was jailed on trumped-up charges. "What's wrong?" He glanced at Micki, who had a look of question on her face.

"I'm sorry to disturb you so late at night," the officer was saying, "but this is important. It's about your daughter, Erin."

"What about her? She's asleep in her room. She wasn't feeling well tonight."

"No, sir, I'm afraid she's not. That's why I'm calling. She's in jail. She's been arrested."

Gary listened in shocked silence as the officer explained what had happened and added that, other than being shaken, the girl was fine.

"Do you know a Marc Lindemeyr?" Officer Bigelow asked.

"He's my brother-in-law. Why? What's he got to do with this?"

"Your daughter was driving his car. She claims she was on her way back to where he works when she went off the road. She was pretty upset and said she wasn't sure how to reach him. You may want to contact him."

Chapter 5

Twenty minutes later, Gary pulled up outside the radio station. It seemed strange, seeing it at this hour – with only one light on outside the front entrance and the rest of the building dark.

"It's just me," he called as he unlocked the door and stepped inside the building, knowing Randy, the overnight guy, was armed.

At the sound of Gary's voice, Marc poked his head out from the prep room. "Gary? What're you doin' here?"

"Driving you home," his brother-in-law replied grimly.

He wore a confused expression. "Wh-why? Where's Erin?"

"In jail. I'll explain in the car. C'mon."

"The police called," Gary told him as they left the station's parking lot. "It seems Erin had a bit too much to drink at a party earlier tonight and wrecked your car."

Marc's breath caught in his throat. "Is she okay?"

Gary shrugged. "I honestly don't know. She's spending the night in jail."

"What happened?"

"She ran off the road, hit something. We're not far from the crash site."

The wrecker had just arrived when Gary pulled up to the accident scene minutes before midnight. The crumpled remains of Marc's vintage Saab rested against a stone bridge abutment, its front tires cocked to the right. A nearby police cruiser's blue lights wig-wagged eerily in the chilly October darkness.

"This your car?" the tow-truck driver asked.

Marc nodded.

"Got the keys?"

He patted his pockets, then shook his head and groaned. "My niece has 'em. And apparently she's in jail."

The driver shrugged and swaggered back to his truck. "Not a lot I can do without 'em," he told Marc over his shoulder with abrupt gruffness. "Call us back when you got the keys."

Meanwhile, Gary assessed the wreckage. Despite his underlying anger, his dad instinct kicked in as he envisioned how shaken Erin must have been, involved in her first serious wreck. His insides clenched and his knees wobbled.

As the tow-truck driver left, Marc went to talk to the officer in his cruiser, confirming his identity as the owner of the vehicle. Then he assessed the wreckage. The front end was crumpled, its windshield shattered but intact. The driver's-side window had been rolled partway down, so he slid his hand in to unlock the door. He retrieved his registration and insurance papers from the glove box. Having no other belongings to remove, other than a pair of sunglasses, Marc rolled up the window, locked the door and shut it.

"I'm sorry," Gary told him as they got back in the Camaro.

His brother-in-law gave a halfhearted shrug. "It's not your fault."

"No, but it was my kid who did this. And she did it while she was grounded."

Marc stared at him in alarm. "She told me you said it was okay for her to borrow my car."

Shaking his head, Gary expelled an audible breath. "That's just great. So on top of everything else, she lied to you."

The rest of the drive to Seymour was peppered with brief, sporadic conversation.

Gary told Marc about the unexpected appearance of his half-brother.

"That must've been quite a surprise."

"That's one way to put it. It was the craziest thing, coming face to face for the first time with someone who looks *exactly* like me."

Marc whistled. "I can't even imagine what that must have been like." He paused. "Does Marie know?"

Gary shook his head. "Not yet. I'm gonna talk to her next week. I expect she'll be excited. I mean, we've suddenly got this whole new family member neither of us knew about. I know she'll want to meet him and get to know him."

"Shit," Marc hissed as they turned onto Washington Avenue. "I can't get in. Erin's got my house keys, too."

Then he noticed lights on in the first-floor apartment and recalled Marie had asked Val and Tim to watch the twins 'til he got home. They'd be able to let him in.

It was nearly two when Gary swung the Camaro into the driveway.

Micki met him at the door. "Where's Erin?" she asked, surprised at seeing him arriving home alone.

He shrugged. "In jail, I suppose."

"You didn't go get her?" she squawked.

His withering look said, *That's kind of obvious, isn't it?*

Michaela followed him inside. "Gary! You can't leave her there."

"Why not?"

"I can't believe you didn't go pick her up and bring her home!"

Gary didn't want to argue. "Micki, it's late, I'm exhausted. I've been up since three and I just want to go to bed." He maneuvered past her and headed for the stairs.

She grabbed onto his arm. "If you're not going to go get her, then I will." She reached for his keys.

Gary held the keys out of his wife's grasp. He caught her steely gaze and kept his tone measured, even. "You'll do no such thing," he replied with a slow headshake, his voice firm. "How'll she learn to be a responsible grownup if she's not held accountable for her behavior?"

"Gary, for crying out loud, she made a mistake."

"No, Mick. Pouring orange juice instead of milk into your coffee 'cause you're half asleep is a mistake. What she did was a carefully executed series of bad decisions – starting with, 'Mommy, I don't feel well. May I be excused?'"

"But, Gary, she's just a kid."

"A kid who not thirty-six hours ago begged me to treat her like an adult. So I'm granting her wish. I'm letting her take responsibility for her crappy choices."

"You can't leave her in jail!"

Exhausted and irritated, he responded with a cranky fierceness Michaela seldom heard from her husband. "Look, she demanded to be treated like an adult, so that's what I'm doing: letting her face her consequences like an adult. And not swooping in to save her – no matter how much it pains us to do that. And if that means she gets to spend a night in jail, then maybe that's what it'll take." The expression on his face told her he was finished discussing the matter. "I'm going up to bed and praying I can get some sleep. You coming?"

She stared after him, aghast. "I can't believe you won't bail out your own daughter."

Gary stopped on the fifth stair. He didn't turn around. "Believe it. I'd leave *you* in jail, too, if you drove drunk. Good night, Michaela."

Chapter 6

In the Middlebury police department's juvenile lockup, it was a typical Friday night. But for Erin Sheldon, it was anything but typical. She huddled in a corner of the cage, trying her best not to cry. She had to pee, but there was only that one metal toilet out in the open. She hated the idea of peeing in front of everybody... but she couldn't hold it anymore. She went over to the side of the lockup and summoned an officer.

"What is it?" he asked, sounding weary – or bored.

"I have to use the bathroom."

He shrugged and motioned to the metal toilet. "Help yourself."

"I can't go *there*," she protested weakly. "It's all... open. Isn't there somewhere else...?"

"Listen, princess," the officer snapped, "that's the pot. Use it or piss down your leg. I don't really care one way or the other."

Stifling a sob, the petite teenager approached the stainless-steel toilet and unzipped her jeans.

Before she could squat over it, a huge shadow fell across her upper body.

"Who said you could use that?" a booming voice slurred.

Erin looked up into the face of the meanest-looking creature she'd ever seen. There must have been some mistake – this couldn't be a teenager! It looked more like a professional wrestler. Or an escapee from the gorilla pen at the zoo. Her scowl terrified Erin – and the powerful stink of alcohol on her breath was enough to peel paint off a freighter.

"I uh... I *really* have to go," Erin told the drunk behemoth in a frightened voice, pressing her knees together in an attempt to hold back the pee.

"Guess again, sweetcheeks," the hulking girl boomed, her breath nearly making Erin gag. "I gotta take me a dump, so you'll have to wait your turn."

"Please," Erin begged. "I *really* have to go."

"Sorry, kid," she said, sounding not sorry in the least. She shoved Erin aside like a pesky mosquito. Several of the other teens in the lockup laughed.

"Please," Erin implored, her legs crossed awkwardly. "It'll just take a minute." She looked around. There was no sink where she could wash her hands. No toilet paper, either.

"Tough luck, girlie," the big drunk told her with a caustic laugh.

Erin thought she could hear the toilet creak when the huge teen settled her bulk onto it. As the hulk made awful noises over the next few minutes, filling the lockup with noxious odors, hot tears coursed down Erin's cheeks, and a warm stream of pee made its way down her leg and into her sock and sneaker. Mortified, she returned to her corner of the hard metal bench, doing her best to ignore the jostling of the other teens crammed inside a lockup that grew more and more crowded as the night wore on. Her post-asparagus pee stank, making Erin feel terribly self-conscious. As it cooled, the wetness chilled her leg. And her soaked panties made her even more uncomfortable.

When she was brought in, the officer who arrested her had offered her a phone call… but she had no idea who she'd even want to call. She couldn't call her parents – and for sure she couldn't call Uncle Marc! Besides, because she was a minor, the officer said, they'd contact her parents anyway. Erin figured she had about half an hour before Daddy arrived to kill her.

But that was more than two hours ago… and Daddy still hadn't shown up.

The girl tried to find a comfortable position on the metal bench, but there was none. All she wanted was a hot shower, some dry underwear, clean pajamas and her bed! But it didn't look like she would get any of those anytime soon.

At 4 a.m., Erin was still awake, exhausted beyond words and miserable in her still-wet jeans. And by 6:15, she was certain Daddy was never coming to get her. She felt almost relieved over that.

"What time is breakfast?" she timidly asked the morning guard sometime after 7:30.

"You must be Princess," he scoffed, shaking his head. "The others told me about you, but I thought they were kidding. Look around you, girlie. This isn't the Hilton. Aside from the corn muffin, breakfast ain't included in the room rate."

Little by little, the lockup cleared out. The three underage hookers were released; the wiry little sixteen-year-old who'd been arrested after a bar fight had also been sprung. And by 8:30, just six of them remained inside the cage. The huge drunk teen lay sprawled across the metal bench, snoring. Three other girls slumped against walls, trying to get in a bit of shuteye. And the sixth girl, probably still high on something, rocked side to side and talked to the cinderblock wall at the back of the lockup. Erin huddled in her corner. Exhausted and fighting tears, she dozed on and off.

By 11:45, even the toilet bully had been released. Now alone and seemingly abandoned, Erin wept openly in a corner of the lockup, not caring about what the officers thought.

One of them took pity on her and offered her some tissues and another corn muffin. After wiping at her tear-streaked face and blotting her tears, Erin thanked him and wolfed down the muffin. It was now nearly 1 and she hadn't eaten a thing since a few mouthfuls of dinner last night. Oh, and some lousy pizza, chips and beer at Sue's party. And vodka. Plenty of vodka. The memory of it sickened her. She ran to the filthy metal toilet and threw up.

Broken, Erin sat on the hard cement floor and sobbed, leaning her throbbing head against the befouled commode.

Chapter 7

Gary awakened well after 10. The house was quiet, so either Micki had corralled the whole crew and taken them grocery shopping – which he doubted – or she'd somehow managed to keep them from creating a ruckus.

Ambling downstairs, he found her reading to the twins in the living room. And Amanda and Michael were watching a movie in the family room. "Hi honey," he greeted his wife, leaning over the back of the couch.

She tipped her head up to meet his kiss. "Hi. Sleep okay?"

"Not really, thanks to the knot in my gut," he admitted, stroking her cheek. "I'm sorry I was so short with you when I got home last night."

Micki smiled. "That's okay. I've had time to think it over, and you're right: We can't always rush in to save Erin. At some point we have to let her face her consequences." She patted the couch. "Come sit and read with us."

Eagerly accepting her offer, Gary scooped up their baby boy, sank onto the couch beside his wife and cuddled close to her as she read Polly Cameron's *"I Can't" Said the Ant* for about the fifth time that morning.

"I love this book! It was one of my favorites as a kid."

"I know. Your mom brought it over a few weeks ago. I think this corner's even got gnaw marks from when you were teething."

"Let me see that." Gary plucked it from her hands. Examining it closely, he grinned. "So it does."

"She said nothing was safe with you around. You used to chew on everything. Books, toys, clothing. Even crayons. Apparently the great big orange one was your favorite."

Gary shook his head. "Not so. The orange crayon tasted nasty. But the green one – that was *exquisite.* I was quite a connoisseur of crayons in those days."

Josephine wriggled in her mother's lap and grabbed for a corner of the book. She whined and thumped at it with a tiny hand.

"Mama, that was an unacceptable – and unauthorized – break," Gary chided, interpreting the little girl's meaning. "Time to get back to reading the delicious book."

That afternoon, Gary waited in the nearly empty church for his turn in the confessional room. He had gone to Father Dave for reconciliation the second and last Saturdays of every month for eight-plus years. Today as he sat with his pastor, he discussed his half-brother's sudden appearance in his life in the past few weeks, as well as the upheaval Erin's arrest the previous night had wrought.

"Sounds like you've got a lot on your plate right now," Father Dave said. "How can I help you deal with that?"

"I get the sense accepting a new brother will take a lot more of an emotional toll in the long run – and I'm certainly open to having him in my life," Gary admitted, "but dealing with Erin is my immediate forest fire. Michaela was pissed at me last night because I made Erin spend the night in jail. And now, even though she said she agrees with my decision, I'm beginning to wonder whether that was the right thing to do."

"It's a difficult spot," the priest agreed. "You don't want to be a jerk, but you also don't want to come to her rescue before she's learned whatever lesson she's got to learn. How do you suppose you'll handle this situation? I mean, on one hand, she just snuck out of the house… but on the other hand, she did something illegal, got caught and will, in all likelihood, end up with a criminal record. That's tough stuff. You've got to walk kind of a fine line there."

"I know. I know I can't let this go as if it's nothing – but I also can't lock her in her room 'til she's twenty. Still, I'm seriously ticked off at her. I can't believe she was so stupid and irresponsible!"

Gary grew uneasy during the priest's extended silence. "What're you thinking, Father?"

"It sounds to me like you're more ready to be accepting of the brother you scarcely know than the daughter you've loved and nurtured the past eight years," he mused. "Perhaps you could start by bringing her here for reconciliation. I'm sure she's feeling a swirl of emotions surrounding what she's done: the lying, the sneaking out and wrecking her uncle's car – plus anxiety over how you'll react. Not to mention she's clearly in need of sacramental forgiveness."

Gary nodded. "That's a good idea. Thanks, Father."

"Now, as for you…" Father Dave gave Gary some specific Scripture readings to reflect on – about brothers and welcoming strangers – and suggested he spend some time in prayer before going to bail out his errant daughter. "Be gentle with her," he cautioned the emotionally tattered father.

"We'll see," Gary grumbled.

After absolving him, the priest added, "Your sins are forgiven, Gary. Go in peace."

***

Gary stood. He'd spent the past half hour praying before the Blessed Sacrament, seeking wisdom and guidance. His knees felt rickety and they'd begun to ache. Genuflecting in front of the tabernacle as he exited the pew, he left the church and drove to the police station.

There, he paid the $2,000 cash bail and signed the necessary paperwork.

An officer went back to the lockup. "Princess," he called, jangling the keys as he unlocked the cage, "your dad's here."

When Erin emerged from her confinement, she ran to her dad for a hug, crying.

Still talking with the desk sergeant, he held the teen at bay.

As he finished, she tried again to hug him, but he withdrew.

"Let's go," Gary ordered curtly, shoving his wallet into the rear pocket of his jeans.

In the parking lot, Erin blubbered an apology, but he didn't acknowledge it.

"Get in the car."

She eyed him in stunned silence.

"I said, get in the car," he repeated. "You're in enough trouble already, Erin. Don't make me tell you again."

The atmosphere in the car prickled with tension.

"What took you so long?" she grumbled as he drove.

"What about, 'Thank you, Daddy, for bailing me out?'" he scolded, firing a stormy glance her way.

She ignored him and glared out the window.

"Where are we going?" she asked in a tiny voice as he drove away from the direction of home.

It broke his heart, but he held firm. "I figured you'd probably want to go to confession."

Tears filled Erin's eyes at her dad's curt tone. She turned away so he wouldn't see. But her sniffling gave her away.

When they arrived at the church, Gary followed his daughter inside at a discreet distance.

Because no one was waiting, Erin went right in.

She emerged ten minutes later, weeping softly. Father Dave had an arm around her shoulder. He spoke quietly to her for a few moments. She turned toward the priest and hugged him.

When they parted, Erin went to pray in a pew at the back of the church.

Father Dave motioned Gary over. "Let's talk." He gestured toward the empty confessional room.

Gary knew it wasn't a suggestion.

The priest sat facing the troubled dad. "You know I can't divulge what, if anything, Erin and I talked about. But in light of our time together, I wanted to speak with you again."

Gary's tone was guarded. "Okay." He wondered what his daughter had told the priest.

"One thing I'll caution you about, Gary, is not to treat her like a criminal. She's done wrong, certainly. We both know she's spent what had to be a disturbing night in jail. And she'll have to go through the legal system – which can be terrifying in itself. The last thing she needs is to feel ostracized by her family. Home is where Erin needs to feel safe and welcome – and *loved*. As angry as you certainly are with her right now, and as justifiably upset as you may be, she's your daughter. Remember that above everything else. Put yourself in her shoes, Gary. How would you want God to act toward you when you've behaved less than honorably? How *does* He treat you?" He paused to let Gary reflect on his words. "He offers forgiveness. He welcomes you back, time and time again. 'All is forgiven, My child.' He's our Dad and He loves us. Unconditionally. And forever. Right?"

Gary nodded.

"Of course you have to discipline her, but extend mercy. And forgiveness. Understand this, Gary: Jesus calls us to forgive — specifically, 'forgive us our trespasses *as we forgive* those who trespass against us.' So, yes, Erin's done wrong — from both a family and a legal standpoint — but you need to respond to her as her dad, who loves her. Correct her, certainly, but be judicious… and kind. Justice and mercy go hand in hand."

Chapter 8

On the way home, Erin didn't even try to talk to her dad. As soon as he pulled in the driveway, she bolted from the still-moving car. She darted past her mom and into the house before Gary even reached the front walk.

"How is she?"

"She's a wreck, which I think we kind of expected. I'm guessing right now she's just going to want a shower and a long sleep."

"And you're not about to let that happen, are you?"

He considered her question as he climbed the porch stairs. "An hour ago I wouldn't have."

Michaela gave him a quizzical look. "What happened in the past hour?"

"I had a talk with Father Dave."

"Ah, that's right – it's second Saturday."

"Not just that. At his suggestion, I brought Erin for reconciliation after we left the police station. Then he and I talked again afterward. He made a lot of sense."

"He usually does," she said, slipping her arms around him.

Their hug was interrupted by a bellow from upstairs. "Where's my door?!"

A moment later, footsteps pounded down the stairs and a furious Erin appeared, glowering. A terrible odor of stale urine swirled around her. "What did you do with my door?"

"I should think that's fairly obvious," Gary replied, struggling to maintain a stern expression. He tried not to sound amused. "I took it away."

She stood before him, hands poised on her hips. "Where is it?" she demanded.

"I think the more important question to ask is, 'How am I going to earn it back?' And you'll do *that* by proving you can be trusted. In the meantime, little girl, I want to feel confident when you say you'll be in your room, you'll actually be in there."

The teenager's eyes narrowed in fury. "I hate you," she seethed. With a swoosh of dark hair, she stormed out of the living room and tromped back up the stairs.

The bathroom door slammed. A minute later, the shower went on.

Gary's eyes traveled toward the ceiling. "Poor kid. I don't even want to think about what a Friday night in lockup must've been like." He shook his head and sighed. "We're gonna have a lot to talk about this weekend, you and I."

"We may as well start now." Micki nodded toward the family room. "The kids are in there, watching a movie, and the twins are napping."

Seated on the couch in the living room, Gary outlined his plan for addressing Erin's disobedience and breaking their trust.

"That seems a bit harsh," Micki countered. "I mean, taking her bedroom door off its hinges was one thing" – she smiled – "and that really was brilliant. But I think that sends enough of a message. What you're talking about doing, Gary… Do you really think it's necessary?"

"I do. She didn't just blow curfew or sass one of us. This was a serious breach of trust – not to mention the property damage *and* the legal repercussions."

"I suppose," she acquiesced, sinking her head into her hands. "I just wish she hadn't gone and done that."

"Same here. But she did, and we've got to deal with the fallout. As does she."

"Speaking of fallout, what should we do about her birthday dinner tomorrow? I really don't think a celebration is appropriate right now."

Gary nodded. "I agree. We've got to cancel."

"I'll call your mom and my dad. Will you call Marie?"

Michaela and Gary talked for nearly another half hour before Amanda charged into the room and hurtled into her mother's lap.

"Momma, where's Sissy?"

Weary of having been asked the same question all day, Micki stroked the little girl's hair. "She's upstairs, baby."

"Where was she?"

Gary and Michaela exchanged an uncertain glance over the child's head.

"She was out early this morning," Gary responded, caressing the girl's cheek. "She got home a little while ago."

"You missed Sissy today, huh?" Micki asked.

Mandy nodded as she cuddled in her mother's arms.

"I don't think she was feeling well, baby, so I'm pretty sure she's taking a nap," Gary told the little girl. "If you go upstairs, be sure not to wake her, okay?"

"Okay, Daddy," the child agreed, collecting kisses from each of them before skipping out of the room.

Micki made her phone calls, apologizing for the short notice in canceling the festivities. When she explained, both grandparents understood – and agreed with their children's decision.

"You made a wise choice," Michael Conwaye told his daughter. "Under the circumstances, I wouldn't have had a party for her, either."

Meanwhile, Gary called his sister. She was out, so he ended up talking to Marc, who sounded more anxious than Gary had heard him in a long time.

"We've decided to call off Erin's birthday dinner tomorrow – for obvious reasons," he said.

"I'm kind of glad to hear that. I've got five midterms to study for, so I couldn't have come anyway." He paused. "How about we do dinner here next weekend – just the family and your mom. It can be a dual celebration – Erin's birthday and my being able to breathe again, 'cause exams end Friday. Besides, I think Marie wants to sit down with Erin, kinda get inside her head and see how she's doing, emotionally."

Although he knew his brother-in-law couldn't see him, Gary nodded. His sister was a child psychiatrist. "Sounds good. Let me run it by Micki."

Later that afternoon, Gary called Pete. "Hey, chief. I hate to bug you at home, but I've got a family situation to take care of. I'll still be able to do my air shift, but I have to back away from the music stuff for a while. Could be a week, maybe two. I've already talked with Jenna and she's willing to cover for me. I'll take care of paying her – the station shouldn't have to shell out for that."

"Whoa! Hold up a minute, Gar'," Pete said. "What's going on?"

Briefly, Gary explained what happened, and what he had in mind.

Pete whistled softly. "I sure don't envy you. And I *really* don't envy Erin. But I hope it works out. Good luck."

Gary's next call was to Erin's high-school guidance counselor. The two had developed a strong rapport from working together on joint station-school functions for the better part of two decades.

"Hey, Jackie, it's Gary Sheldon. I'm sorry to bother you on a weekend," he told Ms DeMay.

"No bother at all, Gary. Always good to hear from you," she said. "What's up?"

When he told her what he wanted to do – and why, Jackie hedged. "That's kind of a radical plan, Gary. But I commend you for your commitment. I'll reach out to her teachers now so they're aware. You know there's no school on Monday – for Columbus Day. But Tuesday morning, check in at the front office first thing, and you'll be good to go."

Chapter 9

(Monday, October 12)

Gary flipped on the overhead light in his daughter's room. "Wake up," he commanded. "We have to leave in half an hour."

Erin opened an eye and groaned in protest, then rolled over to go back to sleep.

"Oh, no," he said, tugging away the covers. "I said get up."

"What time is it?"

"Five fifteen. Now get up."

"Why?" she whined.

"Because I said so. We leave in thirty minutes."

"Where're we going?"

"You'll find that out when we get there. Now get up and get dressed."

Erin grumbled and tried to pull the covers away from his grasp.

"Don't make me pick up that bed and dump you out of it," he warned.

Twenty-five minutes later, they were on the road. Between still being half asleep and furious at her dad for dragging her out of bed so early – especially when she had the day off from school – Erin barely spoke.

Half an hour later, Gary pulled in to the parking lot of the Congregational church on the Litchfield green. "We're here," he announced to his daughter, who'd begun dozing.

The teen turned toward the sound of his voice and opened her eyes, suspicious. "Where?"

"Your first AA meeting."

"I'm not an alcoholic," she hissed.

"Well, I am," he replied as if it were the most normal thing to say. "And you're here as my guest."

Erin's mouth fell open at his revelation; she stared at her dad as they got out of the car.

Draping an arm over her shoulder, Gary guided his daughter into the building. "You'll be fine, honey," he assured her. "And remember: You never have to say anything if you don't want to."

Inside, Gary approached Paula G., the woman who was serving as leader for the meeting. "Hi Paula, I'm Gary" – he laid his hands on the teen's shoulders – "and this is my daughter Erin. It's her first meeting."

Paula gave the teen a warm smile. "Welcome, Erin. I'm so glad you're here."

Erin smirked. "Thanks."

"Why don't you go on over to the refreshment table and get yourself a glass of juice," Paula invited.

Sullen, Erin slumped away in the direction Paula indicated.

"She was arrested for DUI on Friday night," Gary explained once his daughter was out of earshot. "As far as I know, it was her first time drinking and driving. I don't think there's an alcohol problem yet... but I wanted this to be a cautionary experience for her, kind of a wake-up call."

Paula nodded. "That's not a bad idea. How can we support you?"

His shoulders slumped. "Her mom and I are still reeling. We got a call late that night saying she was in jail after she wrecked her uncle's car."

"That must have been a shock."

"That's putting it mildly. Especially since she was grounded – and we thought she was asleep in her room."

"So how can I help?"

"I'm at a loss as to how to deal with her. Obviously grounding her isn't the answer. I doubt making her pay for the auto repairs will achieve anything more than depleting her college savings."

"Has she seen her uncle since the crash?"

"Not yet. That'll probably happen tomorrow."

"I'd suggest – and again, this is only my opinion – you get her in front of him as soon as is practical. If they've got a good relationship, she'll want to apologize. And help her realize her actions have consequences, whatever you decide those will be. I think it's a good idea, bringing her here – as long as she realizes AA isn't some kind of punishment for bad behavior. It's a support system. Make sure she understands that."

Gary nodded. "Of course. That was my intent."

"Good." Paula glanced at the clock. "We're about to get started, Gary – grab yourself a cup of coffee and have a seat."

***

After the meeting, Gary brought Erin to a diner for breakfast before heading home.

"What did you think?"

"I'm not an alcoholic," she insisted.

"So you've said," he replied evenly, nodding as he replaced his coffee cup in its saucer. "I want to make sure that never happens."

Erin fidgeted with her hands in her lap. "It won't," she lamented. "It was just one time."

When she glanced up, Gary met her gaze and held it. "That's what I always said, too. And little by little, I let that demon in. And it took over and nearly destroyed my life. Right now you may be thinking I'm just a horrendous jerk, but I'm trying to spare you that, sweetheart."

Erin looked down again. Her lower lip trembled. She reached for her orange juice just to have something to do with her hands.

"What did you think of the meeting?"

She shrugged. "It was okay, I guess."

"Did anything about it resonate with you?"

"I dunno."

"Think, Erin. What stuck out to you?"

"I didn't know you were an alcoholic," she murmured after a long silence.

"Neither did I, 'til about a year and a half ago," he admitted.

"Am I?"

"Are you what?"

"Am I an alcoholic?" she worried.

"I hope not," he replied truthfully. "It doesn't happen the same way for any two people. Just like some folks have a low tolerance for alcohol, others have a greater susceptibility to alcoholism. Like I said, I'm trying to spare you what I went through."

At work, just as he began his six-o'clock hour, Gary called his sister.

"You're just a regular Chatty Cathy lately, aren't you?" Marie bubbled. "Two calls in as many weeks? What's up with that?"

"Last week I just wanted to catch up. Today I've got news."

"Oh?" Carrying the cordless handset into the bedroom, Marie kicked off her shoes and slid her tired feet into slippers.

"Yeah, this is pretty big stuff," he assured her. He couldn't wait to tell her about his meeting with James and their long talk over lunch. *Was that only last Friday?*

"Okay, so tell me," she urged as she returned to the kitchen to warm up last night's meatloaf and mashed potatoes for herself and the kids.

"We have a half-brother," he told her excitedly. "I met him."

The phone nearly slid from Marie's hand.

When she didn't respond, Gary said, "Did you hear me?"

"I heard you," she said, bristling. "And I wish I hadn't. I don't want to hear anything about him."

"Why not? I thought you'd be excited."

"I'm not," she snapped. "And frankly, I'm appalled that you'd betray our family this way, by meeting that… that – *outsider!* It's a slap in the face to Mom. How dare you, Gary!"

"What are you talking about?" he sputtered. "He's never done anything to you – or to any of us, for that matter. He just happened to be born with half of our DNA. So how can my meeting him be in any way a betrayal? If you're upset about his parentage, Marie, be upset with Dad. He's the one who betrayed Mom. And just because he was an unfaithful jerk, don't go taking it out on James."

"Oh, so now it's *James*, is it? Getting all cozy with the enemy already?"

"What enemy? Marie, he's our brother."

"*Half*-brother," she corrected in a hiss. "And he's no brother to me. And if you start getting all buddy-buddy with him, *you're* no brother to me, either. So choose wisely."

Before Gary could respond, she hung up. He stared blankly at the receiver in his hand. He knew better than to call her back.

When Marc sailed into the on-air studio, Gary's expression told him the cheery banter he'd heard on the radio was all faked.

"What's the matter?"

Gary scowled. "That wife of yours." He shook his head and exhaled audibly. "Sometimes I don't understand her."

Marc tried to lighten his brother-in-law's mood. "Join the club. What'd she do this time?"

Gary related the gist of their conversation.

"I can't understand why she'd react that way," Marc mused. "If *I'd* just found out I had a half-brother, I'd be excited to meet him. Or at least hear about him."

"I know, right? Anyway, I'm sorry I put her in a mood – 'cause you're gonna have to put up with her tonight."

He shrugged. "By the time I get home, she'll be asleep. I won't have to deal with her ire 'til morning" – he grinned – "and *then* I'll curse you. Seriously, Gar', I have no idea what crawled up her butt and died, but I'm sure she'll calm down. Two, three months, she'll be over it. Tops."

Chapter 10

(5:15 a.m., Tuesday, October 13)
Gary shook Erin's shoulder. "Get up. We're leaving in half an hour."

"Again?"

"Yes, again."

"Why?"

"Because I said so, that's why."

Today's meeting was in Waterbury, in a meeting hall at a Lutheran church. Most of the attendees seemed to be in their teens or early twenties. At 35, Dad was probably the oldest person there.

Erin looked around the room in astonishment. Some of these kids were her age – a few even looked younger! How was that possible – to have a drinking problem at fifteen?

By the time they left to head back to Southbury, Erin was fighting tears.

Gary glanced over at her; she was gnawing at her thumbnail. He'd seen Michaela do that as a teenager countless times, whenever she was anxious. "What're you thinking about?"

"Some of those kids were younger than me," Erin replied after a long silence.

He nodded. "I know."

"Am I gonna end up like them?"

"I hope not, baby."

As her father turned in to the driveway at Pomperaug High School, Erin gathered her books and got ready to hop out of the car. But Dad circled around toward the parking area.

She pointed to the front entrance. "You can just let me out over there."

Dad shook his head. "Oh, no, no, no. Not today, my dear. After that little stunt you pulled Friday night, I can't trust you to be where you say you're going to be. I have no assurance you'll be in school all day. So I'm going with you, to keep an eye on you and make sure you're where you're supposed to be."

Horrified, Erin's mouth fell open. "What?" she blurted. "You can't be serious, Daddy."

"Oh, but I am," he assured her as he parked the car. "I've never been more serious about anything in my life. Ready to go in?"

"Do I have a choice?" she grumbled.

"I'm afraid not." He opened the door and got out, then waited for her.

Erin was ready to die of embarrassment. But Dad acted as if it were the most natural thing in the world — and she hated him for it.

Not only did he accompany her to every class, Gary sat with her and her friends at lunch and waited patiently by her locker between classes — even outside the girls' restroom.

"Why are you doing this to me?" she hissed, her cheeks flaming, as they returned to English class after a bathroom break.

"I think you already know the answer to that."

She turned away so he wouldn't see the tears in her eyes.

After school, she was sure he would drop her off at home, but when he drove right past the turnoff for their street, she grew suspicious.

"Where are we going?"

"I'm going to work. My job doesn't stop because I have to babysit you."

"You don't have to babysit me," she muttered, sinking lower into her seat.

"Oh, I absolutely do," he contended. "You've made that abundantly clear, Erin. You can't be left on your own."

On the way there, Gary stopped at the police station.

As he pulled in to the parking lot, Erin grew apprehensive. "What are we doing here?"

"Retrieving your driver's license — not that you'll be needing it anytime soon."

She glared at him. "Just how long are you planning to punish me for this?"

Raising an eyebrow, Gary turned to look at his daughter. "If you've got a problem with not driving, missy, you can take that up with the State of Connecticut. As I understand it, your license is suspended for at least forty-five days – and possibly until you turn twenty-one."

When she started to balk, he raised a hand, palm forward, to quiet her. "You brought this on yourself. So don't you go getting all pissy at me, little girl."

Erin grumbled beside her dad and dragged her feet on the way in to the police station and all the way back to the car. The entire time they were inside, she didn't make eye contact with anyone.

When they got to the radio station, everyone greeted Erin as if she were a visiting dignitary. Even Charlie, the normally gruff sales manager, was at his genial best, welcoming her warmly and trying to engage her in conversation.

Still dragging her feet, Erin trailed behind her dad to his office.

"Can I stay in here while you're on the air?" she asked.

"No, you may not. I want to be able to keep an eye on you. Every minute."

Gary's boss poked his head in to the music office. "Hey, Gary—oh, Erin, I didn't see you there. It's nice to see you!"

She looked up glumly. "Hi, Uncle Pete," she greeted the program director in as morose a voice as she could manage.

"Gary, Jenna said she couldn't find the weekly music report template on your computer. Could you pull it up for her and leave it open?"

"Sure thing. Hey, anything goin' on I should know about?"

Pete shook his head. "Nothing that can't wait."

Chapter 11

"Twenty minutes to six on Z97-3. I'm Gary Sheldon, thanks for hanging out with me this Tuesday afternoon. It's sixty-two degrees in Middlebury, looks like we're heading for a low of fifty tonight. And, hey, speaking of tonight, my buddy Marc Lindsay's in at seven to hang out with you. He'll have Seventies at Seven and Late-night Love Songs at ten. Stick around."

When he shut off the microphone, Gary noticed his daughter looking horrified.

"What's the matter?"

"I can't face Uncle Marc!"

"I don't see how you can avoid it. He'll be here any minute. And it's not that big a studio."

Her eyes brimmed with tears. "Please, Daddy," she begged, clinging to his arm. "Please don't make me talk to Uncle Marc! I'm too ashamed to face him."

He shook his head. "I'm sorry, punkin. You'll have to face him sooner or later. It's all part of being a grownup. You may as well get it over with now."

"But I can't," she wailed, tears spilling down her flushed cheeks.

(6:22 p.m.)
Erin hovered at the door to the DJ prep area. She watched her uncle cull through stacks of feature stories, looking for topical items to talk about during that night's show.

Chewing her lower lip, she gathered her courage. "Uncle Marc?" she barely whispered.

He looked up. As his eyes met hers, he dropped the paper he was holding and stood.

"I'm sorry I wrecked your car," she whimpered, afraid to venture beyond the doorway.

Without a word, Marc crossed the room, his mahogany eyes filled with warmth. Stopping a few feet in front of his niece, he opened his arms in silent invitation. She fell into them, bawling.

"I'm so sorry," Erin sobbed, trembling.

"I know, honey," he murmured, patting her back.

"How can you ever forgive me?" she asked at last, hiccupping, peering up at him through eyes that still streamed with tears. She'd done stupid stuff before, but never something like this. This was awful! She was certain Uncle Marc would hate her forever.

To her surprise, he wiped away her tears and kissed her forehead. "Shh. It's okay. C'mon, honey, don't cry."

"I'm so sorry I lied to you," Erin went on.

"Well, I would hope so," he replied a shade off of gentle, the closest he would get to being stern with her. "And frankly, Erin, I'm way more upset about that than I am about the wrecked car."

She looked up at him, her mouth falling open in surprise.

"I hate that you lied to me, Erin. How am I ever supposed to trust you again if I can't be sure you're being honest with me? Hmm?"

At Uncle Marc's words, Erin tried to turn away from him, but he held her closer.

"Listen to me," he said, his voice firm but still placid. "You need to hear this, honey."

Erin stopped struggling and went limp.

"It really hurt me when your dad told me he hadn't given you permission to ask to borrow my car. Not only that, but you deliberately lied to me to get your way. You took advantage of my trust in you. And I can't even yet talk about your drinking and driving – not with our family history. How could you do that to me, Erin? And how do you think that makes me feel?"

What remained of Erin's composure fled. She collapsed against him and sobbed.

When it was time for them to leave, Gary bade his brother-in-law goodnight and retrieved his still-crying daughter from his office.

Out in the parking lot, he noted the bright-red Jeep Wrangler in the space Marc's Saab had always occupied.

Erin's sobs tapered off on the way home. When Gary asked if she was okay, she shook her head but either couldn't or wouldn't speak.

When they arrived home, she ignored Micki's request to wash up for supper and ran right up to her room, where she flung herself onto her bed.

After it became clear Erin wasn't coming back down, Micki went upstairs and set a tray with a bowl of chili and a hunk of warm cornbread on the girl's desk. Sitting at the edge of the bed, she stroked her squalling daughter's hair. "What's the matter, sweetheart?"

At her mother's comforting touch, Erin cried so hard she couldn't speak.

"It might help if you talked about it, honey."

The girl turned to look at her. Her cries subsided and for a moment it seemed she was about ready to speak. Then, abruptly, she buried her face in her pillow and dissolved into noisy sobs again.

Giving her shoulder a squeeze, Micki stood. "I'll leave this here in case you feel like eating."

Downstairs, Michaela sat with Gary as he ate his supper. "I've never seen her so upset," she fretted. "How long has she been like this?"

Gary shrugged. "She was fine most of the day – mortified at having a shadow in school, but I think what finally did her in was talking to Marc. She dreaded facing him, and she came back to the studio in tears. I had to send her to sit in my office for the last twenty minutes, because she couldn't pull herself together and stop crying when I went on the air."

Micki's eyes widened. Worry filled her voice. "What did he say to her?"

"No idea. It wasn't any of my business, and I figured if either of them wanted me to know, they'd say something."

"You don't think he yelled at her…"

"Marc? Yell?" Gary shook his head. "Not likely, but I wouldn't blame him if he did. She'd certainly have deserved it."

"Maybe you should call him," Micki suggested, "find out what he might have said that upset her so much. Maybe he doesn't even realize what effect he had on her."

He gave a thoughtful nod. "Good idea."

***

"I really didn't say much at all," Marc told Gary later that night, signing the bottom of the log page for the eight-o'clock hour, "just that I was disappointed in her for lying to me."

"Whatever it was, you really got to her. She went from being sullen and petulant all day to utterly disconsolate. Last I knew, she was still crying."

At his brother-in-law's words, Marc grew pensive. He tapped his pen against the control board. "I'm sorry, Gar'. I didn't mean to make her cry. And honestly, I didn't think what I said would upset her so much. I just told her how I felt."

"Don't apologize. You have nothing to be sorry for. You're the victim in all of this." Gary ran a hand through his hair. "I just wish I knew what to do."

An uncomfortable silence lingered so long Marc thought the call dropped.

"I gotta tell ya, Marc, that's one sweet ride you got there," Gary said at last.

"Yeah, she's a real beaut. Ninety-five. We picked 'er up on Saturday. Low miles, great condition. And she's a stick. Runs like a dream. Marie calls it my pre-seven-year-itch mobile. And Edward's already claimed it for his own once he's old enough to drive. Which he's sure is in a year or two."

Gary conjured a mental image of his five-year-old nephew behind the wheel of his dad's Jeep, perched atop a stack of phone books, with wood blocks on the pedals. "What's Fern got to say about that?"

"She's too busy being a woodland high princess right now," Marc replied with a laugh. "She can't be bothered with trivial things like modes of human transport."

Ten minutes later, when Gary peered into Erin's room, she was asleep. *At least she's stopped crying.* Something tugged at his heart as he continued on toward his room to get undressed for bed.

"I never expected having teenagers would be this… difficult," he lamented, sinking onto the bed.

"Still wouldn't talk to you?"

"Poor kid's finally asleep." He shook his head. "What're we gonna do, Mick? How do we deal with this?"

Michaela came over and sat beside her husband. Angling him away from her, she worked at the knots in his shoulders and upper back.

Arching his back, he responded immediately. "Mmm, that feels good."

"I can't believe how tight your shoulders are," she said, leaning to kiss the side of his throat.

Chapter 12

The next morning, Gary awakened Erin at five thirty. "C'mon, get up, sleepyhead. We've got a meeting to get to."

Groaning, Erin rubbed her eyes. They felt all raw and scratchy – like she had wet sand in them. "It's too early," she protested.

"I let you sleep as long as possible, sweetheart. We leave in twenty minutes. You'd better be ready."

"Or what?"

"Or you go to the meeting – and then school – in your pajamas this morning. Your choice."

Eighteen minutes later, Erin appeared in the kitchen in jeans and a striped sweater. "This is getting old," she groused.

"Well, get used to it. It's your new normal." Gary held out a brown paper bag. "Here. I packed your lunch."

"Thanks." She took it from him and shoved it in her backpack.

"Hey." Gary took his daughter's arm, pulled her toward him and kissed her on the forehead. "I love you, kiddo."

"Yeah, right," she muttered, turning away.

Today they were back to Litchfield. Again Erin only listened, opting not to participate. When Dad stood, identifying himself as an alcoholic, a cold emptiness seeped through her, and her insides twisted themselves into a great big knot.

"Why do you have to say that?" she asked him over breakfast.

"Say what?"

"That you're a" – she gestured feebly with her hands – "you know…"

"An alcoholic?"

She lowered her voice. "Yeah."

"Because it's what I am."

Tears sprang to Erin's eyes. She swiped at them. "But you're so much more than that," she insisted in a low hiss.

"True," he acknowledged, setting down his coffee mug. "But that wasn't a So-much-more-than-that Anonymous meeting, was it?"

She scowled. "You're making fun of me."

"Not at all. Just stating a fact. It wasn't easy to admit to at first, Erin, but I've come to terms with that and I embrace it. I've only been in recovery a year and a half, but it's a new day every day, a new chance to acknowledge and celebrate my sobriety."

"Does it bother you when other people drink around you?"

A brief smile flicked at the corners of his mouth. "Not when they're of legal age, no."

Erin leaned back against the booth and managed a hint of a smile. "*Now* you're making fun of me."

"That time, yeah," he admitted.

"I don't think I'm an alcoholic," she mused, adding, "I just made a bad decision one time."

Gary turned in to the lot and found a parking space.

"You're not coming in with me again, are you?"

"I sure am."

"Da-ad! Don't."

"Erin, we've been through this. You've proven I can't trust you to be where you say you're going to be, so I'm going to keep you in my sight for as long as it takes for me to regain my trust in you. This is a situation of your own making."

Erin glared at her father, tears welling in her eyes. "I fucking hate you right now!" she hissed.

Gary killed the engine. "First of all, little girl, you used up your lifetime 'I hate you' allotment eight years ago. And second, if that word comes out of your mouth once more, you won't be sitting comfortably all morning. And don't you test me, 'cause you know I'll do it. And I don't care one little bit who sees. Or hears."

Furious, but certain her father wasn't bluffing, Erin grabbed her backpack, slammed the car door and hurried to catch up with a group of friends, muttering as she went.

Gary followed several paces behind until they reached the front entrance. Then he caught up and took his fuming daughter by the arm before escorting her to the main office to check in.

All day, Erin refused to acknowledge his presence. She tucked herself into a small knot of her companions as they navigated the corridor between classes and at lunch, and kept her head turned away from her dad as much as possible during classes.

"Dude, you're bein' too harsh. You should really cut her some slack," one of the guys told Gary in the cafeteria while Erin was getting herself a carton of milk.

Really? Gary glanced at the familiar faces surrounding him. He recognized several former CCD students; others were neighborhood kids or longtime pals of Erin's. Now he turned to face the acne-riddled teenage advice giver. "I'm so glad you weighed in on this, Ric. Next time I need parenting advice, I'll be sure to ask you."

"Yeah, man," another chimed in. "You're not being fair to her."

Gary bristled. He turned to face the second teen who'd verbally accosted him. "I'm sorry… Fair? You want to talk about fairness, Trevor? Okay, how about this? Do you think it's fair that my car insurance rates just quadrupled? Do you think it's fair that Erin's uncle had to go out and buy a new car because his got totaled by an underage drunk driver who shouldn't have been out in the first place? And heaven forbid the car had gone off the road twenty feet sooner! She'd have tumbled down an embankment or hit a tree and been killed. Do you think that's fair? Because I sure don't."

A few of the guys backed off a bit.

"And let me tell you, your attempts at bullying me into relenting aren't helping one bit. Erin got herself into this mess and she's going to have to deal with how I choose to address it. And when you have a teenage daughter of your own, I hope her woefully uninformed friends try to interfere – yes, I said *interfere* – and tell you how you should be raising her. Then you let me know how you like it.

"I realize you think you're coming to your friend's defense, guys, but trust me: I know what I'm doing. I've been dealing with kids about as long as most of you have been alive."

When Gary and Erin arrived at the radio station, Pete informed him Marc wouldn't be in that night.

"He called a few hours ago, sounded really panicked about midterms, so I told him to take the rest of the week off to study."

"Yeah, he told me last night he was really worried about the one he had today. Did he happen to mention how it went?"

"He didn't say. But he didn't sound good."

"Okay." Gary nodded. "Rob filling in?"

"Just tonight and tomorrow. I'm covering for him on Friday."

***

"I just don't know what to do about her," Gary admitted in bed that night.

Michaela cuddled close. "Still?"

"I always prided myself on my ability to engage in what I considered creative parenting," he said, "but I'm at an absolute loss here."

"Why not let her decide?"

Gary kissed the end of his wife's nose. "Like we did with Dani that time? That's a great idea, Mick. That way, Erin gets some say in how she wants to make this right, and it doesn't all fall to us."

"You gonna go along with whatever she comes up with?"

He shrugged. "Within reason, yeah."

"Good. Now will you quit fretting over that and not let this perfectly good amorous wife go to waste?"

"Now that's an even better idea."

Chapter 13

"Are you coming in to school with me again?" Erin asked when they got back into the car after breakfast the next morning.

"Yep."

The girl let out a resigned sigh. "How long are you planning to humiliate me like this?"

He turned the key in the ignition. The Camaro roared to life. "I don't know, Erin. As long as it takes, I suppose."

"As long as it takes for what?" she challenged.

Gary shrugged. "'Til I feel I can trust you again."

"When's that gonna be?" He heard the frustration rising in her voice.

"Depends on you. Give me a reason to trust you and we'll see how it goes."

Erin glared at her father. "How'm I gonna do *that?*"

"Well, you figured out how to lose my trust. Try doing just the opposite to regain it."

"How?" she persisted.

"You're a bright girl, Erin. Figure it out."

Erin didn't talk to him for the rest of the ride to school.

That night, after Gary and Erin had eaten supper, Michaela joined them in Erin's room.

Seated on her bed, Erin glanced anxiously at them. "What did you guys want to talk to me about?"

"We've given this a lot of thought, honey," Mom began, her arm around Dad – probably to present a united front. "We never expected to have to deal with one of you kids getting arrested, and we're at a loss as to how to correct you."

"Your mom's right," Dad put in. "We know this hasn't been something *you* ever expected, either. So we decided, since we're all three of us heading into uncharted territory, we'd let you have some input as to how we deal with this."

Erin's stomach tightened and she wished she hadn't eaten that slice of birthday cake after supper. "What do you mean?"

Sitting beside his daughter on the bed, Dad took her hand. "You're going to choose your punishment."

Not sure she heard correctly, she eyed him oddly. "I'm gonna what?"

"Choose your punishment."

"What are my choices?"

He shook his head. "Sorry. I phrased that badly. I meant you're going to come up with your own consequence. And as long as Mom and I agree it's appropriate, then that's what it'll be."

"We realize you're growing up, honey," Mom said, coming over to sit at her other side, "and we felt you should have some say in how we discipline you for this."

Erin looked from one of them to the other again. "Really? Whatever I decide?"

"As long as it's reasonable and appropriate, yeah," Dad told her. "If you decide on being forced to eat a hot-fudge sundae every day for a week, that's not gonna fly. We want you to really give it some thought. It's got to be meaningful and appropriate."

Mom reached out a hand to smooth Erin's hair. "Your dad's right," she said. "We don't mean just forgoing your allowance for two weeks or being grounded for a month. We want you to really think about it and present us a reasonable option."

"How long do I get to decide?"

"What's today, Thursday?" Dad's brow creased. "How about you give us an answer before we leave for Auntie Marie's on Sunday afternoon... say, by three thirty?"

Erin gave a pensive nod. "Okay. I guess that'll work."

Her parents stood.

Dad leaned to kiss her on the forehead. "Better get to sleep, kiddo. Five thirty's gonna come awfully soon."

She groaned. "Again?"

The corners of his mouth tipped downward slightly. "Yes, again."

"How much longer?"

He tweaked her nose. "'Til I decide otherwise."

Erin scowled. "Maybe I'll decide that's not gonna be part of my punishment."

Mom offered the girl a smile. "Remember, Erin, whatever you come up with, it's got to meet with our approval." She kissed her daughter and caressed her cheek. "Good night, honey."

Chapter 14

Saturday evening, Erin hovered at the door to Dad's study. "Can I talk to you for a minute?"

He looked up from his computer. "Sure. C'mon in. What's up, baby?"

Erin shut the door and perched on the edge of the couch. "It's a-about my punishment."

Gary nodded. "Want me to get Mom?"

"N-no." Erin shook her head, toying with something in her hands. "I wanted to talk to you."

"Okay." He came to sit beside her. "What did you have in mind?"

"I've been saving up for a car. For about five years. I saved my allowance, plus birthday and Christmas money. And money from my job last summer. But it doesn't make sense for me to buy a car when I can't even drive it 'til I'm twenty-one, so I want to give this to Uncle Marc to fix his car." Erin held up a checkbook. "I know it won't be nearly enough, but it's a start. I was planning on giving him a check tomorrow. And I figured I'd offer to work off the rest over time. If – if that's okay." She dropped the checkbook into her lap.

He gave a thoughtful nod. "I'm sure he'll appreciate that, Erin. How much is it?"

"A little over forty-two hundred."

Gary nodded, trying to disguise his astonishment. "That'll go a long way toward the repairs."

Erin's hand twisting intensified. She couldn't quite meet his gaze. "Th-th-that'll take care of squaring things with Uncle Marc... but, um... th-there – there's something else," she stammered.

When she told him, he shook his head.

"No."

"Why not?" she demanded. "You said I could choose. And that's what I decided on."

"We said it would have to be appropriate. And I don't think that's appropriate."

"You used to."

The statement stopped him short. "That was a long time ago."

Tears of frustration welled in Erin's eyes. "I need you to do this for me. Please."

"Why?"

"Because of how I always felt afterward. It was horrible, but once it was over, you'd always hug me and tell me I was forgiven." She paused. "And 'cause I can't stand having you angry at me. This whole week you've just been mad at me *all the time*… and I hate that."

Gulping air, Erin swiped away tears. Her mouth twisted as she fought to get her words out without sobbing. "I know I did wrong, but you haven't hugged me since my birthday, Daddy… and it makes me feel like you don't love me anymore."

"Oh, honey!" Gary's arms were around his daughter the instant the words were out of her mouth. "Of course I love you! I'm sorry, baby. I never realized I'd put such distance between us." He rocked her back and forth as she wept. "Shh… Don't cry, punkin."

When Erin's jagged sobs abated, Gary drew back from her. He smoothed her hair and kissed her on the forehead. "Are we okay?"

Erin smeared away her tears. She sniffled and looked up at him. "That depends. Are you going to do it?"

"Let me think about it."

"That means no, huh?" she challenged.

"No, it means let me think about it. You've had days to work this out in your head — so of course it makes sense to you. But you've just hit me with this, Erin. It's big, and I need some time to think it over." He met her gaze. "Okay?"

She sniffled again, then nodded. "Alright."

"Out of curiosity, what made you choose that?"

Erin shrugged. "Like I said… because of how I always felt afterward. That sense of forgiveness. You know when you go to confession — right before you go in, there's that awful feeling of dread and shame in the pit of your stomach? Like what you've done is so big and so terrible, and you're sure God will never understand? But by the time you leave, you feel this huge sense of relief, like it's all better, and you're starting over fresh."

That's exactly how it feels. Gary nodded. "I get that. I guess it makes sense. Okay, honey, let me think about it."

In bed that night, Gary drew close to Michaela. "Erin came to talk to me earlier."

She shut her book and laid it on her nightstand. "What about?"

Gary told her what their daughter had suggested. "She didn't want me to tell you. I guess she felt embarrassed about it and didn't want you to know."

Michaela frowned. "Or she figured I'd try to talk you out of it."

"That's possible."

"Are you going to do it?"

He exhaled slowly. "I told her I'd think about it."

"What did she say to that?"

Gary smiled. "She called me a big chicken. I think she was trying to goad me into it."

Michaela couldn't help grinning as she envisioned her husband with a beak and feathers. She gave him a sidelong glance. "Did it work?"

He gave a little shrug. "As opposed to the idea as I am, I gotta admit I'm leaning toward it. She made a reasoned argument and neatly refuted every objection I raised."

"What made her choose that?"

"She sees it as the biggest possible consequence. When she was little, it was always the great-granddaddy of punishments. Only spoken of in hushed tones – and reserved for the worst of the worst infractions. Now she's got all these swirling emotions bottled up and needs a cathartic outlet."

"That's eloquent. She told you this?"

Gary shook his head. "That's the sense I got from her. She feels so burdened by this, she needs some way to release that guilt. I know you've always opposed it. And as much as I don't want to do it either, Mick, this may be what she really needs. So, for Erin's sake, I think I have to."

Michaela nodded, her blue eyes serious. Her hand curled around his. "I think you're right."

"You do?" Gary had expected her to voice vigorous objection, not give in – especially not so readily.

She shrugged. "You *did* tell her it had to be meaningful. And what you said makes sense. At least, emotionally, for Erin. When are you planning to do this?"

"I was thinking tomorrow, when we get home from Mass."

"Do you want me there?"

As Gary considered this, his brow furrowed. "I think that would embarrass her. Let's not add that layer of emotion. Besides, aren't you seeing Trish tomorrow?"

Chapter 15

After 9:30 Mass, Michaela announced she was dropping Amanda and Michael at Grandma's house. As they jumped up and down with glee and raced to her car, Gary and Erin carried the twins to his car.

On the way home, he broached the subject delicately. "I've given our discussion last night a lot of thought. I talked it over with Mom, an—"

"Daddy! I told you not to!" she squawked, her face contorting in equal parts shame and fury. Her fists clenched and unclenched.

"Let me finish," he said quietly. "Mom and I never keep secrets from each other. We've decided to accept your suggestion."

Her eyes widened in surprise, then narrowed in suspicion. "Are you messing with me?"

"No. We realize this is something you need me to do. For the record, I'm opposed to the idea, but you presented a well-reasoned argument, and I like to think we're fairly reasonable, open-minded parents. That said, I figured we'd get it out of the way when we get home."

"So soon?" she squeaked.

He shrugged. "Why put it off? Like you said – kinda like going to confession, it's awful at the time but you feel so much better afterward."

"And then you expect me to sit and eat lunch?"

Gary considered this. "Good point. We'll do it after lunch."

During lunch, a heavy sense of dread prevailed in the kitchen. To dispel it, Micki chattered excitedly about her visit that afternoon with her long-away friend Trish.

"How long since you've seen her?" Gary asked, eager to chase the awkwardness they all felt.

"Too long," Michaela replied with a wistful sigh as she stirred her tomato soup.

Within weeks of the Sheldons' August 1990 marriage, Trish Deming had impulsively moved to California to be near her boyfriend, a business major at UCLA. Now unattached after a bitter breakup several months ago, she was back in Connecticut this week to see family. She'd called her old friend on Wednesday to arrange a visit.

"It'll be good to see her," Michaela mused. "We've talked a few times since she left, but I haven't seen her in almost nine years."

"Hard to believe it's been that long."

"Who's this?" Erin asked.

"My best friend from grade school. She was maid of honor at our wedding."

"Bringing the twins for show and tell?" Gary teased.

"Of course. Real babies are so much more cuddly than photos." She grinned. "Of course, she'll have to settle for pictures of the rest of the brood."

After lunch, Erin cleared the table, then quietly escaped to her room. Micki bundled up the twins and left to visit Trish. Meanwhile, Gary retreated to his study to pray.

Distressed and anxious, he pocketed his rosary beads partway through the second Glorious Mystery. "I don't know what to do, Lord," he lamented. "This just feels so wrong!"

Getting up, he reached for his book of prayers for troubled times. He flipped through it and, not finding anything to even remotely address his particular fret, returned to the couch, dejected. He recalled something he'd told his religious-ed students: If they had difficulty in praying, they might try setting out a chair for Jesus and inviting Him to sit for a chat.

Gary pulled over his desk chair. "Can we talk?" he asked aloud.

At last, he went up to Erin's room. The girl lay on her bed, reading.

Gary picked up the hairbrush from his daughter's dresser and perched beside her. "Hey."

She sat up. "Hi."

"We need to talk."

Erin swallowed hard. A flutter began in her insides. "Okay." When her father looked at her, the girl's cheeks flushed. Her words came out jittery. "I know this seems babyish, Daddy, but it's important to me."

He said nothing.

Erin watched him, uneasy.

When Dad finally spoke, his somber tone chilled her. "Erin, I want to be sure you know why we're doing this."

She gulped as she eyed him in silence.

He ticked off items on his fingers. "You disobeyed me by going out when you knew you were grounded. You lied to Uncle Marc to get him to lend you his car. You lied to Mom about not feeling well. You snuck out of the house. You were drinking. You got behind the wheel of a car while you were drunk. You wrecked your uncle's car. You lied to the police about me."

Erin gaped at him.

Dad slapped the hairbrush against his palm. It made an unnerving *thwack*. "Didn't think I knew about that, huh?"

Her cheeks flushed with embarrassment. Looking away, she shook her head.

"And you were arrested for drunk driving. Have I covered everything?"

Erin looked down at the floor. A shiver tingled her spine. She nodded. "Mm-hmm."

He tipped her chin upward and met her gaze. His tone turned her blood to what felt like little chunks of ice. "I want to know, young lady, why you did all those things."

She shrugged. "I don't know."

The intensity in his eyes seemed to pierce her. "You don't know. Really?"

Now Erin squirmed. She stood and paced. Seeing Dad palming that hairbrush made her nervous. "I didn't think it was fair that you grounded me... and I really wanted to go out with my friends. It was my *birthday*..."

"So you figured lying and disobeying was a better idea than coming to talk to me?"

"I *tried* to talk to you – but you wouldn't *listen*," she shrilled.

"About going out Friday night, no. However, I was willing to negotiate on the length of time you were grounded – which would have allowed you to go out this weekend. When are you going to learn, Erin? I don't do things just to be mean. I always build in the option for leniency. That's why, when you're grounded, it's usually for a longer time than what you've done would actually warrant. So when your behavior improves, Mom and I can amend it to let you off easier. It's all by design."

Erin considered this. It made sense.

He went on. "And for the record, if you had let it drop after I initially said no on Thursday night, I was ready to relent and let you go out with your friends."

Her lower lip quivering, Erin looked at Dad with questioning in her eyes. "You were?"

"Yes – and I really wanted to! It was your birthday. Do you think I wanted to be a colossal jerk to you on your birthday? Of course not – because I remember how much of a jerk my dad was to me – on more than one of my birthdays, and I hated him for it. But you kept pestering me and wouldn't let it go… so I had to let your punishment stand."

"Oh." A tremor of dread rippled along Erin's spine. Dad was still gripping that hairbrush. Stopping as she reached the far side of her room again – if only to put as much distance between herself and that wooden weapon as possible – she shifted foot to foot.

Eyeing her, Gary let the unnerving silence stretch out for nearly a minute. "This *is* what you asked me for, isn't it?" he prompted at last.

"Y-y-yes," the girl stammered, twining her fingers together.

He got to his feet. In two long-legged strides he stood beside her. Gently taking Erin by the wrist, Gary guided her back toward her bed, where he sat again, facing her.

She stood before him, her downcast eyes brimming with tears. Her diminutive stature, slight build and quivering lower lip made her seem way younger than her seventeen years.

He sat the girl beside him and wiped at her tears. "Sweetheart, there's an old Bible quote that says, 'No discipline seems pleasant at the time. But later it yields a rich harvest.'"

Erin sniffled. "What's that mean?"

"It means this is gonna hurt, and, boy, are you gonna cry!" he told her. "But you'll remember this lesson for a long time – and learn from it."

"Why do you have to use that hairbrush? You've only ever used your hand."

Reaching for the brush again, Gary shuddered as he recalled the sting of his mom's wooden hairbrush from his youth. "This is different. What you've done is serious, and it demands a serious consequence."

"But I didn't want—"

"Shh." He put a finger to her lips. "Erin, you got to decide on your punishment. I never said you'd get to specify how it's carried out."

Her lower lip trembled fiercely. "But Daddy…" she warbled.

"Honey, know this: I love you. I would never give you more than I know you can handle."

"You promise?"

"I promise. No one's ever been spanked to death – and you won't be the first."

Erin managed a wan smile. She stood, still twisting her fingers together, eyeing him in uncertain silence for several long seconds.

Before Erin could step forward to accept her punishment, Dad tossed the hairbrush back onto the bed. Shaking his head, he looked his eldest daughter in the eye. "I'm sorry. I can't do this."

"Why not? You threatened to the other day."

"Yes, but—"

"But what? Did you not mean it?"

He shot a hand through his hair. "Yes, I meant it. At the time. But… honey. It – it's just not appropriate."

"But it would have been appropriate in the parking lot at school?" she baited him.

"It wouldn't have been appropriate, period. I'm sorry I said that. I – I wasn't thinking straight."

Erin's mouth fell open. She stared at Dad in disbelief. "But…? Y-you said…"

"I know what I said. But, Erin, I *can't*. You're practically a grown woman. It would be" – he gave an adamant headshake – "all kinds of wrong."

Tears of frustration welled in her eyes. Uncomfortable silence swirled around them.

"What's wrong about it?" she asked at last.

Aside from being like something out of a bad porno movie? "For months you've been badgering me to treat you like an adult – and now you're asking me to discipline you like a little girl." Dad looked everywhere in the room but at his teenage daughter. "Geez, Erin, do I have to spell it out? It would constitute improper and wildly inappropriate contact."

"And it wouldn't if I were Aaron with two As instead of an E?"

She's right. Gary stood. Shook his head again. "I'm sorry, Erin. I can't have this conversation with you."

"You weren't here for a conversation," she reminded his retreating back.

Down the hall, Gary shut his bedroom door. The rule was if a door was open, you could come in, but if it was closed, you knocked and didn't enter without permission. He didn't want to continue this discussion and he felt this was the only way – cowardly though it was – to avoid it... and Erin.

Troubled and agitated, he reached for the Bible on his nightstand. As he sank onto the bed, the book fell open at Hebrews 12. "God deals with you as with sons; for what son is there whom his father does not discipline?"

Further along in the chapter, he knew, was the passage about discipline he'd paraphrased for Erin. Smirking at the coincidence, he shut the Bible then reopened it. Now his eye caught a passage in Proverbs 3: "My son, do not reject the discipline of the Lord or loathe His reproof. For whom the Lord loves He reproves, even as a father corrects the son in whom he delights."

He looked toward the ceiling. "Okay, now you're just showing off."

Shutting the Bible with a labored sigh, he returned it to the nightstand.

Why do you not turn to Me in the first place, child?

Gary whipped around. Surely the voice wasn't just in his head. He couldn't have imagined it. "I-I'm sorry... *me?*" he stammered.

The voice continued, speaking now to his heart. *This* was the conversation he needed to be having, he realized.

In the end – reluctant but in a spirit of obedient trust – Gary emerged from his room.

72

Chapter 16

Just after 3, Erin ventured downstairs and found Dad in the living room, engrossed in a magazine.

Gnawing at her lower lip, she slumped onto the couch beside him. "Daddy?"

He laid aside the new issue of *Radio & Records*. "What's up, punkin?"

"Do I have to go?"

His brow furrowed, as if he didn't comprehend her question. "Of course you do. It's your birthday dinner. It'd be kind of pointless if you weren't there."

Her eyes welled with tears. "Please don't make me go, Daddy. I can't face Uncle Marc. It was hard enough to have to see him that night at the radio station," she wailed, "but now, having to face him in his home – surrounded by his family? And eat dinner with him? I can't do that, Daddy!"

Dad lifted her chin and turned her head to face him. "It'll be fine, honey. Uncle Marc loves you. He's one of the most forgiving people I know. It might seem a little awkward at first, but he's not going to—"

"And what about Auntie Marie?" Erin moaned.

"What about her?"

"She's gonna hate me…"

"She's not going to hate you, punkin." *Of course not. It's me she can't stand right now.*

Erin turned away from her father and sniffled. Her shoulders slumped.

He gave her ponytail a playful tug. "Honey," he cooed. "It'll be alright. I promise."

The teen stiffened at his touch. "I can't face them, Daddy," she lamented, shaking her head. "I just can't. Please don't make me go there. Please let me stay home."

"You'll have to see them sometime, baby," he reasoned.

"I will. But not today, Daddy. *Please!* It's too soon." She turned back toward him, her eyes filling with tears. In the silence that followed, Erin's tears spilled over and she dissolved into sobs.

Gary's heart ached for the girl… but this was a mess of her own making, and she had to face up to it. Deciding a firm but gentle approach was best, he glanced at his watch. "We're leaving in ten minutes. Pull yourself together and prepare for an uncomfortable first few minutes. But I'm willing to bet it'll be a lot easier than you're worried it'll be." Now he wrapped her in a long, reassuring hug.

"Go on upstairs and wash your face," he instructed when he drew back from her. "It'll help you calm down, and you'll feel better. Okay, honey?"

Sniffling, she nodded and did as he said.

On the way to Seymour, conversation between father and daughter flowed easier than at any time in the past week. Still, large patches of uncomfortable silence intermittently filled the car.

"I'm really sorry, Daddy," Erin said, breaking one especially awkward silence.

He reached for her hand. "I know, sweetie." The comforting rub of his thumb against the back of her hand soothed her. "All you've got left to do is square things with your uncle. And the state."

"What's the state got to do with it?"

"Erin, we've been through this. You were arrested for DUI. From what I've read, you'll lose your license for at least forty-five days – probably a lot longer. And you'll have to go to court."

"But I'm only seventeen. Won't they charge me as a minor?"

"I dunno. We'll find that out when we go to court November second."

"Will I go back to jail?" Fear trembled her voice. Visions of her night in lockup filled her head.

He squeezed her hand comfortingly. "Probably not. But they'll almost certainly send you to an alcohol-education program. It'll likely work in your favor that you've been attending AA meetings. And, according to Officer Bigelow, when you do get to drive again, you'll only be allowed to drive a vehicle equipped with an ignition interlock. It's a gizmo that makes you pass a breathalyzer test before you start the car. You'll have to buy one and pay to get it installed. And they're not cheap."

Erin fell silent. Her eyes grew misty.

Gary figured she was pondering his words and silently lamenting the countless hours she'd have to put in – and missed outings with friends – to work off the rest of her debt to Uncle Marc. Not to mention the crimp this would put in her Sisters Adventure Days with Amanda.

It was several minutes before Erin spoke again. "What am I gonna say to him?" she asked in a fragile voice.

"To Uncle Marc? I always find 'Hi' is a good way to start."

Fifteen minutes later, they pulled up to the blue two-family house on Washington Avenue.

"Ready?"

She gave a hesitant headshake.

Gary squeezed his daughter's hand. "You can do this."

As they approached along the walk, the front door burst open and Edward and Fern flew out to greet them.

"Uncle Gary! Cousin Erin!" the five-year-olds exclaimed in unison, clamoring for the new arrivals' attention.

Erin bent down and the twins rushed into her arms, nearly tackling her. She laughed at their exuberance as she hugged them.

Gary watched, a smile playing about his face. This was precisely the diversion his daughter needed.

By the time they got upstairs and trooped through the living room, Erin was so engrossed in entertaining her young cousins, she scarcely noticed her uncle.

"Hey guys," Uncle Marc greeted them with a broad grin. "I see the welcoming committee's been out in full force."

Erin's face paled; her eyes filled with worry.

He strode over to his niece and gave her a hug. "I'm so glad to see you." He felt the teen's body tense. As he released her, Uncle Marc planted a kiss on her forehead. Taking a step back, he added, "I love that sweater. The color looks great on you!"

***

Twenty minutes later, as her uncle reached into the upper oven to pull out the lasagna, Erin ambled back into the kitchen.

"Uncle Marc?" She spoke his name tentatively. "Can I talk to you for a second?"

"Sure." He shut the oven door with his elbow and set the pan across two trivets on the counter. Then he tossed the potholders aside and gingerly pulled away the foil from the top of the steaming pan. "What's up?"

Erin pulled the check from the pocket of her jeans and fidgeted with it. "Here" – she held it out – "I want you to have this. I'd been saving for a car. But I want you to have it, to pay to get your car fixed. I don't even know if you *can* get it fixed… If not, it can go toward paying you back for your new car. It's not a lot, but it's a start. And I promise I'll give you the rest as soon as I can."

Marc accepted the check with a gracious smile. "Thank you. I appreciate that, Erin. And, yes, I am getting it fixed. One of my classmates works on cars and he said he should be able to get it looking – and running – like new again."

Erin let out a sigh of relief. "Oh, good!" Tears welled in her eyes as she hugged her uncle. "I'm so sorry, Uncle Marc. I really am! And I swear, I've learned my lesson – I'll never drink and drive again."

He patted her back. "I'm glad to hear that. And that, right there, made my day. Thank you."

As a wedding present, Marc's sister Emily had given him and Marie a gift that would reflect their core values and stand as a reminder of those values for years to come. She'd painted eight ladder chairs a different vibrant color, with a single word painted in white across the topmost slat of each one. For each of their two subsequent anniversaries, she'd gifted them four more chairs.

The chairs that normally sat around the dinner table were Love, Encouragement, Gratitude, Patience, Kindness, Understanding, Grace and Comfort. With so many chairs and only eight seats at the table, the extras (Laughter, Joy, Hope, Peace, Faith, Forgiveness, Truth and Humility) lived along a wall in the dining room.

Rather than having a regular place around the dinner table, each night the Lindemeyrs – and any guests at their table – would sit at an appropriately designated seat. It had become a family ritual for

Marc to assign each person a seat, based on a particular attribute or need at that specific meal.

"Where do you want us to sit, Uncle Marc?" Amanda asked, sailing into the kitchen to hug her godfather.

In anticipation of so many guests tonight, Marc had brought out a small folding table to abut the dining-room table. With the pocket doors retracted, the small table jutted into the living room.

Reaching down to caress her cheek, he smiled at his adoring niece and pointed to Laughter.

Giggling, she skipped over to take her seat at the kiddie end of the table.

"Do me next," Michael insisted, jumping up and down.

"Ahh, my little jumping bean," Uncle Marc said, tousling the eager little boy's hair, "you get Patience."

"What about me, Daddy?"

"You sit here – Kindness," he said, stroking his son's cheek tenderly. "And Fern, today you get Truth." The twins scurried over to their respective chairs; Fern hauled hers away from the wall and dragged it over to the far end of the table, near her cousins.

Marc sidled over to Erin, who looked as if she might cry at any moment. Taking her by the hand, he led her over to Forgiveness, situated at the cusp of the adult and kiddie sections.

"Could there possibly be any other one for you, darlin'?" he asked as new tears spilled down her cheeks. He gently wiped them away, then folded the teen in a hug.

Before taking her seat, Erin darted into the bathroom to collect herself.

Marc selected Grace for his mother-in-law; Faith and Gratitude for Gary and Michaela; and Encouragement for Marie. After watching her husband's loving interaction with Erin, Marie chose Understanding for him.

Chapter 17

When everyone was almost finished eating, Erin set down her fork. After dabbing at her mouth with her napkin, she fidgeted with it in her lap for a few moments. Then she looked around the table at the faces of the people she loved best.

"Can I say something?" she asked timidly.

Nine heads turned in her direction.

"Of course," Uncle Marc said.

Auntie Marie rested her fork against her plate. "What is it, sweetheart?"

Erin looked toward the head of the table, where her uncle sat. Then she twisted around to look behind her, indicating the attribute painted on her chair. "I'm fully aware of why I'm sitting in the Forgiveness chair tonight, and I just want to tell Uncle Marc again how sorry I am. I know what I did last week was wrong and I'm really, really sorry, Uncle Marc. I promise I won't ever do it again. I just feel so awful that I lost your trust. And I really need you to forgive me." She wiped away tears from her eyes when his gaze met hers.

"Of course I forgive you, honey," he said, his words as tender as the look in his eyes. "I told you that days ago. You just need to accept that forgiveness... which is why I chose that chair for you tonight."

Erin's eyes brimmed with fresh tears; she smeared them away.

"What did you do?" Mandy asked innocently, her blue eyes wide.

Before Gary could reply that it wasn't something they really needed to discuss right now, Erin spoke up.

"I lied to Uncle Marc so he'd let me borrow his car," she admitted as her little sister's mouth dropped open. "Then, after I was drinking with my friends, I crashed his car and wrecked it. And I got arrested for drunk driving and had to spend a night in jail."

Amanda's eyes widened even further. "Really?"

Erin nodded in response to her little sister's question. "And the worst part is, Uncle Marc had trusted me… and I destroyed that trust." She glanced at her uncle, tears shimmering in her eyes again. "I'm so sorry, Uncle Marc."

Marc met his eldest niece's gaze again and offered her a nod and a sympathetic smile.

The eight-year-old child gaped at her sister. "Wow! That's *really* bad. It's a good thing you're a big girl, Erin. If you were a little girl, I bet Daddy would give you a spankin' for sure," she observed bluntly.

The adults in the room smiled in amusement at the child's innocent comment. Michaela squeezed Gary's hand under the table. Gary, who had just taken a sip of water, nearly spit it out, trying to stifle a guffaw. He managed to swallow it as he glanced first at his plate, then at Micki before his gaze darted away.

Erin's cheeks flushed pink as she recalled leaning across her bed earlier that afternoon while Dad delivered five token swats of her hairbrush across the seat of her jeans. Afterward, he'd hugged her and consoled her as she sobbed, from remorse rather than any actual pain.

Accustomed to sharing all manner of secrets with Mandy, Erin forgot she was in a roomful of family. "He already did," she admitted at a volume intended only for the younger girl.

Amanda's mouth fell open. "He did?" she gasped in astonishment. The girl turned toward her father in alarm. "Daddy! You gave Erin a spankin'?"

Every adult head in the room swiveled toward Gary.

"Are you nuts?" Marie hissed at her brother. Abruptly, she stood and gathered dishes and cutlery, thumping one plate atop another. "What kind of pervert are you?!"

Marc fired a warning look at his wife, then spoke in his customary understated way. "Marie, easy with those plates, huh? Kids, why don't you go play a game in Edward's room. We'll clean up in here and I'll call you back when it's time for cake." While quiet, his tone indicated it wasn't simply a suggestion.

The four youngest children obediently got up from the table and scurried away to the little boy's bedroom, the one furthest from the dining room.

Erin remained behind.

Giving her a stern look, Auntie Marie pointed down the hall. "You too, Erin. Go on."

The teenager looked first at her dad, then at her aunt. "Actually, Auntie Marie, I think I'll stay. You're going to be talking about me, and I believe I have a right to stay and defend myself."

Marie aimed a fiery glare at her brother, as if demanding he back her up.

Gary held up his hands and shook his head. "Don't look at me. She makes an excellent point. I say we let her stay. What do the rest of you guys think?"

Micki shrugged. "I don't have a problem with it." She looked at her mother-in-law. "Mom?"

"She's old enough to make reasonable contributions to the conversation," Diane said. "And I agree, since the discussion's clearly going to be about Erin, she should be included."

Marc nodded. "I agree. Let her stay."

Marie shot a blistering glare at her husband. "Fine."

She assailed her brother the instant Edward's door clicked shut. "I can't believe you'd think that was anything other than a ridiculous option! It's totally unreasonable."

"No, Auntie Marie, it was perfectly reasonable," Erin rebutted calmly. "Mom and Dad gave me the option of choosing my own consequence. They said as long as it seemed reasonable and appropriate, they would go along with it. And—"

"You thought *this* was reasonable and appropriate?" Marie seethed at her brother and sister-in-law.

Erin continued speaking as if she hadn't been interrupted, her voice slightly more forceful. "*And*, Auntie Marie, you may not think so, but I gave my options a lot of thought. In fact, that was practically all I thought about for two days and I figured it was the only thing that felt meaningful enough for what I'd done. For them to ground me would have been a joke, because I was already grounded when I snuck out. And giving Uncle Marc the cash I'd saved to buy my own car, to pay for repairs to *his*, made sense because it's a real way to make up for what I did. But it still didn't seem like quite enough. That's why I told my dad I thought a spanking would be an appropriate – if really oddball – additional consequence."

"You always let your teenage daughter dictate what you do?"

Gary remained unruffled by Marie's baiting. "Not at all. But while I was strongly opposed to the idea at first, her reasoning made sense, so we agreed with her decision."

"It's not like this was something I *wanted*," Erin added. "But I knew it would be effective and make me not want to repeat it… as if I'd actually ever go and do something that stupid again."

"Oh, hush, Erin," Marie snapped. "This isn't about you."

The teen folded her arms. Her chin jutted upward just the slightest bit. "I'm sorry, Auntie Marie, but it *is* about me. This is as 'about me' as it gets. And frankly, how he chooses to deal with my behavior is between Dad and me. I don't know how this involves you in any way. It was something my parents and I agreed on, and that's all there is to it. We don't require your permission – or your approval."

"That was unbelievably rude!" Marie scowled at her niece in a combination of irritation and disbelief. She turned to her brother "I can't believe you're not going to reprimand her for that."

"Why would I? It was well reasoned, nicely stated – and commendably reserved," he replied, a decided edge in his voice. "Plus, she was far more polite than I would have been."

Michaela laid a restraining hand on her husband's arm. "Enough," she murmured when he turned to look at her.

Gary didn't heed her advice. "And anyway, you know as well as I do, Marie, this attitude of yours hasn't got a thing to do with my having disciplined my daughter in a way you don't approve of. This is one-hundred percent, completely and entirely, about James."

Letting out a sharp gasp, Marie shot a horrified look at their mother before staring down her brother again. *"How dare you!"* she sputtered. "How dare you mention that name in this house – and with your mother sitting right there!"

"It's the truth," Gary replied evenly, as Erin turned a perplexed gaze toward him. "That's why you're getting so upset, Marie. That's at the root of your little outburst. You wouldn't care about any of this if James weren't in the picture."

"I don't want that name mentioned in this house ever again," Marie raged, her fists clenched. A vein in her temple throbbed.

Marc laid a calming hand on his wife's arm. *"Querida*, get ahold of yourself," he cautioned in a gentle undertone. "He's three feet away; there's no need to shout."

Marie shook him off, her eyes flashing with rage. "It *is* about her. Quit trying to change the subject, Gary. Erin's practically a grown woman – you can't punish her the same way you would a six-year-old child."

"Oh, for Pete's sake, Marie," Gary exclaimed, "don't go getting your panties in an uproar."

"Hey!" Now Marc's voice held a strong reproving tone as he pointed a cautionary finger at his brother-in-law.

Gary eyed him briefly, his eyes dark with growing fury.

"Leave my wife's panties out of this, huh?"

Scowling, Gary ignored his brother-in-law's exhortation. His eyes narrowed as he continued his tirade toward his sister. "I didn't come here to be lectured about how Micki and I choose to parent our children," he said, his tone carefully controlled. "And especially not by you."

Marie bristled. "What's that supposed to mean?"

He waved away the question. "Never mind. Just drop it."

"No. I want to know what you meant by that 'especially not by you' crack."

"Drop it, Marie. Just forget it."

"I won't forget it, Gary," she persisted. "What did you mean?"

"You may be some high and mighty child psychologist, but I don't have to sit here and defend my parenting decisions to you."

"Psy*chi*atrist," she corrected indelicately.

"Whatever," he spat back. "Potato, potahto."

"Kids," Diane interjected in a cautionary tone, casting a nervous glance at Erin, then eyeing her son and daughter, who glared venomously at one another. "Now is not the time for this conversation."

"I agree." Gary tried not to let his anger flare. He pushed his chair back and stood, gathering more plates to carry out to the kitchen. "I think it's safe to say it's not time for *any* conversation."

Marie folded her arms and glared at her brother. "Well, you know where the door is. Why don't you just get out!"

"Marie!" Marc gaped at his wife. He turned to his brother-in-law and best friend. "No. Don't listen to her, Gar'," he implored. He reached toward the stack of plates Gary had gathered. "Look, let's finish clearing the table and I'll put on a pot of coffee. Then we'll set Erin's cake on fire."

Ordinarily, that comment would have garnered laughter. Today no one so much as smiled.

The air bristled with hostility.

Gary set the stack of dishes on the table with a quiet thump. "It's nearly the twins' bedtime. I don't want to disrupt their schedule."

"One night won't throw them off," Marc interceded.

"Yeah. But you know how unreasonable I can be, Marc – I might just start letting them stay up 'til midnight, swilling beer and watching the late show."

Marc recognized the hurt in his voice. "Gary…"

Ignoring him, Gary continued. "It certainly wouldn't be good for their routine. And heaven forbid I do anything to incur the wrath of your resident child-rearing expert. So I'd better nip this in the bud and get them to bed on time."

One at a time, he plucked the happily gurgling twins from their high chairs and settled them into their carriers. "It's been a lovely time. Thanks ever so much. We simply *must* do it again soon," he droned with sarcastic blandness.

"Gary, don't be stupid," Marie said with an exasperated sigh.

"Oh, so I'm not just a barbarian. Now I'm stupid, too," he shot back. "That's good to know. I'll add it to my resume."

He gave Michaela a kiss. "See you and the rest of the kids at home."

"Daddy." Erin stood. "Wait."

Gary turned, not relishing an argument with her, too.

"I'm going with you."

"Erin, you don't need to…" Auntie Marie began.

"Erin, don't," Uncle Marc said at the same time. Then, ever the appeaser, he turned to his best friend. "Gary, stop it. Stay."

He shook his head. "I appreciate what you're trying to do, Marc, but you're not the one to make that call." His eyes still locked on Marc, Gary pointed at his sister. "That's on her. And if Erin wants to come with me, that's her choice. We've already established she's capable of making decisions."

Marie gave an annoyed sigh. "Look, Gary, if you want to leave, that's fine. But there's no need to uproot any of the rest of them. They're having fun."

He turned to face his sister. "This is *not* about what *I* want, Marie. It comes down to simple math. I need to bring two kids in car seats home with me. And Mandy and Michael are having fun playing with their cousins, so it wouldn't be fair to tear them away. Chris and Josie can gurgle and drool anywhere. You can send cake home for them with Micki."

Without further discussion, Gary picked up Christopher's carrier and handed Josephine's to Erin, who looked like she was trying not to cry.

When they reached the sidewalk, Erin felt the cool night air against her face as she took her dad by the arm. "Daddy! I can't believe you'd let Auntie Marie order you around like that. Don't do this. Go back up there – *please!*"

Gary turned toward his daughter, fuming. It took him several seconds to compose himself enough to speak. "Sweetheart, let me school you on the fine art of getting thrown out of someone's home: Your permission to go back ultimately rests on whoever it was who threw you out. You don't get to make that decision. Once you're out, you're gone. That's it. End of story. If they want you back, it's on them to come after you. Or to reach out after the fact. I'm done here."

"But, Daddy, she's your sister!"

"I know that, baby. And he's my best friend. Which just makes it even more difficult. But" – he shrugged – "it wasn't my call."

"Maybe not, but you didn't have to go and antagonize her."

Gary glanced away, acutely feeling the sting of truth in his daughter's words. "Perhaps not," he acquiesced. "But what's done is done."

Tears filled the teenager's eyes. "This is gonna ruin things between you and Uncle Marc. Don't let Auntie Marie do that to you, Daddy."

"She's not going to ruin anything. Uncle Marc and I are fine. We've been friends longer than you've been alive. We'll be okay."

Erin gave a vehement headshake. "No. You'll see. Things are gonna be different. You may have been friends a long time, but Auntie Marie's his wife. Even if he thinks she's not gonna have any effect on him, she will. It's gonna ruin your friendship, Daddy. And I don't want that to happen. Please go back up there – *please*, Daddy!"

Gary sighed aloud. "Erin, I love that you're paying such close attention in psychology class, but don't be melodramatic, huh? This is a silly little family squabble, that's all. It's not going to mess up my friendship with Uncle Marc."

"You're always telling me how important family is," the teen continued as if he hadn't spoken. She swiped at her tears. Her face crumpled with her growing anguish. "Don't wreck it, Daddy. Go back up there. *Please*."

"Erin, this discussion is over. Get in the car. We're going home."

Without further argument, the girl opened the front passenger's door. Slumping in her seat, she folded her arms and sniffled as tears of silent misery wended their way down her cheeks.

After Dad secured the kids in their seats, he got in and started the car.

Chapter 18

The first several minutes of the ride home were largely silent, except for Erin's occasional sniffles.

"Is Auntie Marie seeing somebody?" the teen asked abruptly.

"What?" Gary blurted, astounded by the question. "Why would you ask that?"

"Is she?"

"Not that I know of. Why?"

"Then who's James? If he's not her *paramour*, why'd she get so flustered and upset when you mentioned him?"

James. Gary exhaled audibly. He hadn't wanted to tell her about him yet. But now he had no choice. "James is our half-brother."

She squinted at him. "Half-brother?"

Man, this isn't going to be an easy talk. Gary was glad he had to focus on the road and wouldn't need to make direct eye contact. "Yeah, we have one parent in common. Like you and Mandy, before Mom adopted you."

Erin nodded. "Okay. So you and this James guy had, what? The same dad?"

"Exactly. Look, remember when I told you, all those years ago, your grandpa didn't exactly used to be the nicest guy?"

"Uh-huh." She sounded worried.

"I kind of understated things because you were so young and you'd just lost him and I didn't want to destroy your memory of him, because I knew he'd been good to you and you'd loved him."

"Does that mean you're going to tell me the truth now?"

For more than the first time tonight, her words stung. Gary glanced at Erin; she was eyeing him with challenge. "Yeah, I am. The truth is, sweetie, he was a louse. And while he and Grandma were married, he was sleeping with other women."

"Wo*men*? Plural?"

"Yeah."

The teen recoiled in revulsion. "Eww! That's disgusting. Why did Grandma even stay with him?"

"Those were different times, honey. Wives didn't just up and leave their husbands in the mid Sixties… even if they were being cheated on – especially when kids were involved. Things were just different then."

"So what happened?"

"He got one of those other women pregnant… and her baby was born just two months after me."

Erin remained silent for a long time, processing the information. "So that means Grandpa was sleeping with that other woman while Grandma was pregnant? What a jerk! Did that woman know he was married?"

Gary nodded. "I'm sure she did. Some years later, she ended up in jail and our dad wasn't about to raise their love child – besides, even if he wanted to, I doubt your grandmother would have stood for that. So James was put into the foster-care system. And his foster parents adopted him a year or so later."

"How did you find out about him? And when?"

"Someone he knew saw the billboard that used to be up on the highway and mentioned how much I looked like him… and he reached out to me at the radio station."

Erin's brow wrinkled in confusion. "But… hasn't that billboard been down for ages?"

"Yeah."

"So why did he wait so long to contact you?"

"Timing doesn't always work out how we want it. But the important thing is, he got in touch with me. We met. And we talked.

And we talked. And we talked some more. We talked an awful lot, actually. We shared photos. There's no denying he's my brother."

"Well, with all that talking, I don't doubt it either," she deadpanned. "Do you get along?"

"Yeah." A smile spread across his face. "Yeah, we do."

Excitement built in her voice. "Can I meet him?"

Gary nodded. "Yeah, I suppose. Someday."

"When?"

"I don't know, Erin. Someday."

Silence settled between them for a long moment while Erin pondered the sudden appearance of a new uncle.

"So, what's Auntie Marie so honked off about?"

"In her eyes, for me to have established a relationship with James is somehow being disloyal to your grandmother."

"That's ridiculous!" Erin blurted.

"Thank you."

"I mean, how is it your fault that your dad was a cheating scumbag – even before you were born?"

"It's not. But for some reason Auntie Marie thinks I'm being deceitful to your grandmother by getting to know him. Consorting with the enemy, so to speak."

She folded her arms resolutely. "That's just stupid. Has anyone bothered to ask Grandma how she feels?"

Dad shook his head. "Not that I'm aware of. Although, yeah, that would make a lot of sense. I guess where emotions are running so high, neither of us considered doing the sensible thing."

Now she gave a confident nod. "I bet she'd be fine with it. Especially after all this time. I mean, it's not your brother's fault Grandpa was cheating on her. Or that he had another child. Auntie Marie's just being silly."

After an awkward silence, Dad continued. "Your aunt's been angry about this all week – and apparently she was looking for some way to vent that anger. I'm really sorry you ended up in her line of fire."

Erin gave another slow, thoughtful nod. "I'm sorry I put a target on your back, Daddy. I had no idea she'd freak out like that over a simple spanking."

"Apparently, there was nothing simple about it," Dad replied with a wry smirk. "What made you bring it up, anyway? This afternoon you were all concerned about my not telling anyone – and then you go and spill the beans at a family dinner. What's with that?"

"I'm not really the one who spilled the beans," Erin reminded him, twisting her hands together. "Mandy did that."

"True, but why'd you even tell her?"

The teen shrugged. "We tell each other everything. It's a sister thing. No secrets between us. I just answered her question. Guess I wasn't thinking." She looked anxiously at her dad. "I'm sorry it got you in trouble with Auntie Marie."

Gary waved off the apology. "Don't worry about it. It'll all blow over soon enough and life'll get back to normal... whatever 'normal' is." He grinned and Erin grinned back at him.

Later that night, Erin looked up from reading in bed when she heard a tap at her door.

"C'mon in."

The door opened. "I saw the light from under the door and figured you were still awake," Dad said.

As she put aside her book, he came in and crouched beside her bed. "I wanted to make sure you're not blaming yourself for what happened tonight with your aunt and me."

Erin gave a halfhearted shrug.

"You are, aren't you?"

When she didn't respond, Gary sighed quietly. He reached out to stroke her hair. "I know it feels to you like it's your fault, but honey, it goes way beyond that. Auntie Marie and I" – he shook his head – "it's complicated. Just, please, trust me when I tell you not to lose any sleep over it."

Erin rolled onto her side to face her dad. "But, Daddy… if it hadn't been for—" she stopped when she saw Dad shaking his head. "What?"

"This wasn't ever your fault, Erin. It's something my sister and I have to work out in our own time." He gave the girl a moment to consider that. "Okay?"

Erin obliged him with a small nod.

As he was about to stand, she put a hand on his arm. "Daddy? Thank you for giving me back my door."

Leaning in, he kissed her on the forehead. "You're welcome, punkin."

She wrinkled her nose. "Are we going to a meeting tomorrow?"

"Not unless you particularly want to."

"So, what time do I have to be up?"

He gave a slight shrug. "I'd suspect at least in time to catch your bus."

Erin wrapped her arms around her dad and hugged him tight. "Thank you, Daddy!"

"You're welcome, sweetheart." He stood, then leaned to kiss her forehead. "Now get some sleep."

***

After everyone left, Marc and Marie cleared away the empty cake plates, coffee mugs and milk glasses. Because Marc had done the cooking, Marie washed the dishes. While she did, Marc got the twins ready for bed.

After he tucked his son into bed and was about to kiss him goodnight, the little boy asked, "Daddy, what's a pervert?"

Marc's shoulders stiffened. His voice sounded strained. "That's not a nice word, Edward, and I don't want to hear you saying it."

"What's it mean?"

"Never mind. It's a terrible, awful word, and you shouldn't be using it."

His eyes widened. "Why did Mommy call Uncle Gary a bad name?"

Marc crouched beside his son's bed. "You know how sometimes you and your sister get mad and call each other names?"

"Like doo-doo head, moose breath and turkey face?"

Suppressing a grin, he nodded. "Yeah, like that."

Edward sat up. "What's that got to do with Mommy calling Uncle Gary a pervert?"

Marc sighed at his son's use of the banned word but didn't make an issue of it. "Nothing. It's got everything to do with Uncle Gary and Mommy being brother and sister. Sometimes even grownup siblings call each other stupid names."

"Do you call Auntie Emily stupid names?"

This was not going as smoothly as he'd hoped. "Go to sleep, Edward."

The child lay down again. "You *do*, don't you?"

Marc grinned as he ruffled the boy's hair. "Sometimes," he admitted. He leaned to kiss him on the forehead again. "I love you. Now go to sleep."

The little boy snuggled under the covers. "I love you, too. Goodnight, Daddy – I mean, doo-doo head."

Marc stood. "Goodnight, moose breath."

Chapter 19

(8:43 a.m., November 2 – Tuesday)

The court clerk announced the next case on the docket. "State versus Erin Sheldon, driving under the influence and underage consumption of alcohol."

As her attorney had instructed her earlier this morning, Erin stood. The toes of her brown loafers perfectly aligning with each other on the marble floor, she stared at the judge seated behind his massive oak bench.

"Prosecution?" the judge droned, sounding bored.

"On the evening of October eighth, after crashing into a bridge abutment, the defendant failed a range of field sobriety tests," the prosecuting attorney said, "and twice blew a point-oh-five on a breathalyzer test – two and a half times the acceptable limit for an underage driver."

Erin's stomach clenched. Her knees trembled. She fought the urge to flee. She knew Dad was seated almost directly behind her in the gallery. Erin remained facing forward. Just past the lower edge of her navy blazer, the tips of her fingers brushed the textured wool of her plaid skirt. The back of her neck tensed. She took a deep breath and willed herself not to pass out.

"How do you plead?" Judge Kenneth Nelson intoned with a frown.

The court stenographer's fingers danced lightly over her steno-type machine, recording the proceedings.

"Guilty," Erin responded in a tiny voice.

"Speak up," he prodded. "I couldn't hear you."

The girl cleared her throat. She took a quarter step forward and forced herself to repeat her plea more audibly.

The judge appraised the teenager standing before him. "How old are you, Miss Sheldon?"

Erin shifted foot to foot. "Seventeen, your honor."

"Are you aware of the legal drinking age in this state?"

She nodded. "Yes, your honor. Twenty-one, sir."

"Yet you drank and drove anyway."

Her head drooped. Her side-parted hair fell forward, obscuring her face. She tucked it back behind her right ear. "Yes, your honor."

"And what have you got to say for yourself?" he asked in a chiding tone.

Now Erin twisted her hands together. "I um… I'm sorry, your honor. I won't do it again – I promise! I've surrendered my driver's license and I've been attending AA meetings with" – she gestured backward – "with my dad. And I've paid to have my uncle's car fixed. I'm really, really sorry!"

"This is a first offense, your honor," her attorney offered, referring to the file folder in his hand. "Miss Sheldon is a straight-A student at Pomperaug High School who's due to graduate in June. She's editor of her high-school newspaper and is involved in youth activities at St. John of the Cross Parish. Her parents, Gary and Michaela Sheldon, are both upstanding members of the community who are invo—"

"Mr. Langton, I don't care who her parents are or what they do." The judge directed a withering glare at the defense attorney. "They're not the ones who drove drunk. I don't care about Miss Sheldon's grades or her activities – and I certainly don't care whether she's homecoming queen. I want to be assured this won't become her pattern of behavior, going forward."

Erin shook her head vehemently. "No, your honor!" she exclaimed, her brown eyes wide and pleading, and glistening with tears. "I swear."

Judge Nelson's stern expression seemed to soften as he eyed the contrite teen before him. "Very well. That'll be a five-hundred-dollar fine, two weeks in jail, suspended, and license revocation until the defendant's twentieth birthday. In addition, Miss Sheldon will attend alcohol-education classes and pay to have ignition-interlock devices installed on any vehicles she drives for a period of one year following license reinstatement." He banged his gavel to signal the end of the proceeding.

***

Gary and James began meeting weekly for lunch at a series of quaint little cafés between Middlebury and Litchfield. While their discussions were largely amiable, James occasionally found – and pushed – his brother's buttons.

(1:35 p.m., December 2 – Thursday)

After they'd finished eating and paid their bill, the two lingered over refills of coffee. James asked whether his brother had made any progress in resolving his spat with Marie.

Gary grew wary. And evasive. His gaze darted away. "Why do you ask?"

James gave a half shrug. "Just wondering. I hate conflict and I'm compelled to fix things. I was always the peacemaker among my siblings, growing up."

"Well stop it," Gary warned, eyeing his brother over the top of his coffee mug. "Don't try to fix this. Don't even go there."

"Don't you think you should get this resolved? I mean, I totally understand sibling misunderstandings, believe me… but this spat of yours has gone on for over a month now, Gary… and that's way too long."

Gary shrugged, trying to come across as nonchalant. He set down his mug. "Six weeks. But that's her problem. I don't care."

"Oh, but you do. You care far more than you're letting on."

"No. I really don't," he insisted, toying with his spoon. Irritation rasped at the back of his throat.

James eyed his half-brother carefully. His words remained calm, measured. "I'm telling you, Gary, you do. And, truth be told, you're doing a lousy job of hiding it. You try to tell yourself this issue with Marie isn't affecting your relationship with Marc, but it is. It *is*."

Gary tightened his grip around the spoon's handle. "You leave Marc out of this."

With a slight headshake, James continued, as if he hadn't heard his brother's warning. "You're guarding every word you say around him. You're not being your most authentic self with your best friend. How is that good for your relationship?"

"I said, leave him out of this," he hissed. "You don't know him; you've barely even met him. And you don't know shit about our relationship. So stop trying to use him as a pawn to guilt me into backing down with Marie."

Now James' headshake became more pronounced. "I'm not trying to guilt you into anything, Gary. But whether you like it or not, Marc's already involved. He's stuck in the middle, between the two of you."

Gary scowled. "Let me guess: clowns to the left of him, jokers to the right?"

"Exactly. Thank you, Stealers Wheel. And that's a really uncomfortable place for him to be." He paused for a moment. "I'm telling you from experience, it's not fair to put him in this spot."

"I don't want to hear this."

"I know you don't want to hear it," James replied gently. "Which is precisely why you've *got* to hear it, Gary. It's for your own good – and the ultimate good of your relationship with Marc. You may not want to, but you're going to hear it."

Gary stood, intending to leave. Then, rankled by the other man's intrusion, he turned to face James again. "Look, just tell me one thing, okay? I need to know who I'm dealing with here: Are you my brother or are you my priest?"

James paused a moment before responding. He looked hurt. "I'm your brother. And it pains me deeply to watch you put such a treasured relationship in jeopardy… particularly when it's over me. Frankly, Gary, besides everything else, that's a whole other bunch of guilt I don't need. I've got enough going on right now."

Question clouded Gary's countenance. "What've you got going on?"

James shrugged. "Just some health stuff."

Eyeing his brother, Gary sat. "What kind of health stuff? Here I thought we were being honest with each other. Now I find out you're holding out on me. What's going on?"

He shook his head. "Nothing. Don't worry about it."

"You don't get to play that card." Gary looked him dead in the eye. "Clearly it's *not* nothing. And I *am* worried about it, James. I want to know what's going on with you."

James looked away for a long time. In his mind he replayed a snippet of conversation from late last year.

"The experimental stem-cell treatments aren't working."

James had suspected as much. "That's disappointing."

"It's beyond disappointing," Dr. DiFusco's voice sounded grim. "It looks like a transplant may be your only remaining option."

He nodded in acknowledgment. "I was afraid of that."

The doctor met his gaze. "Medical advances have made this surgery safer than ever before."

The assurance had done little to comfort James then and it didn't make him feel much better now. When he looked back at his brother, his expression exuded guilt. "I don't want you to get the wrong idea," he prefaced, fidgeting with his spoon.

Gary's left eyebrow arched. He tried to keep his tone light. "About what?"

"About us… about why I reached out to you."

He cocked his head. "Go on."

"That parishioner I mentioned, the one who told me about that billboard on 84…" James began.

"Yeah?"

"He's not just some random parishioner. He's a lead transplant surgeon at Yale-New Haven. And when he saw that billboard, he figured you had to be my brother."

Gary held up a hand. He shook his head. "Hold up. What are you getting at? I'm a little slow on the uptake sometimes, so you may have to spell it out for me. What's that got to do with" – he shrugged – "well… with *anything?*"

"I don't want you to think the only reason I wanted to connect with you is because I need something from you. That's not it at all." James splayed his hands before him on the tabletop and looked down at them. "The truth is, I really *was* curious about you… *and* I have an ulterior motive."

Gary's brow furrowed as his gaze intensified. "Which is?"

"My kidneys are failing. I've been on dialysis twice a week. And stem-cell treatments didn't work. So I need a transplant. And when this parishioner saw that billboard, he figured you could be a potential donor candidate. I'm so sorry I wasn't upfront with you about this from the start."

Gary absorbed his brother's words in silence. When he spoke, James had to strain to hear. "You want me to get tested to see if I'm a match? Is that what you're telling me?"

Looking away, James nodded, ashamed. He braced himself for an onslaught of fury from his brother – and he told himself he couldn't blame Gary for being rightfully irritated.

"You tell me where and when and I'll be there."

He stared at his brother in combined fear and amazement. "Y-you mean you're not mad at me?"

Confusion crossed Gary's face. "Why would you think that?"

James looked down at his hands before him on the table. He gave a guilty shrug. "Because I showed up in your life under false pretenses?"

He shook his head; it felt like he was moving in slow motion. "You've got it all wrong. You showed up in my life. End the sentence there. You showed up." A broad, unstoppable smile spread across Gary's face. "That's what matters. I can't believe you think I'd be mad at you about this – you goofball!"

The other man took a sip of his now-cold coffee.

"Just tell me what you need. If you want me to talk with your transplant surgeon, fine. Give me his number. I'll call him today and find out what I need to do, what my next step should be."

James' hand shook so badly he nearly spilled his coffee. "Are you for real?"

Gary shrugged. "Well, I should probably talk this over with Michaela before I gallop headlong into donating body parts… but, yeah, I'm not opposed to it."

Overwhelmed by his brother's reaction to his confession, James set his mug down, shaking his head in disbelief. "And to think, for weeks, I've agonized over how to approach you about this – all the time terrified you'd tell me to get lost." He swallowed hard, forcing back a sudden swell of emotion. "I had no right to even dream you'd be receptive. Let alone willing."

Chapter 20

(10:22 a.m., December 15 – Wednesday)

Gary's physician's brow creased as he reviewed the file on the desk before him. His mouth formed a thin line. "I don't see anything amiss here, Gary. You're young, you're healthy. You're in terrific shape, physically. No prior family history of kidney disease. The ultrasound indicates both kidneys appear sound. While your blood type isn't an exact match, it's compatible; and a good chunk of the HLA markers are there. You're as close to an ideal match as he's likely to get."

Despite the positive assessment, Gary still didn't feel confident. "But given everything in that file – and everything you know about me – am I a suitable candidate to be a donor?" he pressed.

Dr. Caron closed the file and folded his hands atop it. "I see no reason you wouldn't be an excellent candidate," he assured Gary. "I'm ready to sign off on this."

Gary nodded, trying to absorb the news. He took a deep breath and let it out slowly. "Okay. That's good enough for me."

"I can tell you're anxious about this. Frankly, I'd be concerned if you weren't at least a little apprehensive. It's a big decision, not one everyone would be willing to make. Part of me wants to reassure you, Gary, the risk is minimal – for both of you. At the same time, I feel like I need to remind you that you don't have to do this… not if you don't want to."

"I do want to. And I guess I *am* kind of nervous," he admitted. "I've never had surgery – not even to have my tonsils out."

"Well, don't worry; that won't happen now. Your tonsils are nowhere near your kidneys," the doctor joked, at last getting a weak smile out of his longtime patient.

"And honestly, like I said, I'd be concerned if you weren't anxious," Dr. Caron continued. "Because, really, it's a bigger deal for you than it is for him. They're just going to tuck your kidney in alongside his other internal organs and connect some tubing. There's a whole lot more that has to happen for the donor – and the surgery itself takes about an hour longer."

Noticing his apprehensive expression, Dr. Caron reiterated, "But you're in excellent health, Gary. I wouldn't be willing to sign off on this if you weren't. And all the pre-op compatibility testing has come back fine. It's an excellent match and it should be a relatively smooth procedure."

(7:12 p.m.)
"Will you be joining us for Christmas?"

Marc gave his brother-in-law a sidelong glance as he prepped his first set of commercials and jotted notations on the program log. "Highly doubtful. Not after…" He gestured feebly as his words trailed away.

Gary released an audible breath. "Really? She's still on about that? It's been nearly two months."

The other man shrugged in a gesture of futility. *I don't see you making any move to resolve this, either.* "What do you want me to say, Gar'? She's the most stubborn woman on the planet. And when you throw in chronic PMS" – he rubbed his temples – "let's just say you don't want to be around when she's in one of her moods. It's a *joy*, let me tell you."

Dark silence passed between them.

"Ya know, you could extend an olive branch," Marc suggested a minute or so later.

"You're funny."

"I'm serious, Gar'. Just reach out to her. Apologize."

"For what? Having an opinion? Or for wanting to have a relationship with my brother? Neither of which is any of her business."

Marc gave him a defeated look.

"Besides, I'm not the one who threw *her* out of *my* home. That's entirely on her."

"Well, it's my home, too, and *I'm* asking you to come back."

Gary shook his head. "I appreciate it. But I can't accept that. No offense, Marc, she's got to rescind that ouster."

"Isn't there *anything* I can do to change your mind?"

Another headshake. "Not unless you can persuade her to invite me over for coffee, which I don't see happening anytime soon, either."

***

Christmas Eve at the cottage felt subdued. Michaela and Gary both commented on how quiet, even empty, it seemed without the five-year-old twins' added giggles. And Amanda and Michael expressed their displeasure over not getting to see their cousins.

Even Martha Johnson, spending her first Christmas as a widow, mentioned how much she'd looked forward to – and missed – the usual level of merriment.

Gary wrapped her in a warm hug. "I'm so glad you decided to be here with us tonight." He kissed the elderly woman on the forehead, still keenly feeling the loss of Grandpa's dearest friend and longtime business partner four weeks earlier. "I remember how hard it was, that first Christmas without my grandfather. All I wanted was to be alone. But Sam reminded me it was so much better to surround myself with people who'd loved him, because they were all grieving, too."

As he hugged his surrogate grandmother, Gary's mind reeled through the days that led up to Sam's wake. The sweet old man died the day after Thanksgiving – or, more likely, late Thanksgiving night – in his sleep. He'd suffered from Alzheimer's disease for several years, so his eventual passing had been as much a relief as a heartbreak to those who loved him.

Early that Friday morning Martha had called Gary in tears after discovering her husband's cold body. He'd rushed over to console her and to summon the coroner. He stayed to offer support and comfort while she called her family. Finally, after Gary returned home to the cottage, he called Marie. Thankfully, she was out, so he broke the sad news to his brother-in-law.

At Sam's wake Monday night, Gary and Marie never spoke; they barely acknowledged one another's presence. Tuesday morning, at the funeral Mass, Gary and Marc served as pallbearers, along with Sam and Martha's four grandchildren. Erin sat with Michaela behind the Johnson family. Marie sat several pews back, alone. Mom had offered to stay home to mind the babies.

Martha drew back from Gary. She took a deep breath, inhaling the piney aroma of the fresh-cut balsam in the corner of the living room. "Thank you, dear," she said, doing her best to smile at the young man. Her expression turned somber. "I take it you're still on the outs with your sister?"

His gaze darting away briefly, Gary looked down at her and nodded.

She patted him on the arm. "Don't let it drag out too long, sweetheart. You never know how much time you'll have to make things right again." When she saw him about to offer resistance, she urged, "Do it. Don't let your relationship sour, Gary. Family means too much to do that."

***

Meanwhile, Marc, Marie and the kids spent Christmas Eve at his parents' house. Emily and Clive were there with Felicity and Elliot, so the twins would get to play with one set of cousins. Still, it wasn't the same as their customary raucous, fun-filled holiday celebrations with the Sheldon side of the family.

"It's so good to have you all here for Christmas Eve," Fernanda Lindemeyr crowed, hugging her elder son when his little family arrived. She graciously accepted both an affectionate kiss and the loosely wrapped and still-warm *Bolo Rei* from her daughter-in-law and stooped to kiss her wriggling grandchildren.

"Mommy's mad at Uncle Gary, so we can't go to their house anymore," Isabella announced firmly, fixing her mother with an impertinent glare.

"Oh, hush!" Marie hissed, with an equally stern glower at her precocious daughter.

Fernanda pretended not to have heard her granddaughter's spontaneous pronouncement and instead ushered the children into the kitchen to ply them with treats.

Chapter 21

(January 9, 2000 – Sunday)
Just before the end of Mass, Father Aiden Reilly, pastor at St. Anthony of Padua Parish in Litchfield, asked parishioners at the 10:15 Mass to be seated.

"Our prayers have been answered. Praise God, a suitable living donor has been located, so Father James will be going into the hospital for surgery Monday after next," Father Reilly told the congregation. "I ask for your prayers on his behalf – as well as for his donor – for a successful surgery and a favorable outcome."

When Gary and James met Thursday for their weekly lunch, both seemed subdued.

"Are you nervous?"

"I'd be lying if I said I wasn't," James replied with a shrug. "How 'bout you?"

Gary gave a wary nod. "The same."

"It's gonna be okay."

"I know. I keep telling myself that."

James tilted his head. "But?"

He sighed, anxiety behind his eyes. "But anything can happen."

Now James shrugged. "True. But think about this: Either way, you'll wake up surrounded by people who love you."

At his brother's words, Gary's jaw fell slack. Nodding slowly, he stared at the other man for a moment before speaking. "I never thought of it that way," he admitted.

(January 14 – Friday)

"It's five minutes to seven on Z97-3. I'm Gary Sheldon and it's time for me to pick up my toys, hop in the Garymobile and head on out of here. Marc Lindsay's up next to take you through 'til midnight. I'll leave you with Giorgio Moroder and Philip Oakey, 'Together in Electric Dreams.' I'll see you in your electric dreams, and normally I'd say, 'I'll see you Monday at three,' but not tonight. I'll be embracing my inner brown bear and hibernating for the next several weeks, so Rob Tyler's gonna be takin' good care of you 'til I get back to the ol' air chair. Not exactly sure yet when that'll be, but you be nice to him, huh? – and make it a good night now. Bye."

Immediately, the request lines lit up, with regular listeners wanting to know where he was going and when he'd be back.

Gary stuck around awhile to field calls.

He thanked the callers for their concern, assured them he was fine and graciously accepted all offers of prayers on his behalf.

Eventually the onslaught tapered off and he relinquished phone-answering duties to Marc to take requests for Seventies at Seven.

During a lull in phone calls, Marc and Gary chatted briefly about mundane things. When it got awkwardly silent, Gary gathered up his headphones and other belongings and, weary and a little anxious, bade his brother-in-law goodnight.

(7:43 a.m., January 17 – Monday)

Before dashing out to meet her bus, Erin tapped at the door to her dad's study.

Gary looked up from his computer. "Hi sweetie. All set for school?"

Coming in, she nodded. "Uh-huh. She bent down and gave him a kiss. "Good luck with the surgery. I hope everything goes well today. I'll be praying for you – and Uncle Jim. I also wanted to wish you a happy birthday – I know it's not 'til tomorrow, but I doubt I'll be able to see you."

He smiled as he stood to hug his daughter. "Thank you, sweetheart. I'm sure everything'll be fine. I really appreciate the prayers. And the early birthday wishes." When he drew back, he kissed her on the forehead. "I love you, baby girl. Have a good day."

***

The phone rang as Marie packed lunch for the twins. Marc was overseeing the brushing of the kids' teeth, so Marie answered it.

"Marie, it's Michaela."

"Oh, hi. What's up?"

"I wanted to let you know Gary's having surgery this morning. At Yale-New Haven."

Marie stiffened at the mention of her brother's name. "Why? What's wrong?"

"Nothing's wrong. He's donating a kidney to your brother James."

Irritation prickled in her voice. "That man is *not* my brother. And I'd appreciate it if you'd please stop calling him that."

Michaela sighed audibly. "Look, I just thought you'd want to know. Would you pass that along to Marc, too?"

"Fine. Thanks for calling."

When Marc emerged from the bathroom with a pair of giggly kids, he noticed Marie in what looked like a much grumpier frame of mind than when he'd left her a few minutes earlier. "Who was on the phone?"

"Micki. Something about Gary donating a kidney to that brother of his."

Marc eyed her critically. Aware the twins were in the room and not wanting to alarm them, he kept his voice down, but he couldn't repress the underlying tension in his tone. "Really, Marie? We're back on this again? It's bad enough you're still not speaking to Gary, but I don't know what you've got against James. He's a perfectly nice guy, and I think you'd really like him if you gave him half a chance."

The children eyed their parents in silence. They'd been bickering a lot lately.

Marie stood. Her tone turned as icy as her gaze. "I'm not going to discuss this with you now, Marc. Micki said he's having the surgery this morning at Yale. She figured you'd want to know."

He nodded. "Yeah. I've known for a couple weeks."

She poised her hands on her hips. It was a challenge posture Marc knew well. "So why didn't you say anything?"

Taking charge of the situation the only way she knew how, Fern put an arm around Edward and steered him toward their bedrooms. "C'mon, let's go get our stuff," she whispered.

"Didn't think you'd care," Marc replied, keeping his tone as light as possible. "I had a feeling you'd react about as you did, so I figured I'd spare myself the outburst." He kissed his wife on the forehead and went to help the kids on with their coats and mittens.

Chapter 22

(9:12 a.m. – Yale-New Haven Hospital)

From his wheelchair, James eyed the woman approaching from up the hall. "I'd know that smile anywhere." He reached to take her hand. "You've got to be Diane."

"James." His name was a smile on her lips. Diane bent to kiss the cheek of the stepson she'd just now met. His resemblance to Gary was uncanny. "It's so good to finally meet you," she added graciously. "I wanted you to know you have family here for you during your procedure – other than Gary, that is. I mean, someone who'll be waiting here for you when you wake up."

"I really appreciate that," James said around the lump in his throat. "Thank you."

"Don't let her fool you," Gary piped up. "She's here to see me."

Diane gave him that pursed-mouth look he and Marie used to jokingly refer to as 'Mom lips.' "Will you behave?" she scolded, shaking her head. Then, to James, she added, "I'm here to see *both* of you. Is there anyone here with you?"

James shook his head. "My pastor dropped me off – Father Reilly. He prayed over the two of us and administered the Sacrament of the Sick."

"Is that what that was?" Gary kidded, trying not to let his nervousness show. "I thought they called that Last Rites. It was startin' to freak me out."

"Same thing, different name," James reassured him with a shrug. Then he cracked a grin. "It's like calling a turnip a rutabaga. So in case anything goes sideways, you've got a reasonable shot at not sitting in the un-air conditioned section for eternity."

Diane laughed. The two brothers even seemed to share a sense of humor.

"Thanks. That's so comforting. I think." Despite Gary's joking tone, his laughter sounded forced.

A tall man entered the room. Dressed in blue scrubs with what looked like a gauze shower cap covering his hair, the two loose ends of his untied mask dangled down the front of his chest. "Gary?" He looked from the occupant of one wheelchair to the other.

Gary raised a hand. "That would be me."

"You two could be twins," he marveled, shaking his head. "I'm Cameron DiFusco. They're just about ready for you. Father Jim, they'll get you prepped in about fifteen minutes. I wanted to come out and let you both know what to expect."

Diane gave her son's shoulder an unobtrusive pat. "I'll leave you two now. Good luck. Take good care of my boys, doctor." She leaned and kissed her son, then his brother, on the forehead. As she left, she turned to wave. Both men waved back.

"Thought she'd never leave," Gary intoned when his mother was halfway down the corridor, a smile dancing about his lips.

James socked him in the arm. "Don't be fresh. Be thankful your mom's still around."

"Father Jim!" Dr. DiFusco exclaimed. "I've never seen you hit somebody."

"Then you've obviously never been to one of my parish stewardship meetings," he quipped.

The surgeon gave a hearty laugh. "This is true." Then, regaining his professional demeanor, he checked the IV line in Gary's right arm. "Gary, we're about to take you back now. They're going to give you something through your IV to relax you. And if you haven't already, you'll meet with the anesthesiologist and the rest of your surgical team. I'll be performing your surgery this morning. I want you to know it's normal to feel a little anxious. After all, it's your first transplant surgery. But don't worry; you're in good company. It's my first one, too."

Gary paled, then offered a wan smile as the surgeon broke into a broad grin.

"You had me goin' there, Doc."

James laughed and shook his head. "You had that comin', Gary. You been cracking wise all morning. I'm glad you finally got yours." He clasped his brother's hand and drew him in for an awkward, wheelchair hug. "Seriously, though. Thank you — from the bottom of my failing kidneys. They're further down than my heart" — he flashed a grin — "I don't know what I would've done without you. Godspeed, bro. I love you."

Chapter 23

Susan Conwaye smiled as she opened the front door. "Thank you for coming," she greeted the tall, dignified-looking man on her porch. His dark hair was greying at the temples, but he looked as handsome as ever. Susan swallowed hard around the pasty lump in her throat. Her heart thudded giddily. It felt almost as though he'd never left.

"How could I *not* be here?" Michael's smile was genuine as he greeted her. He leaned to kiss her cheek. "What time is your appointment?"

She stepped aside so he could enter. "Eleven thirty. We've got some time. Do you want to sit down for a bit?"

He shed his black wool topcoat and unwound the scarf from around his neck. He laid them over the back of the couch and sat beside his former wife.

They engaged in stilted small talk until Susan, her fidgety hands restless in her lap, could no longer tolerate sitting still. "Maybe we should go now." She stood. Sliding her arms into her quilted jacket, she shrugged it on.

Michael stood. "You might need a heavier coat than that, Suz. It's brutal out today."

The two remained largely quiet on the ride to the medical center. Occasionally, Susan would let out a tremulous sigh and tighten her quaking grip on her shoulder bag's leather strap. From time to time, Michael glanced in her direction. At seeing her worried expression, he'd furrow his brow and chew his lower lip. Their divorce had been finalized nearly a dozen years earlier, but he still felt affection for Susan. They had a connection. They had a daughter. Even grandchildren, for goodness' sake… although he doubted she'd ever met them. From everything he knew from talking with Gary and Michaela, neither of them had seen her in years. She might not even know she had grandkids.

Once at the medical arts building, Susan paged through magazines from the selection on the table in the waiting room. Periodically, she'd glance at Michael, who looked as serene and steady as he always had. As their eyes met, he reached over and took her hand.

A breath snagged in her throat. His touch felt so comforting! It was no surprise, really. He'd always been the strong one, the one who could meet illness and adversity with grace and tranquility. All those years ago, while Michaela was so sick, Michael had been the one to comfort and care for their daughter. She'd never been able to summon that kind of nurturing spirit.

And now, here he was, offering that same sense of comfort to her – when she had no right to expect that from him.

When a young woman in blue scrubs called her name, Susan put down the magazine she'd been flipping through, gripped the strap of her purse and stood.

"Do you want me to come in with you?"

Susan looked into Michael's serene eyes. That fluttery feeling returned. Unable to speak, she just nodded.

Michael stood and, resting a hand against the small of her back, accompanied his former wife through the door the young medical assistant held open.

"I wish I had better news for you," Dr. Brenna Dandridge told Susan, her tone somber as they sat in the oncologist's private office. "The scans show your cancer's spread and it's metastasized to your liver. As it stands now, we have few options."

Susan gripped Michael's hand and eyed him in fear. "But there *are* options… right?"

The oncologist's expression turned grim. "Nothing that will cure it. The available treatment options might prolong your life by a few months" – she shook her head – "but the overall prognosis isn't good."

Michael cleared his throat. Susan's hand in his felt so cold – and small! He tried to keep his voice from wavering, to appear composed for her benefit. "Is she a candidate for surgery?"

The doctor shook her head. "I'm afraid not. The cancer's so widespread it would be nearly impossible to get it all. The best we can really do at this point is palliative measures."

"What kind of time are we looking at?" he asked, dreading the answer.

Dr. Dandridge remained quiet for a moment. "Probably eight to ten months, tops."

Michael and Susan eyed each other in dismay. Tears filled her eyes.

Seeing her look of shock, Michael felt helpless, and certain this day couldn't get any worse.

Chapter 24

"We're losing him!"

At those words, a rush of activity began around the operating table. Behind the transplant surgeon, the heart monitor flat-lined, its steady tone demanding the immediate attention of everyone in the room.

"Oh, not today, Satan," Dr. DiFusco muttered. "Not today. And *not* this one." He began CPR, deftly applying chest compressions. As he worked, he recalled snippets of his conversation with the two brothers earlier that morning.

He'd found Gary to be a gregarious young man – just a day shy of 36 – with a wife and large family. Five kids, he recalled. And he was donating a kidney to a brother he'd only recently met. *How many guys would do a thing like that?* He couldn't let that act of kindness be this man's last. He couldn't let James awaken in recovery to learn his brother had died during surgery. And he for sure couldn't bear to tell the two women in the waiting area their husband and son wouldn't be coming home.

The rest of the surgical team stood by, awaiting instructions. One readied the defibrillator, to administer a shock to Gary's heart, if necessary.

After several rounds of chest compressions, they got a faint, unsteady pulse. When the surgeon signaled to her, she handed him the paddles.

"Charging," she declared.

"Clear!"

The team backed away as the surgeon positioned the paddles and discharged a shock.

Gary's body flopped with the jolt. The heart monitor blipped momentarily, as his heartrate accelerated into tachycardia. The lead surgeon withdrew the paddles.

"Charging," the surgical assistant called out again.

The others looked on in silence.

"Clear," Dr. DiFusco barked, positioning the paddles a second time.

Again Gary's body jerked at the shock, and his heart stopped again.

The surgeon tossed aside the paddles and resumed chest compressions. "Come on," he urged. "Beat, dammit!"

Chapter 25

As Michael navigated the familiar route to his former wife's house, he reflected on all they'd been through these past thirty years – the good and the bad. He knew no words that could offer comfort to her now.

Susan sat, equally silent. *Eight to ten months.* The thought of dying – of dying alone – filled her with ceaseless dread. Nothing Michael might say now could give her any measure of comfort.

Finally, he cast a glance toward her, weighing his words. "You shouldn't be alone now. I think I should move back in."

She stared at him, scarcely believing she'd heard correctly. *Is he reading my thoughts?* "You what?"

"I want to move back in – to take care of you."

Susan shook her head. "You don't have to do that."

"I know I don't have to. I want to, Susan."

She stared out the window as house after house went by. "What, because no one should die alone?" Something prickled in her voice. Was it sarcasm? Hurt? Fear? It was all of them, she realized.

"No." He faltered. "I mean, that's not what I meant. But no, no one *should* die alone."

Susan sighed, twisting her hands in her lap. "I don't want your pity, Mike."

"I'm not offering it. I just think it'd be better for you to have me around. I don't want you to go through this alone. And I" – he hesitated – "I still love you, Suz. I want to come back."

She said nothing as houses turned to blocks turned to miles.

"Did you hear what I said?"

"I heard you," she replied woodenly. "Do you really think that's wise?"

No response.

Another mile slipped past, during which neither of them spoke.

At last, Michael pulled to a stop outside the white colonial where they'd been so happy all those years ago. He recalled the day they'd first walked through it together – he a young attorney, she five months pregnant. Years of memories here sped through his mind… the day they closed – they'd celebrated with lunch at Friendly's because it was all they could afford at the time… painting the nursery on weekends and setting up the furniture in there… bringing their baby girl home from the hospital… unending sleepless nights… laughter-filled holiday and birthday celebrations… presents galore for Kayla… the swing set they put up in the backyard for their giggling toddler… his first promotion… her excitement at getting her real-estate license – then selling her first home… more birthdays and holidays… then six-year-old Michaela's leukemia diagnosis… three years of illness and treatments… long hours at the office for both of them to pay the medical bills… and the beginning of the end. Liquor bottles hidden in the kitchen cabinets, stuffed behind chair cushions in the bedroom, under the living-room couch. The screaming… the fights… and finally the separation and divorce.

So much failure. So much regret. But after all of it, he still loved her.

Michael parked the car but left it running so the heat would stay on. For what seemed like an hour, no one spoke.

At last Michael turned to face his ex. "Marry me, Susan."

"What?" The word was an explosion from her lips. "Are you crazy?"

He shook his head. "Not at all. Listen to me. It makes sense. I want to be there to care for you. Let's do this, Susan. While there's still time."

"Are you serious?"

"I've never been more serious. And anyway, where's the harm? Let's make it work."

"Make it work? For what? Six months? Ten, tops? What good will that do?"

"Then it'd be ten more months we'll have together."

"Don't be ridiculous."

"What's ridiculous about it? I never stopped loving you, Susan, and I know you still love me."

"So you'll marry me all over again to – what? – lose me in less than a year? Is that what you want? Aren't you taking this whole "til death do us part' business to an extreme?"

"If it means we get to spend the rest of our lives together, yes."

Chapter 26

From a corner of the room, Gary silently observed the frenzied activity unfolding beneath the blinding overhead lights. Moving closer, he craned his neck and saw the surgeon performing chest compressions as the rest of the surgical team looked on. He watched as the surgical assistant grabbed the defibrillator paddles and handed them to Dr. DiFusco. The back of his neck prickled as the lead surgeon positioned the paddles and delivered the shock to his chest. Gary felt current surge through him… and then nothing. He watched in impassive silence as the frantic bustle around his lifeless body intensified. He stepped still closer, curious. Another sense of electrical buildup and then discharge. Another shock to his body. Another searing pain jolted through his chest… and nothing.

Then it all faded to black.

Waves crashed.

Gary felt the salt spray on his face. Looking around, he realized he was standing at the end of the jetty. The operating room was gone. All the machines, instruments and monitors – all gone. The entire surgical staff, also gone. And he stood alone on the seawall.

No. Not alone.

At first he felt more than saw the other presence. He inhaled the sweet aroma of cherry pipe tobacco mingled with salt air. He hadn't smelled that particular combination in nearly fifteen years. Along with realization of who it was came a bubbling excitement at their reunion.

"Grandpa!" Gary exclaimed, turning to greet the old man. "It's really you!" Tears blurred his vision as he wrapped his arms around his beloved grandfather, as sturdy and solid – and alive! – as ever.

Edward Sheldon enfolded his eldest grandson in a mighty hug. "Gary! It's so good to see you, my boy," his voice boomed as he thumped the younger man heartily on the back.

"You're looking well," the old man said as they broke their embrace at last. "Not even the slightest bit dead."

Gary's breath caught in his throat at his granddad's teasing words. "Am I?" His question came out in a fearful squeak.

"Of course you are. How else could you be here?"

Dread rose in his chest as he looked around. "I thought it was a dream."

The old man shook his head.

Fear snagged in Gary's throat. "So this is it? I'm done?"

Grandpa patted him on the shoulder. "It's not as simple as all that. And it's not necessarily over, either. Not yet. You can still decide to go back… if you want. After all, Gary, you've got so much left to do down there." He wagged a chiding finger at his grandson. "Including fixing things with your sister."

Gary shook his head. "I don't want to think about her. Not now. Not here."

Grandpa frowned. "Still that stubborn little boy, I see. When are you going to learn, Gary?"

He looked affronted. "Learn what? What's that supposed to mean?"

"It means the two of you are acting like a couple of pouty kids. And what kind of example is that setting for your own children?"

"I never thought about that," Gary admitted. He glanced down, avoiding Grandpa's piercing blue gaze.

"You need to make it stop. Your sister's marriage is headed for trouble, Gary. *Deep* trouble. Pray hard. Marc is going to need your support more than he's letting on."

"Over this?"

Grandpa nodded. "It's caused a huge divide between them; and while I would never blame you for their breakup, just know this: Despite their underlying issues, the rift between you two over James will be the primary catalyst in the breakdown of that marriage."

Suddenly cold and empty inside, Gary considered this tidbit of information as they walked along the shoreline. Grandpa puffed at his pipe, and sweet cherry tobacco smoke swirled around to envelop them.

"So I need to go back…" It was part statement, part question.

The old man gave a noncommittal nod. "Seems that way."

"But if I want, I can stay?"

"You could…" Grandpa waved a hand in front of him and an image shimmered into view before Gary, as if on a movie screen. "But do you really want to leave your family like this?"

The scene that unfolded wrenched Gary's heart. Doubled forward in grief, Michaela sobbed, mourning over his lifeless body on a gurney in the stark, sterile environment of the operating room. One by one he was shown the faces of his three eldest children, their eyes red and streaming with tears, at his wake. Amanda and Michael looked tiny and vulnerable in oversized upholstered chairs in the funeral home. Their eyes looked vacant, bewildered and sad. Meanwhile Erin, her face contorted in anguish, tried her best to maintain a brave façade for Mom and her younger siblings.

Now the scene before him shifted and he saw his sister and brother-in-law, their faces filled with resentment and wrath, arguing bitterly. As they turned away from one another, Gary sensed simultaneously the internal feelings each was experiencing. A bolt of white-hot pain shot through his heart. He flinched.

"Make it stop," he whispered. "Please."

Grandpa swished his hand again and the images dissipated like smoke. The old man's voice filtered back to him. "You could stay here, Gary, but is that what you're ready to leave behind?" He rested a hand on his grandson's shoulder. "You've got more to do, my boy. Way more."

"What more can I do?"

"Ah, what, indeed? For starters, you can fix your relationship with your sister… and then you can be instrumental in her and Marc healing their relationship."

The statement took Gary aback. "I didn't realize things had gone bad between them. He never said anything…"

"There's a lot he doesn't say, and a lot you didn't know. But they have. And in the coming months, Marc is going to need your prayers and your support in a big way — ways you can't even imagine. You need to be there for him. And you can't, Gary, if you don't go back."

"What about Marie? That surprises me. I should think you'd say I need to be there for my sister."

Edward Sheldon shook his head slowly. "Marie's got her own issues; I'm not disputing that. But she's stronger than you realize. It's Marc you need to worry about. Take care of him, kid. He's a good man, and he needs you."

Gary gave a pensive nod, taking this all in. "I guess that's reason enough for me to go back, huh?"

Grandpa nodded. "That's only one part of it. You want to watch your babies grow up, don't you?"

Tears stung at Gary's eyes. "Of course." He tried to envision his year-old twins at age five, at ten, at their high-school graduation. Another jolt of pain stabbed through his heart. He winced. "Of course," he repeated, his voice choked with emotion. "What kind of dad would I be if I didn't?"

"Good," Grandpa replied. His eyes sparkled. "I'm also going to give you a challenge to help you flex and strengthen your generosity muscle. Are you up for it?"

Gary looked at him, his gaze serious. "Absolutely," he replied without hesitation.

"I want you to give away a ton of money."

He nodded. "Done."

Grandpa raised a cautionary finger. "But you haven't heard the details yet."

"Doesn't matter," he asserted.

Grandpa's left eyebrow arched.

Now Gary looked worried. "Okay… what are they?"

"You're going to find some way to give away a thousand dollars a week."

After a pause, Gary gave another, more definitive, nod. "I can do that."

"For twenty years," Grandpa added.

Gary looked astonished. "That's a long time," he mused. "Different people each week?"

Grandpa shrugged. "That's up to you. It sounds like a lot, but it only comes out to just over a million dollars." He gave his grandson a knowing look. "Besides, you've invested your inheritance well over the years… and I assure you, you'll not even miss it. Will you do it?"

"Will I have twenty years?"

The old man gave him a meaningful look. "I can't make any promises."

Chapter 27

When Michael returned home after dropping Susan off, he knew he'd have to call Kayla. This was not a call he looked forward to making.

He listened to his messages as he shook snow from his coat and hung it on the wooden rack by the front door. Then he punched in Michaela's number.

Getting no answer at the house, he tried her cell phone. As it rang, he remembered she was probably at the hospital. Gary was having surgery today.

She answered on the third ring. Her "Hello?" sounded shaky, like she'd been crying.

"Hi Kayla, it's Dad," he greeted her. "Are you okay? How's Gary doing?"

Michaela's hand shook as she gripped the cell phone. A sob escaped her lips. "Gary died on the operating table," she blurted, numb. Part of her needed to speak the words aloud, needed to make it real.

Michael gasped. The phone nearly fell from his hand. "Oh my goodness! Sweetheart! Where are you? Do you need me to come—"

"N-no. I'm okay, Daddy. I – I mean, he's okay. He— they were able to bring him back. But he… he died on the table."

Michael knew with all his daughter was dealing with right now his news would have to wait.

Chapter 28

A squeezing sensation around his right arm tugged Gary into consciousness. His eyelids fluttered open and he looked around. From what he could tell, he seemed to be in a small room with glass walls on two sides and floor-to-ceiling curtains that could be drawn around the bed. At the moment, though, they were pushed against the back wall. He felt the familiar tightening of an inflating blood-pressure cuff. Behind him, machines whirred on both sides.

"Oh, good. You're awake."

That voice! It's so familiar. Gary cast his gaze in the direction it had originated from. He forced himself to pay attention to its warm, soothing sound.

"How do you feel?"

He rubbed at the left side of his chest. It felt like someone had dropped a piano on him. "Hurting," he admitted, confused. "Why does my chest hurt?"

The nurse drew closer.

Now he could make out her features. It was Amanda Petersen, the ICU nurse who'd cared for Michaela all those years ago. *Why would an ICU nurse be in the recovery area?* "Where am I?" he asked, befuddled, before she could answer his previous question.

"You're in ICU, Mr. Sheldon," Nurse Petersen confirmed as the blood-pressure monitor beeped and released the pressure on his arm. "There were complications during your surgery and…" There was no delicate way to say this. "You died on the table. The team had to use some pretty aggressive measures to bring you back —

that's why your chest hurts. Also, they had to use the defibrillator, so it'll feel like it's burning for a while."

He felt himself nodding. "I remember that," he said, the words coming out slower than he thought he'd spoken them. "I was standing behind them for a few minutes. I saw them working on someone… and I heard them talking. I kept hearing them say, 'We're losing him,' and it made me wonder who they meant. Then I leaned in closer and realized they were talking about me.

"I watched them work and it didn't seem like what they were doing was helping any. Then all of a sudden I felt like I'd been sucked through a tunnel… and I was at the beach."

The nurse didn't seem surprised by that statement.

Gary rubbed a hand over his face to clear the mental cobwebs. "How long was I…?" He paused. "Dead?"

"Two, three minutes."

A memory shimmered into view. He shook his head. "It seemed like an awful lot longer than that," he murmured.

Nurse Petersen took hold of his wrist and checked his pulse. When she was finished, she squeezed his hand and gave him a tender smile. "It often does. I'm glad you came back to us. Was it beautiful?"

Gary nodded numbly. "I can't even describe it. The colors, the sights – even the smells – so vivid! It almost made my eyes hurt. But yeah, it was beautiful." Then he smiled. "My grandfather was there."

She rested a hand on his shoulder. Her placid smile was as beatific as he remembered from years ago. "Well, of course he was."

"How did the surgery go? Were they at least able to do the transplant?"

The nurse's smile broadened. "It went fine," she reassured him, nodding. "And even having to monitor you after your momentary demise, you should be good to go home in three to five days. Your brother came though the transplant with flying colors. He'll probably be released in four to seven days. He's in the next room."

Gary felt himself perk up at that news. "Can I see him?"

She shook her head. "Not 'til we're certain you're out of the woods. Perhaps tomorrow. We just want to be sure you're not experiencing any unusual heart rhythms or adverse effects from their efforts to revive you."

"Is Michaela here?"

"She's in the waiting area. I'll let her know you're awake and asking for her."

"Wait."

Amanda turned back toward him. Her brown eyes reflected her deep concern. "What is it?"

"This is Yale. What are you doing here? You were at Saint Raphe's."

The Hospital of St. Raphael was the Catholic hospital in New Haven, where Gary and Michaela's kids had been born – and where he'd first encountered this extraordinary nurse. While Micki lay in a coma, and their three-months-premature infant daughter was hooked to all sorts of machines and monitors in a NICU Isolette, ICU nurse Amanda Petersen had been there to comfort and reassure Gary – even staying long past the end of her shift to pray with him in the hospital's chapel.

The nurse gave a quiet sigh. "They had cutbacks. Fortunately, a position opened up here and some friends on staff recommended me. I got hired a few weeks back. Just before Christmas." Amanda smiled again. "There's no such thing as coincidence, Mr. Sheldon. You know that."

He reached for her hand. "I'm glad you're here. When they told me the transplant had to be performed here or up at Hartford Hospital, I knew it made sense, but part of me hoped I could've had the surgery at Saint Raphe's." Suddenly exhausted, Gary let his hand fall away from hers. At the same time, his head dropped back against his pillow. He offered a weary smile. "It's such a relief to see you."

The nurse rested a hand on his shoulder. "It's good to see you, too, Mr. Sheldon," she told him with a warm smile. "Now you get some rest so you'll feel well enough to visit with your brother tomorrow. I'll go find Michaela."

***

Nurse Petersen went out to the waiting room to let Michaela know her husband seemed to be doing well, but he was sleeping at the moment.

"You might want to go get some coffee or a snack from the cafeteria and come back to see him in an hour or so. He might be up for a short visit then."

Chapter 29

(January 18 – Tuesday)

Just before 2, Gary was moved to a semi-private room. Having no roommate, he took advantage of the quiet to get in a short nap before Michaela arrived. While he appreciated her coming to see him, he didn't know how to tell her he didn't want visitors. All he really wanted was sleep… and another shot of morphine or whatever it was they had him on to take away his pain at the incision site.

Later that afternoon, he was deemed well enough to venture downstairs for a brief visit with James. A hospital volunteer wheeled Gary to the entrance of the ICU.

"Remember, when you're ready to leave, go back to the nurses station and let them know you need transport back to your room," the volunteer told him, "and someone'll come to get you."

Gary thanked the man and maneuvered his wheelchair over to the nurses station.

"Hey." James brightened as his brother wheeled into the curtained room. "It's so good to see you!"

"You're only saying that 'cause I look exactly like you," Gary kidded as he scooted over to his brother's bedside. "How're you feeling?"

James nodded and reached for Gary's hand. "The doctors tell me I'm doing well. The new kidney's already starting to work. I can't thank you enough."

"Consider it an early birthday present." He grinned. "Sorry I didn't get a chance to wrap it."

"Speaking of birthdays, isn't today yours?"

Gary had to stop and think for a moment. "Yeah, it is."

James squeezed his brother's hand. "Happy birthday, bro. I hope you're not mad I didn't get you anything."

"You kidding? You got me this all-expenses-paid weeklong get-away at the sumptuous Yale-New Haven Hospital. Five-star service, non-skid socks, all the Jell-O I can stomach and not a moment's sleep… except those few minutes when I flat-lined on the operating table."

"Don't even joke about that," his brother chided.

Gary shook his head. "I'm not joking."

James paled.

Marc made it a point to stop by to visit with Gary on his way either to or from class. He knew better than to stay long – usually just popping in to say hello and ask if he needed anything.

Gary, who missed their daily interactions at work, looked forward to these visits. He wished Marc would stay longer, but figured the other man didn't want to unnecessarily tire him.

Wednesday, Marc brought him a child's puzzle book and two dozen fun-size Mounds bars hot-glued to twigs and arranged with greenery in a vase.

"It was kind of a group effort," he explained as his best friend laughed, then winced at the pain along his incision site. "I asked the kids what they thought Uncle Gary needed to help him get better, and Edward insisted on a book of Sesame Street word-search puzzles. I told them I wanted to give you medicinal chocolate, so Fern said we should make it a candy bouquet. With – of course – ferns all around it." He placed the vase on the bedside table.

"Thank you! I love it!" He didn't ask whether Marc had sought Marie's input. Probably not, he decided, because the curious array didn't include any giant hissing cockroaches.

"Stay awhile?"

Marc glanced at his watch. "Okay, but only a few minutes. I've got class at eleven." He sank into a chair beside Gary's bed. He couldn't think of anything he wanted to say.

"How's school going?"

"Unless I flunk out this semester, I should graduate in May."

Gary chuckled. "Now, there's a confident attitude. Why would you think you'd flunk out?"

"Who knows?" he replied with a shrug. "Anything can happen."

Against his better judgment, he asked, "How are Marie and the kids?"

He sensed Marc's smile was forced. "Kids're great. Growing like weeds. Of course, they miss their Uncle Gary. I'll tell them you were asking about them. That'll thrill them to no end."

"What about Marie?" he asked cautiously.

Marc checked his watch again. "Would you look at the time," he said unsubtly, standing. "I gotta run, Gar'. Don't wanna be late for class and end up flunking out."

"Marc."

He turned back to Gary. Shook his head. Said nothing. But the depth of the sadness in his eyes revealed everything he wasn't saying.

"Come back again, huh? And stick around awhile. We haven't really talked in a long time." He paused, then met and held Marc's gaze. "We need to talk, Marc."

He gave a dismissive headshake. "I gotta go. Feel better, huh? Don't eat all that candy at once."

"Come back tomorrow?" he pressed.

Marc shrugged. "No promises."

Gary nodded in acknowledgment. "None expected."

Marc didn't return the next day. Or the day after.

Gary wondered how he could reach out to Marc when he was being so evasive. It wasn't like he could just show up at his doorstep and make him talk. But Grandpa's words echoed in his heart: "Take care of him, kid. He's a good man, and he needs you."

(January 22 – Saturday)
"I hear you're getting sprung today," James said.

Gary's smile gave the other man the only response he needed. "That's what they've said. I can't wait to get home and just get a good night's sleep. This is the worst hotel I've ever stayed in."

James' smile mirrored his brother's. "I know what you mean. The other night they actually woke me up to say they were giving me something to help me sleep."

Gary's discharge paperwork included strict orders not to return to work for at least four weeks – possibly even twice that… or more.

When he asked what would determine whether his return to work date would be eight weeks or ten, the nurse managing Gary's release told him it depended on how his healing progressed and whether he experienced any additional issues or setbacks with his heart.

James was set to be released two days later. Because he would need peace and quiet – and a steady stream of well-meaning, casserole-toting parishioners concerned for his healing process was not high on his doctor's list of people he needed to see – Dr. DiFusco strongly advised Father James to secure arrangements for his first eight to twelve weeks of recuperation somewhere other than the rectory. Preferably something without stairs.

"You'll stay with me," Diane Sheldon declared in her no-nonsense voice when she learned of his predicament.

"I'm sorry… what?" James stared at her in astonishment. This woman he'd barely just met – and who had every reason to despise him – insisted upon opening her home to him in his time of need. "You heard Dr. DiFusco. It's going to be as much as three months. You're gonna get sick of me real quick. Are you sure about this?"

"Of course I'm sure. That's what family does," she replied, her tone firm but kind. "And no, I don't mean the getting sick of you part" – now she flashed a grin – "Besides, you can't be left alone to fend for yourself all that time."

"I – I can't… I don't have adequate words to thank you," he stammered, overwhelmed by her generous offer.

(10:47 a.m., January 24 – Monday)

Diane Sheldon drove up to the front entrance of the hospital. She helped her new houseguest out of the wheelchair and into her car.

"Thank you so much," James told her. "I can't tell you how much I appreciate your doing this for me."

She smiled. "I told you, James. We're family. And family takes care of each other. Now get in the car; we're goin' for a ride."

When she pulled into her driveway, Diane led James slowly up the walk toward her front porch.

When he stopped partway, she patted his arm. "Do you need to stop for a moment to catch your breath?"

James shook his head. "I'm not that out of shape – at least I hope not. I just…" He gazed upward at the sprawling slate-blue colonial with white trim and black shutters. "What a beautiful house," he murmured in admiration, wondering what the inside must look like.

"Thank you," she replied, holding on to his arm at the elbow. "It'll be nice to have someone here with me for a while."

"You live here alone?"

Diane gave a diffident shrug. "Seems a waste, doesn't it, such a big home, for just me? But I purposely bought a large house so the grandkids could come and stay." She gave him a warm smile and patted his arm again. "Or a guest, of course."

At the foot of the stairs, she stood behind him as he took hold of the railing and painfully eased himself up the four steps to the covered porch.

Once he reached the top, James stopped for a moment to catch his breath. "I can't believe how much effort it takes just to climb four measly stairs."

"You've just had major surgery, James. It'll take time to recover. And once you're inside, you won't have to worry about stairs," Diane reassured him as she unlocked the house. "Your room's on the first floor and just about everything you could need is within about twenty feet."

She held the storm door open as James stepped into the foyer.

He looked around the entryway in amazement. "This is glorious," he exclaimed softly as he admired the gleaming hardwood floors and the airy feel of the open living and dining areas with their nine-foot ceilings.

"Let me show you to your room," she said, shutting the ornate wooden entry door after he stepped inside.

Diane led James to the first room on the right. The door stood open and the bed, already made up, looked soft and inviting. A coverlet in shades of blue and green matched both the floor-length drapes and the braided rug by the bed. An upholstered chair in one corner of the room stood by a reading lamp, and the dresser sported an array of framed family photographs.

"I hope you'll be comfortable in here." Then she added, "If not, there's always the garage."

James burst into hearty laughter but instantly grimaced and hunched forward.

"Sorry," Diane said, a playful grin lighting her face. "I forgot it would hurt so much to laugh right about now. I promise I won't say anything else funny 'til you get your stitches out."

He fixed her with a grave look. "I find that hard to believe. And besides, I wouldn't ever want you to. Laughter's a great healer – plus it'll help firm up these saggy abs." He gingerly patted his bandaged yet still-lean middle.

"Oh, you are *such* a liar," Diane scolded. "If you're flabby, I'm Mother Teresa."

James grinned. "Well then, you look pretty good for an octogenarian nun who's been dead more than two years."

Diane rewarded him with a broad smile, then patted him affectionately on the arm. "We are quite a pair, my boy, aren't we?"

Chapter 30

At home, Micki and Erin wouldn't let Gary do anything for himself. For his first three days back, he was only allowed to nap and watch TV – and get up, with assistance, just to use the bathroom. They brought him all his meals – along with plenty of water, to ensure his remaining kidney continued functioning at optimal levels.

(January 29 – Saturday)

Just before 10:30, a small truck pulled up in front of 45 Mapleside Drive in Middlebury. Three men in moving-company uniforms made short work of unloading the furniture and boxes they'd loaded into the truck at Michael's apartment in Waterbury forty minutes earlier.

When they were finished, Michael generously tipped the trio. As soon as they departed, he and Susan sat on the couch in the living room with mugs of coffee.

"I guess that makes it official," Michael said with a smile. "We're living in sin." He winked at his former wife, who responded with a tired smile.

"I guess we are. What'll we tell the kids?" she joked.

"I say we let 'em find out on their own," he replied with a shrug. He slipped an arm around Susan and kissed her on the temple.

"I see you had them bring your bedroom furniture up to Kayla's old room. Does that mean we're maintaining separate bedrooms?"

"That's entirely up to you, Suz. Whatever you want is fine with me."

Susan settled comfortably into his arms. "I've always wanted a guest room," she mused. "And that queen bed feels pretty empty when I'm the only one sleeping there."

Late that night, a searing pain slicing across his lower abdomen jolted Gary from a heavy, drugged sleep. Disoriented, he cast about in the darkened room to assess his surroundings. As his eyes adjusted, he could make out the bookcase against the far wall, and the floor lamp over by the couch.

Gary shifted position, tugging at the blanket Micki had laid over him when he dozed off earlier. A slight heaviness against his lower legs disturbed him momentarily – until the weight stood, stretched and walked up his left leg, purring.

Attila.

Grandpa had given him the tabby kitten fifteen years earlier, as part of Gary's college graduation gift.

The cat gingerly navigated Gary's midsection, avoiding the spot where his kidney had been, and settled on his chest. Tucking his paws in beneath himself, Atilla continued purring. The familiar rumble soothed Gary, oddly alleviating his pain.

The rest of the house seemed quiet, and his pain meds had worn off some time ago, so it must be around 10, Gary reasoned. He also needed to pee. That would take some doing, getting up.

In slow, careful movements, he eased first one leg then the other off the hassock in front of his wingback chair. Once both feet were flat on the floor, he petted the cat still tenuously perched on his chest.

"Hey, buddy," he murmured. "Sorry, but you're gonna need to move."

Stretching, Attila got to his feet, then stepped onto Gary's shoulder and up to the back of the chair.

"Good boy."

Steeling himself for the anticipated surge of pain, he braced his hands against the chair's arms and slowly hoisted himself to his feet.

That wasn't so bad. Part of the blanket slid onto the hassock; the rest puddled around his feet.

Wincing as he reached down to pick up the fallen blanket, Gary gathered it into a heap on the chair. Inching forward, he made his way toward the bathroom. Apparently, his remaining kidney was working just fine.

When he returned to the living room, Michaela – who'd been snoozing on the couch – had his next dose of pain meds and a glass of cranberry juice ready for him.

"How are you feeling?"

He shrugged. "Okay, I guess. That was a good idea you had, sleeping in the chair. I don't think I'd be able to get in and out of bed yet."

"Why didn't you wake me up when you needed to use the bathroom? I would've helped you."

"I forgot you were there," he admitted sheepishly.

"I'm sorry. I should have stayed awake."

Gary smoothed her hair. "And what? Watch me sleep? No. You need your rest. I'm fine, honey. I just took it one little step at a time and stopped when I needed to."

"Are you in pain?"

"Some. I'll feel better once the meds kick in." He hobbled over to his chair and Michaela helped lower him into it. She got his feet propped up on the hassock and arranged the blanket over him again.

"Thank you," he said, pain evident in his voice. "What time is it?"

"A little after two." She leaned to kiss his forehead. "Get some sleep."

He squeezed her hand. "You get some sleep, too. I love you."

In his second week home, Gary was allowed to navigate the stairs once a day, but was still confined to the house. To Michaela's relief, a fierce snowstorm made it impossible for her stubborn husband to venture beyond the covered front porch. He couldn't risk slipping and falling.

By his second weekend, Gary was permitted to go for short rides in the car. That meant he could visit the public library and attend Mass, but he still wasn't allowed to sit at his computer or resume teaching his weekly CCD class at church. Through his third full week of recuperation, he wasn't allowed to drive.

His CCD students mailed him get-well cards. Reading their sweet, caring sentiments and well wishes in sloping first-grade printing made Gary smile. The parish staff and his fellow teachers sent cards, too – in the same big envelope with the kids' cards.

At the start of his fourth week, his doctors said Gary could drive short distances, but only within Southbury, which precluded his going in to the office.

By the start of his fifth week, Gary was in full jitter mode from not being allowed to roam at will. Someone always seemed to be watching him, whether it was Micki, Erin or one of the younger kids ready to rat him out for lifting a fireplace log or taking a gallon of milk out of the refrigerator.

Chapter 31

(2:15 p.m., February 7 – Monday)

"Have you given it any more thought?" Michael asked as he drove Susan to her followup medical appointment.

"You mean getting married? Not really."

"I wish you would."

Susan sighed. "I'll think about it," she promised.

"Don't think too long," Michael cautioned.

(5:47 p.m., February 14 – Monday)

"This is silly," Susan insisted as Michael helped her on with her coat, "two adults carrying on like a couple of teenagers."

"I don't think it's silly at all," he replied, handing Susan her gloves. He pressed a tender kiss against her temple. "Going out together on Valentine's Day is a time-honored tradition."

She made a face. "You're a hopeless romantic."

"Is that so bad?"

Susan shook her head. "I suppose not. But you sound like Gary."

He shrugged, beaming at her comparison of him to their son-in-law. "Again, is that so bad?"

Now she smiled. "Of course not."

Over dinner, the two avoided discussing her terminal condition. Instead, they reminisced about their early years, when they enjoyed a happy family life.

"What happened to us, Mike? Where'd we go wrong?"

Michael reached across the small table and patted his former wife's hand. "Life happened, Suz. Kayla's cancer... both our careers" – he shrugged – "we drifted apart."

Looking down at her broiled salmon, Susan ventured a glance in Michael's direction. Her cheeks flushed. "And my drinking," she mumbled, remorse in her voice.

Michael's fingers closed around hers. "Let's not go there," he consoled. "That's water under the bridge."

"But it's what broke us up, Mike. I can't deny that." Now she looked up and met his gaze. "Can you ever forgive me?"

His gentle smile was all the answer she needed. "Sweetheart... I forgave you long ago."

"I can't tell you how much that means to me." Tears misted her eyes. She looked away again and fell silent, blinking away tears. When at last her eyes met his, Susan wore a trace of a smile. "Then let's do it, Mike. Let's get married again, and see if we can make it work this time."

"In that case..." Michael reached into the pocket of his suit jacket and withdrew a small velvet box. Not wanting to create a stir in the crowded restaurant by getting down on one knee, he placed it beside Susan's water glass and opened it. "Would you please do me the honor, Susan, of becoming my wife again?"

She let out a little gasp.

Inside, cradled in deep-blue velvet, lay a spectacular diamond solitaire ring, one that by far dwarfed the engagement ring he'd been able to afford nearly thirty years earlier.

Michael picked up the ring and slipped it onto Susan's left ring finger. Then he drew her hand to his lips and kissed it.

Three days later, with a pair of bored municipal employees as witnesses, Michael and Susan appeared before a justice of the peace at Middlebury City Hall to be remarried in a civil ceremony.

(February 24 – Friday)

At the end of Gary's fifth week post-surgery, doctors Caron and DiFusco cleared him to return to work. He was still recuperating from major surgery, they cautioned, and neither of them wanted him doing more than four hours of light-duty work per day. That edict restricted him solely to his daily air duties. But because he insisted he couldn't host a proper radio shift without some form of show prep, the doctors consented to let him work an extra hour and a half a day. They agreed he could drive to the station every afternoon at 1:30 and leave right at 7.

For his part, simply grateful for the opportunity to return to work, Gary never strayed from the DJ prep area. He didn't go near his office or even answer music department-related phone calls.

After eight seemingly interminable weeks, Gary at last got the go-ahead to resume most of his normal daily activities. To his relief, that permission included driving to work, resuming his daily music-director duties, hosting his four-hour show and getting to hang out for a while to talk with Marc. But more often than not these days, Marc seemed disinclined to chat.

Little by little, Gary noticed, Marc started coming in later each evening until, by the beginning of April, he was sailing in at ten minutes to seven with the excuse he was way too busy to talk. And if Gary happened to stick around after his shift, Marc would immerse himself in the show prep he hadn't done beforehand to avoid getting drawn into conversation. If he spoke at all, it was to ask about weather updates, station promos or giveaways he needed to do.

And the past three months, he'd avoided the monthly poker game with some of the staff. He didn't even bother making excuses anymore, just stopped showing up.

Chapter 32

(7:15 p.m., April 25 – Tuesday)

Gary leaned in the doorway to the on-air studio. "I thought you were planning to give up the seven-to-midnight shift once you were ready to graduate."

Marc glanced up, then returned his attention to the program log. "Mmm," he mumbled.

"When do you take your state boards?"

No reply.

"Marc?"

"What?" he snapped more sharply – and far more abruptly – than he intended.

"When do you take your state boards?"

Distracted, he shook his head. "I dunno. Look, Gary, I don't feel like talking right now."

"Yeah, I know. You haven't felt like talking in weeks."

"I got a lot on my mind, alright?"

Without response, Gary left the on-air studio, stowed his headphones in his desk drawer and headed home.

When Marc arrived home that night, he found Marie asleep on the couch. She hadn't merely dozed off while reading; she had a blanket and pillow and was down for the night. A shaft of light from the front hallway shone on the cascade of auburn hair flowing across her blanket-swathed body. Marc shut off the hall light and gently shut the front door. He threw the deadbolt as quietly as he could to avoid waking her. Then, a pang hitting him in the gut, he crept past her to the bedroom.

The next morning, Marie bustled about in the kitchen as though nothing were amiss, her blanket and pillow stowed in the bedroom. When Marc entered the kitchen, he found the twins sitting at the table, eating breakfast.

"Hi, Daddy," they chorused.

"Good morning," he replied, coming over to kiss them both.

"Good morning," Marie greeted him cheerfully. "Breakfast will be ready in a few minutes, sweetheart. Coffee's on."

Marie didn't talk much during breakfast — and when she did, it was mainly to the kids.

When Marc complimented her on how fluffy the scrambled eggs were, she replied with a tense-sounding, "Glad you like them." But when she engaged the twins in conversation, her smile returned and her tone grew light and animated.

After breakfast, Marc herded the kids into the bathroom to brush their teeth before heading out with them to wait for the bus.

When he came back inside, Marie's demeanor had shifted. Her smile had vanished, replaced by a sullen, almost angry expression. When Marc attempted to engage her in conversation, she pretended she didn't hear him, then got up and left the room.

She returned a few minutes later, keys in hand. "I'll be home by five thirty," she informed him curtly.

He kept his tone chipper. "Okay. Have a good day, *querida*. I love you."

The only response was the door clicking shut.

That night, when Marc arrived home from work, Marie was again asleep on the couch.

Next morning, the same thing: Smiling, cheerful wife and breakfast as usual, but stony silence the instant the kids were out of the apartment.

After Marie left for work, Marc sat at the kitchen table, head in his hands, trembling.

Before he left for class, he placed a distressed call to his AA sponsor.

"Hey Robin, it's Marc. I hope this isn't a bad time."

"Not at all. What's up, kiddo?"

"I'm on the edge. I mean, I'm *really* on the edge."

"What's the matter?"

"The past several weeks, things have been crumbling. And all this week, Marie and I have barely spoken to each other. Then the last two nights, when I get home from work, she's sleeping on the couch. And this morning I noticed her wedding and engagement rings are on her right hand." He forced back a swell of emotion. "Whenever the kids are around, she acts like everything's fine between us, but the moment we're alone, she won't speak to me. No, that's not quite right. She'll pass along all sorts of ordinary information – like when she'll be home, or whether we need milk or eggs – but there's no real connection between us anymore. We aren't communicating."

"Oh, Marc, I'm so sorry to hear that. What happened with you two? And when?"

He wiped a mist of tears from his eyes. "It's been a series of little things over time. They've built up and built up, and now it feels like I'm living inside a pressure cooker."

"Where are you?"

"At home. I'm about to leave for class. Finals start next week, and I can't focus, Robin. All I want is a drink. I can't think about anything else."

"Marc, no," she counseled. "That's just your emotions talking. Okay? Listen to your better self. You don't want a drink. You can get through this. If you'd like, I'll drive out and stay with you 'til the urge for that drink passes. Or I'll stay on the phone with you. Whatever you want. I'm here for you, Marc. You know that."

"I know." His voice was a whisper. A tear slid down his right cheek. He swiped it away. "I don't know what to do," he admitted.

"Have you reached out to your therapist?"

"I can't. She's friends with Marie. How's that gonna go over? 'Hey, Doc, I think your pal's gonna ask me for a divorce. Have you got some time to talk?'"

"Okay, then what about your friend Gary?"

"He's her brother!" Marc wailed in despair. "When it comes down to it, who do you think he's gonna side with?"

"Is there someone else you can reach out to? There's got to be a counseling center on campus. Maybe you can talk to someone there."

"I dunno." He ran a hand through his hair. "I hadn't thought about that."

"Do you think you'll be okay to drive?"

"I… I guess so."

"What time do you have to leave?"

Marc checked his watch. He drew in a shaky breath. "Ten minutes."

Robin exhaled softly. "Okay. Listen to me, Marc. You can get through this. You can. You're stronger than you think, and you can do this. You're stronger than your desire for alcohol. Take it one hour at a time, Marc. One minute at a time if you have to."

She kept him on the phone until it was time for him to leave, talking him past his initial crisis point.

Marc's hands shook on the steering wheel as he backed out of the driveway. He shifted the Jeep into first gear, taking deep breaths to calm himself. On a desperate impulse as he drove up the road, he veered into the church parking lot. He sprinted inside to the small chapel. Kneeling in one of the rear pews, he offered a quick prayer for strength and guidance before heading off to class.

Needing quiet to clear his head, he switched off the radio and prayed, sometimes silently, sometimes aloud. And amid the steady hum of the engine and the drone of the road sounds, he listened for answers.

Marc found a parking space near the building where his classes were, grabbed his books and ran for the entrance. He made his way to his classroom and slipped inside. He'd arrived six minutes late. But fortunately, the professor was also running late and hadn't shown up yet.

After a full day of classes, and a quick mile in the practice pool, Marc went online in the student center and found an AA meeting close by that would be starting soon. He jotted down the address and looked it up on the college's mapping software. It was only twenty minutes away. And it was on his way to work.

When the meeting ended, he pulled out his mobile phone and punched in Robin's number.

"Hey, it's Marc," he told her as he walked back to the Jeep. "I just wanted to follow up with you. I was able to get in a swim – and I went to a meeting after class, so I'm feeling a little less jittery now. I think I'll make it through my air shift without running out for a beer."

"I'm relieved to hear that. And I'm glad you called. You had me worried. I've been praying for you. I know what it's like to be the one making that call you made this morning. I know it's not easy… but I am so proud of you. Now go take on that next hour."

When he got home to find his wife sleeping on the couch a third consecutive night, Marc knew he couldn't let this continue. She was cocooned in a blanket, so he scooped her up, blanket and all, and carried her into the bedroom.

Marie awakened as he placed her on the bed. "What are you doing?" she asked sleepily. Too much so to speak sharply.

"You're my wife," he replied. "I'm bringing you back to our bed." *Where you belong.*

Before she could protest, he continued.

"Please, Marie. Don't shut me out. This isn't helping either of us. Whatever's wrong between us, we need to talk it out." He reached for her hands. "I *love* you. And I'm prepared to stay up all night and talk with you if that's what it takes."

Snatching her hands away, Marie sat up and faced him, indignant. "*Whatever's wrong?*" she parroted, as though she hadn't even heard the remainder of her husband's plea. "Don't try to tell me you don't know, Marc."

"*Querida*, please," he begged, feeling his composure slipping. "Talk to me."

Marie arranged the covers around herself and lay down with her back to him. Her tone was brittle. "No, Marc. As far as I'm concerned, we're a couple in name only. I'll sleep here if that's what you really want from me, but that's as far as it goes."

Marc stared at the rigid lump on his wife's side of the bed. He eyed her for a long time. At last, resigned, he shed his clothes, turned off the light and slipped into bed, careful not to make even the slightest contact with her. He rolled onto his side, his back to his fuming wife, as a cold ache swept through him. He knew he couldn't go on like this. He couldn't endure for much longer this chilly reception from the woman he loved.

They'd had their issues in the past – all couples did… but this particular problem had arisen suddenly. Its onset had coincided with the arrival of James Griffin in their lives.

Regret swirled through Marc. If only he hadn't voiced his unwavering support of Gary's position in the ugly dispute between his wife and her brother! If he'd taken her side, this might not have blown up in his face… and he wouldn't be facing the disintegration of his marriage.

But he felt strongly that Gary was right, that his brother-in-law held the moral high ground in this matter. He couldn't help how he felt. When it came down to it, Marc knew he had to be true to himself. And if Marie couldn't understand that, well…

He let out a tremulous sigh. Unable to get comfortable, Marc punched his pillow into a more suitable shape and tried to sleep.

Chapter 33

(9:47 a.m., May 3 – Wednesday)

Marc slipped into the classroom and found a seat; he took a deep breath to settle his nerves and ran his hands through his hair. He'd submitted the last of his two end-of-term projects a few minutes earlier and was about to sit for his last final. He felt less jittery now than he did when he left home, and was glad he'd thought to stop in at St. Mary's for a few minutes to pray before he headed over to campus.

Nearly two hours later, once he'd turned in his exam booklet, Marc exited the classroom and quietly shut the door on his college career, so as not to disturb those students who hadn't yet finished. He leaned against a wall in the cool, semi-dark corridor. Sighing, he rubbed his temples, feeling almost numb with relief.

Returning to his vehicle, Marc grabbed his bag and took a brisk walk to the pool, eager to rid himself of his nervous energy. While he walked, he looked up. The sky was overcast; it'd be raining before too long.

As he swam, he delighted in his smooth forward movement through the cool water and easy, playful dolphin-like flips at each end of the pool. Climbing out of the pool after completing a mile and a quarter, he shook the water from his hair.

Marc showered, dressed and left the locker room feeling energized. As he headed toward the facility's exit, he gave a jaunty wave to the lady at the front desk. A light rain began as he returned to the Jeep.

When he'd climbed inside, he pulled out his phone and called Marie.

"What's wrong?" she asked.

"Nothing's wrong," he told his wife, enjoying the emotional buoyancy, the freedom to breathe again, now his exams were over. "I finished my last final. I can't tell you how liberating that feels!"

"That's great, Marc," she said, sounding almost as if he'd simply said he had a good visit to the dentist.

"Are you okay?"

"I'm fine," she replied, in that same distracted manner, like she'd rather be doing anything other than talking to him.

Marc quickly made an excuse to disconnect the call, but for the rest of the afternoon, he couldn't shake that niggling sense of unrest about Marie's tone.

On his way in to work, he stopped for a celebratory Snickers bar and five one-dollar scratch-off lottery tickets. It didn't even bother him that he didn't win anything.

After work, he drove home with the windows down, delighting in the brisk night air against his face. At home, he took the stairs two at a time. He hoped Marie would still be awake, but she was dead asleep. Surprised at how disappointed and alone he felt at having no one to share his sense of relief with, Marc brushed his teeth and undressed, then fell into bed to enjoy his best night's sleep in months. In less than three weeks he would graduate. At the end of next month, he'd start his full-time apprenticeship at Einhorn Sloan Associates. In three years, he'd be eligible to sit for his state boards. Provided he passed those, he'd be a registered architect by the end of '03. And then they'd begin building their dream home.

Chapter 34

The following morning, after the kids clambered aboard their school bus, Marc waved to them and watched as it lumbered down Washington Avenue. He returned upstairs to find his solemn-faced wife seated at the kitchen table. Her eyebrows were drawn together in concern, as if she'd just gotten bad news.

"What's wrong?"

"Sit down," she directed, her voice expressionless. "We need to talk."

Worry in his eyes, he sat beside Marie and reached for her hand. She pulled away.

"What's the matter?"

"I think we should separate."

"What?" Marc couldn't feel his lips move. His insides clenched. His breath came in shallow gasps. He looked down at his hands on the table. "Wh-why?"

She gestured vaguely, then twisted her hands in her lap. "I didn't want to do this while you were studying for finals. I didn't think it was fair to you, to hit you with this then. But now, with your exams out of the way" – she shook her head – "there's no sense putting it off any longer."

Stunned by her sudden announcement, Marc dropped his head into his hands, then looked up again to meet his wife's cold, unblinking gaze. A shiver ran through him. "Why are you doing this? I *love* you, Marie. Doesn't that count for anything? Don't I get a say in this?"

She gave a slow headshake. "I'm sorry, Marc. You had your chance."

"What? What chance? What are you talking about? How can you do this to me – to… to *us?* To our *family?* How can you toss aside seven years of marriage and two beautiful kids… for *what?*"

Shaking her head, Marie looked away. "Don't put this on me," she warned, her teeth gritted.

"How can I not? You blindside me with 'I think we should separate' and won't even tell me what it is I've supposedly done."

"What you've *done*, Marc," she snarled back, "is failed to support me!"

"How have I failed to support you? Other than financially, which for some reason you seem to enjoy reminding me of periodically."

Marie's fists clenched in her lap. "That's not fair!"

"So how else have I failed to support you?" he demanded again.

"Emotionally, you ninny! About James," she spat out. It looked like just speaking his name tasted awful.

"Here we go with this again!" Marc sputtered. He leapt to his feet, knocking his chair backward. It crashed to the floor.

"Oh, that's just great. Now Val and Tim are gonna think we're—"

"Who gives a crap what they think?" he practically howled. "Our marriage is falling apart and all you care about is what Tim and Val will think about a little noise? What is *wrong* with you?!"

"Marc, I didn't want this to get ugly," Marie said calmly. "I thought we could discuss it like reasonable adults."

Marc quit pacing. He gave a caustic laugh. "Like reasonable adults? You mean like how you were so reasonable and adult in your glib announcement a few minutes ago? Well, I've got news for you, Marie. There's absolutely nothing reasonable about your wanting to end our marriage."

"I never said anything about ending it," she corrected. "I wanted us to do a trial separation, without having to go through the ugliness of filing a legal petition. I don't want to take that step, Marc. You're jumping to conclusions."

"Oh, so this *trial separation* is for what? For us to get along better?"

"No, to work on what's wrong in our marriage."

"And how do you propose we do *that*, Einstein? How can we 'work on what's wrong in our marriage' if we're separated? And when I don't even know what's 'wrong' because there's – *obviously* – not a lot wrong! Doesn't it make more sense for us to stay together to work things out?"

She folded her arms. "I need some space."

"So then, I take it you'll be moving out?"

Marie shook her head. "Don't be ridiculous. I'll be living here with the kids. I'm their mother. After all, this is their home and I'm their primary caregiver. I'll stay with them. I figured you'll move out."

Bile rose in the back of Marc's throat. "Hold on a second. Let me get this straight: *You* need space, so *I* have to move out. That's brilliant. And what do you suggest we tell the kids about why Daddy's got his own apartment now?"

She sniffled. "Kids are resilient. They'll be fine. Especially at their age. Besides, this way they don't have to be uprooted or change schools so late in the school year."

"Well, what about this? You're at work all day, so if I'm not around, who's gonna be here when the kids get off the bus in the afternoon?"

Marie's lips tightened briefly into a slim line. "That's already been taken care of. They'll go home with friends and I'll pick them up there. Oh, and in case you get any funny ideas, I've alerted the school never to release them to you," she bluffed.

Marc stared at his wife, defeated. "You can't do that. I'm their father!" He shook his head in disbelief. His shoulders slumped. "You've got it all figured out, haven't you? Just how long have you been planning this?"

Her icy tone shot through him as painfully as her next words. "Months. And the simple fact you have to ask that, Marc, just proves how clueless you are! You can just pack up your things and get out – and not worry about the kids. They'll be fine."

"Oh, so you think it's just that easy, do you?" He shook his head. "I'm not about to let you tear our family apart, Marie, and leave our kids wondering what *they* did to make Mommy and Daddy hate each other. Because you know that's what'll happen. And then, when you arbitrarily decide it isn't working out and we *do* end up getting a divorce, they'll blame themselves for that, too. You know it as well as I do. Is that what you want, Marie? Because you can't separate from me without ultimately separating both of us from our children."

Doing her best to retain her calm façade, Marie placed her palms flat before her on the table. Her words came out slow, measured. "Look, I need this, Marc. I just need you out of my face right now."

Turning away, Marc sighed deeply, absorbing her words. Then he swallowed hard and nodded in capitulation. "Okay. I don't understand any of this, Marie, but out of respect for you *and our marriage*, I'll give you the space you need – for as long as I can." He shook his head. "I just don't know how long I can keep this up."

Rolling her eyes, Marie heaved an audible sigh. "Are you done?"

Something snapped. "No, I'm not done," Marc seethed. "I can't believe you just asked me that. As a matter of fact, I'm just getting started. *This* was supposed to be the time when things got easier, Marie. Or had you forgotten? After eight years – *eight years!* – of juggling work and classes – and then babies – I'm about to graduate. So after my apprenticeship and exams, when I get into a decent firm, we can start building the home I've spent the past year and a half in there designing" – he flung an arm in the direction of the back bedroom – "the dream house we've talked about for years. Remember that, Marie? *Now* was when all that was supposed to have started happening. But you've unilaterally decided it made more sense to pull the plug on everything. Why?" His fists clenched and unclenched at his sides. His breathing grew erratic. "And why wait 'til just now, Marie? Why couldn't you have dropped this little bombshell years ago and saved us all this time?"

"I told you: I didn't want to do this while you were studying for your finals. I knew how important it was to you, and you were already under a lot of pressure and I didn't want this to be a distraction for you."

"How fucking considerate of you!" Marc spat out. He turned away abruptly to hide the tears that sprang to his eyes. Unwilling to give her the satisfaction of seeing him get even more emotional, he gritted his teeth to fight back a sob. His back rigid, he spoke around the lump in his throat. "If you didn't mean forever, Marie, why'd you even marry me in the first place?"

Without waiting for an answer, he stalked into the bedroom. Shoving his keys and wallet into his jeans pockets, he returned to the kitchen. For a chilling moment, he stood over Marie, resisting the overwhelming temptation to point a menacing finger in her face. Not wanting to come across as intimidating or threatening, he positioned his clenched fist behind his back.

"I can't talk to you right now, because I don't want to say something I'll regret later, but this discussion is *not* over," Marc cautioned. He started to leave, then turned back to level a parting shot at his wife. "And don't you go and do anything shitty like changing the locks – or draining the bank account. At least for the moment, I still live here, Marie. And this could probably go without saying, but don't wait up."

He yanked the door shut behind him.

Fumbling with his keys, Marc unlocked the Jeep and got in. His breath came in ragged gasps as he slammed a fist against the steering wheel. And again. Then a third time.

With trembling hands, he fastened his seatbelt and turned the key in the ignition. As he did, he noticed Tim emerging from the house with Sebastian and Trouper, heading out for their morning walk before work.

Stomping on the clutch, Marc shifted into first and tore off down the street. He didn't want Tim to see him like this. He shifted rapidly into second and then third.

Anguished and distracted, he careened through town with no idea where he was headed. When he blew through a stop sign, the driver of the Blazer he nearly T-boned leaned on his horn, then shook a fist at Marc's retreating Jeep and shouted expletives at him through his open window.

Shaken, Marc realized he shouldn't be driving. Not like this. He pulled off to the side of the road, yanked the hand brake and killed the ignition. He took several deep breaths in an attempt to settle himself down. Marc reached into his jacket pocket and pulled out his mobile phone, an old Nokia 5190. It was a dinosaur, but he liked it. It was reliable and familiar. Jabbing at the numbers he'd long ago memorized, he called his sponsor. Particularly vulnerable right now, Marc knew he didn't want to turn to alcohol – no matter how badly he longed for a drink to dull the horrible throb in his heart.

"Hello," Robin's soothing voice came through the little phone's tinny speaker against his ear.

The familiar voice triggered his tears.

"Robin, it's Marc." A sob caught in his throat. "I'm so sorry to bother you this early, but I didn't know what else to do."

Overwhelmed with emotion, Marc tried to explain what had happened, but his words came out in a jumbled mess.

"Hold up, Marc," she said. "Slow down. Slow down. I can barely understand you. Where are you, kiddo? Are you safe?"

"I – I'm – I'm…" he cast about, looking for a familiar landmark. "I don't even know where I am," he admitted, sounding like a lost child in a department store. "I'm in the car. And I – I don't know how long I've been driving."

"Okay, listen to me, Marc," Robin told him, doing her best to keep her voice serene. "You need to calm down. I know that doesn't seem possible right now, but I want you to take a few deep breaths and pull yourself together.

"I need to know you're not going to take a drink, Marc. I know that feels like the easy way out right now, but we both know that's not true. Promise me you won't drink."

Marc only sniffled in reply.

"Marc," she prompted. "Did you hear me?"

"Mm-hmm," he mumbled at last.

"Promise me you won't drink," she directed. "I know it feels like your world's been upended right now, but you're going to get through this. I promise. And you'll get through it without alcohol. But I need you to say those words, Marc: 'I promise I won't drink.' Say it, Marc. Promise me."

Gradually, his ragged breathing slowed. "I won't drink," he said at last.

"That was only three words," she reminded him, her voice gentle.

Marc rested his head against the steering wheel. "I promise I won't drink," he mumbled thickly.

"Alright, good. Now, when you're able to drive— uh, do you have a speakerphone?"

"Umm… n-no."

"Okay, listen to me, Marc. I want you to call me back when you get to a familiar landmark and you know where you are, alright?"

He nodded. She was making so much sense. His hand holding the phone trembled. "Okay."

"I'm not going anywhere," she reassured him. "I'll stay right here and wait for your call. And when you do call back, I'll come find you. Okay?"

"Okay," he said again. "Thank you."

Five minutes later, Marc called back. "I'm on Route 34 in Orange, near St. Anthony's Book and Gift Shop. I don't know how I got here." He sounded jittery and frightened.

"That's okay," Robin assured him, her voice low, steady and comforting. "Listen to me carefully. I want you to stay on 34 'til you intersect with Route 121. You're a little over a mile from there right now, Marc. Then I want you to turn left onto Route 121. When you come upon Grassy Hill Country Club, you're almost there, okay? Eisenhower Park will be a mile and a half ahead on your right. I'll be there waiting for you just inside the entrance."

"Thank you." Marc felt a sudden sense of calm sweep over him. "I don't know what I would have done if you didn't answer."

"You don't have to think about that. I'll see you in a few minutes. Hang in there, kiddo. You'll be fine."

Marc turned in at the park entrance and pulled in behind Robin's Honda. He killed the engine and stumbled out of the Jeep.

Robin wrapped him in a long, comforting hug. "I'm glad you made it," she said, keeping her voice as reassuring as she could. "Everything's going to be okay, Marc. You're going to be just fine."

When she drew back from him, they walked over to a nearby picnic table to sit and talk.

"Tell me what happened," she prompted.

Little by little Marc pieced together the morning's events, and the confrontation with Marie, right up to his frenzied departure from the apartment.

Robin nodded in acknowledgment. Her brow furrowed deeply in concentration as he spoke. It didn't sound good.

When he finished relating the story, Marc looked at his sponsor, desperation in his eyes. His voice carried a tremor. "What am I gonna do?"

Robin took his hands; they trembled fiercely. "I'm not sure what you should do right now, Marc, but what you're *not* going to do is drink," she told him, her voice both placid and reassuring. "I don't want you to let this overwhelm you. Don't try to absorb it all at once. Take it one piece at a time, okay?"

Robin remained with Marc another hour, talking with him, letting him retell the story of how that morning's sudden and unexpected unraveling of his marriage had unfolded. Together the two of them unpacked the elements that might have led up to Marie's decision to ask for a separation.

"All I keep coming back to is James. She's mad at me for siding with Gary about him."

"Has she ever met James?"

Marc shook his head. "Never. And she says she doesn't ever want to. She just hates him on general principle – just because her dad got some other woman pregnant."

"And because you're siding with your best friend over their relationship," Robin added.

He nodded glumly. "That too."

"So what do you want to do?"

He shrugged in resignation. "I don't know what I can do. My guess is if I try to go back to the apartment, she'll either make it so unpleasant for me that I end up leaving on my own, or she'll call the cops… and I don't want that. I really don't want the kids caught in the middle of a custody battle. That won't be good for anyone – least of all, them."

Marc's eyes welled with tears at the thought of how bewildered his two children would be to find Daddy not there to sit with them at breakfast, help them with applying toothpaste to their Cookie Monster and Big Bird toothbrushes, or put them on their school bus the next morning. "I don't even want to think about what this'll do to them."

Seeing the tears in his eyes, Robin drew Marc close again and held him for a long time.

Finally, he pulled away, embarrassed. "I'm sorry," he told her, shaking his head and swiping at his eyes. "I shouldn't be falling apart like this…"

"Of course you should. You've had your rug of normalcy torn out from under you. You're entitled to feel upset over it – and to react in any way you wish… except for drinking. *That* I'm not gonna let you do."

After he left Robin, Marc got into the Jeep and drove – along one back road after another, letting the peaceful, bucolic scenery calm him – until his heart stopped clattering in his chest and his breathing returned to almost normal. More than an hour and a half later, he pulled off to the side of the road, uncertain where he was. He couldn't recall having recognized any road signs. None of the street names and nothing in the area looked familiar. He drove until he found a small convenience store at the far end of a strip mall.

"Can you help me?" he asked the clerk behind the counter, sounding befuddled. "I have no idea where I am. What town is this, please?"

The young man looked up. "Plainville." He smiled. "As in ordinary. Boring. Bland. Nothing exciting ever happens here."

That meant nothing to Marc. He shook his head. "Am I east or west of Waterbury?"

"About twenty miles northeast."

"Which way to I-84, please?"

The young man gave him directions.

Marc shook his head again, this time accompanied by a blank stare. "I'm sorry. Would you mind terribly writing those down for me? I'm… I'm having a brain-like-a-sieve kind of day."

The young cashier smiled at Marc's phrasing. "Never heard it put quite that way, but I totally get it, man. I'd be happy to write 'em down for you." He retrieved a small notepad from beneath the counter and wrote out the directions. When he finished, he tore off the sheet and handed it to Marc with a cheerful grin. "Happy landing."

Marc forced a return smile. "Thanks."

As he was about to exit the store, he reached for his wallet and turned back, having noticed a beer poster in the window and a side-by-side cooler down at the end of the aisle. "Let me get a six-pa—"

he shook his head. "Nah, never mind. I'd like ten bucks in instant scratch-off tickets. Those, over there, please," he said, pointing to the ones he wanted.

"Good luck," the clerk told him as he tore off ten tickets and exchanged them for Marc's ten spot.

Tucking them into his back pocket, he headed for the door.

"Aren'cha gonna scratch those?" the clerk asked. "Don't you wanna see if you won?"

Marc stopped, turned around. Shrugged. "Nah. I just didn't wanna buy beer. This was a safe alternative." He gave a slight wave. "Thanks. Have a good night."

(12:02 a.m., Friday, May 5)
After relinquishing the controls in the on-air studio to Randy Lear, Marc crashed in the DJ prep area, rather than risk driving all the way home to encounter a combative and quarrelsome Marie.

When the morning guy and news director arrived at 4:30 to prep for their morning-drive shift, they found him lying in a heap on the ratty old couch. Ken and Barb spoke in low voices to keep from awakening him, but it wasn't long before he stirred.

"Sorry, Marc," Barb told the nighttime jock softly, standing over him. "Didn't mean to wake you. Are you feeling alright?"

Marc stretched. His back ached from sleeping on that lumpy couch. Lord knows how long it had been there – or what kind of activity it had seen in its day. "Yeah, I'm fine," he lied. "I was just really tired after my show and didn't relish driving all the way… home." The last word caught in his throat.

He groaned as he hauled himself to his feet. "Guess I'd better get to it."

"I hope you called Marie," Barb said. When Marc shook his head, she said, "She's gotta be worried sick about you."

He twisted to one side, held the position for a moment, then twisted in the other direction. His neck cracked in protest. *I doubt it.*

Marc started the Jeep and pulled out of the station parking lot. It was still dark, but the night was clear and the moon shone brightly overhead. The eastern sky was interspersed with faint streaks of light. He rolled down the window and breathed deeply as the refreshing coolness of the night air blew against the left side of his face and ruffled through his hair.

Along his route was one of those commuter lots where carpoolers could meet. He pulled in there, killed the engine and reclined his seat enough to facilitate sleeping.

Marc stirred just before eight. The lot had begun filling up with commuters on their way to work. He lay his head back against the headrest and drifted off to sleep again.

It was after nine when he woke up. For sure by now the kids were on their way to school and Marie had left for work. His heart ached at the thought of his children getting on the bus this morning without their usual hugs and kisses from Daddy. They must have been bewildered by his absence. Ever since they arrived home from the hospital as newborns, he'd never *not* been there to greet them in the morning.

Tears stung his eyes as he started the engine and headed back to the apartment. Marc didn't feel comfortable thinking of it as 'home' anymore. He marveled at how quickly that had happened — it had scarcely been twenty-four hours since Marie asked him to leave.

He unlocked the back door and crept up to the second-floor apartment. He felt like a thief, sneaking around in here — not the slightest bit like a legitimate resident whose name had been on the lease paperwork for the past nearly seven years.

Marc looked around. The apartment already felt cold, unfamiliar to him. Almost as unfamiliar as Plainville had seemed yesterday afternoon. Yet, he thought wryly, at least he'd been welcomed when he showed up there.

When he went into the bedroom, he could tell Marie hadn't slept well last night, either. The covers were rumpled and unkempt — she hadn't bothered making the bed before she left. Going to her side of the bed, Marc picked up her pillow and hugged it to himself, inhaling her lingering scent. Still clutching the pillow, he sank onto the bed and slumped forward, elbows on his knees.

Marc sat that way for a long time. At last, he stood up and cast his wife's pillow aside, muttering a curse in Portuguese.

Roused from his morning nap, Oscar looked up and eyed him evenly. Marc reached over and gave the little cat a scritch behind the ear. "Hey, buddy. Sorry to bother you. Go back to sleep."

After fighting the urge to make the bed – or at least straighten the covers, Marc took several days' worth of underwear, socks, t-shirts and jeans from his dresser. And from his side of the small walk-in closet, he selected half a dozen shirts. He grabbed a small suitcase from an upper shelf in the closet and unzipped it on the bed, away from where Oscar lay curled up. The last time he'd used this case was on their honeymoon. It still bore the tags from Lisbon Portela Airport and their return flight to JFK. Forcing aside the memory, Marc shoved his clothes inside. The shirts could stay on their hangers.

In the bathroom, he packed his deodorant, comb, toothbrush and electric shaver into a small zippered toiletries kit and added that to a corner of his suitcase. Cotton swabs, ibuprofen, toothpaste and any of his and Marie's other toiletries-in-common he could pick up at the drugstore. No need to be vindictive and take those things. After all, he loved Marie – why would he want to do something so spiteful and petty to her?

With a quick look around the room, he decided there wasn't anything else he really needed from in here. *Nothing except Marie, that is.* Forcing back an unbidden cry, he took a deep breath and tried to calm himself.

Marc contemplated taking down his Portuguese fishing-village painting from the living room wall, the one his sister had painted for him years back. But that would only make it official he didn't live here anymore – and that notion was too heart wrenching to think about.

Still holding out hope of returning someday, he locked up the apartment and lugged his things downstairs. If he needed to get anything else — or to shower, he could come back in the middle of the day, while no one was home. After tossing his suitcase into the back of the Jeep and hanging the shirts down the back of the head-rest's chrome support post, Marc got in and drove away.

Chapter 35

Late that morning, Marc drove to a convenience store to buy local and regional daily newspapers, along with copies of the newest *People* and *TV Guide* magazines. He went to the public library in Middlebury, where he could do his show prep undisturbed, so he wouldn't have to arrive at work any earlier than necessary.

He showed up at the station a few minutes before seven – just in time to pull music for his Seventies at Seven feature.

When Gary greeted him, Marc pretended not to hear and darted toward the DJ prep area to retrieve his headphones.

When he returned, he greeted his brother-in-law with a cursory "Hi."

"Are we gonna not talk again?"

Marc couldn't tell whether he heard hurt or accusation – or maybe both – in Gary's voice. His insides crumbled to dust as he eyed the facial features that looked so much like his wife's it felt physically painful. Drawing in a gasping breath, Marc shook his head. "Gary, please," he implored. It hurt to talk. "I… I just can't, okay?"

"Alright," he acquiesced, hands raised in capitulation. He gathered his belongings, unplugged his headphones and made way for Marc behind the control board. As they changed places, he patted his brother-in-law on the shoulder. "Hang in there, buddy."

All Marc could do was nod. If he tried to speak, he'd lose his composure. And he needed every bit of that composure to make it through five hours on the air.

(May 6 – Saturday)

When he surrendered the control board to Randy Lear at midnight, Marc again crashed on the couch in the DJ prep area. Fortunately, because it was a weekend, there'd be no morning team coming in at 4:30. The Saturday-morning guy never did much prep. His main duty was to play music, run spots and read the weather and a few community announcements.

It was nearly 9 when Marc awakened. He sat up, disoriented. Looking around the room and remembering where he was, he yawned and stretched, then glanced at his watch. He couldn't recall the last time he'd slept this late.

The weekend midday guy looked up from drinking coffee and reading the local morning newspaper. "Good morning."

Marc jumped at the sound of his voice.

"Sorry – didn't mean to startle you," Jeff Dawson told him. "Rough night?"

Marc shook his head. "Just… not feeling so hot."

Jeff nodded. "I hear ya. You look like you feel awful. Better go home and get some rest."

Marc hauled himself to his feet. "Yeah. Good idea." He dragged himself from the room and out to the Jeep. *Home.* He didn't even know where that was anymore.

He drove to the commuter lot and pulled in. Killing the engine, he pulled out his phone.

"Hey, it's Marc," he said when Tim answered.

"Hi! You wanna go exploring with the four-footers?"

Marc grinned at the wording of his landlord and friend's invitation. "Can't. I'm not there right now."

"Oh."

"Actually, that's kinda what I wanted to talk to you about… not being there."

"Oh?"

Marc sensed the underlying perplexity in the other man's voice. He ran a hand through his hair. "I know you and Val own a number of properties in the area," he began. There was no sense hedging or dancing around the subject. "Any chance you've got one open for short-term rental… maybe a furnished place that's available right away?"

"Yeah, we have a couple vacant apartments. And I think a few of 'em are furnished. At least minimally. You got a friend who needs a place?"

"Uh…" Marc hesitated. "No. It's not for a friend. It's… for me."

Tim's surprise was evident in his gasp. "What? Marc — what happened?"

"Marie asked for a separation," he admitted, ashamed at having to speak those words aloud. "So I need a place to stay. I'm not sure how long." He paused. "I hope not more than a few weeks."

"Oh my goodness! Of course," Tim assured him. "Marc, I'm so sorry. Is there anything I can do?"

His voice caught in his throat. "I — just need a place to stay. Someplace to get my head together while we figure this out."

"Where are you now?"

Marc looked around. "In the commuter lot on 188."

"Do you want to look at a few places today?"

"Can I?"

"Of course. Let me give you an address. Hang on a sec."

Tim gave Marc the address of a three-family house in a nice part of town. "The apartment's on the second floor," he added.

"I can be there in half an hour," Marc told him.

"Sounds good. Or, better still, have you eaten?"

"No. Not yet."

"Why don't we meet for breakfast at the Blue Bell Diner? We can talk awhile and then head over to look at a few places."

Marc sniffled. His composure was slipping. Between classes and his study schedule these past several months, it had been ages since he and Tim had done more than exchange pleasantries in passing. He nodded. "I'd like that."

"Great. I can meet you there in twenty minutes. That work for you?"

After looking at a few apartments with Tim, Marc signed a short-term rental agreement on a furnished one-bedroom place not far from where Marie and the kids lived. He couldn't think of that as home — not anymore. He needed to compartmentalize the past seven years. The mere thought of the separation from Marie made his insides disintegrate like spalling concrete.

"You can move in today," Tim told him.

"That'd be great. It sure beats sleeping on a beat-up old couch in the prep room at work."

"Oh, Marc… you haven't. Really?"

Eyes downcast, he nodded.

Tim motioned toward the bedroom. "I know we've got a few sets of linens that'll fit that bed. I'll bring 'em by later today. No sense in your having to shell out money for sheets you might not have use for once you two get back together."

Marc realized the other man was trying to sound optimistic for his sake. He managed a grateful smile. "Thanks." Then his smile fled. "I don't have the rent money just yet… but I can get it to you by Monday morning."

Tim clapped him on the shoulder. "Don't worry about that, Marc. You're good for it. Now, is there anything else you need?"

Marc blinked back tears. He turned away, shook his head. "Just my wife. And a reason this is happening."

(8:27 a.m., May 8 – Monday)

After he was sure Marie was gone, Marc knocked at his landlord's back door.

Tim and Val were both home. They wrapped him in warm, comforting hugs.

"I hope it's okay I came by," he said, his voice trembling slightly as Val drew back from him.

"Of course it's okay," she replied, her eyes teary as she recognized the anguish in his eyes. "Come on in, Marc. Sit down." She motioned to the kitchen table. "Let me get you a cup of coffee."

"I uh… I brought a check for the first and last months' rent… plus a security deposit," Marc told them as he pulled out a chair and sank into it.

Sitting across from him, Tim waved it away. "We don't need you to pay the last month's rent up front – or a security deposit." He met and held the other man's gaze as Val set mugs of steaming coffee in front of them. "Are you okay?"

Val poured herself a coffee and, after retrieving the milk from the refrigerator, took a seat beside her husband.

"No." Marc shook his head. "I'm not," he admitted, his hands trembling. Somehow, it felt almost good to finally admit that. He looked from one of them to the other. "I can't wrap my head around this. None of it seems real. Things were going so well. I mean, I *thought* they were. Sure, we had our little disagreements, but every couple has those… right?" He stirred milk into his coffee.

Val and Tim glanced at each other.

"Of course," Tim agreed with a slight nod.

Just then, hearing his walking buddy's voice, Sebastian barreled into the room, wriggling with excitement as he hurtled toward Marc. The little dog leapt into his pal's lap, squirming and whining. Wagging his tail in unrestrained exuberance, he licked Marc's face.

Genuinely smiling for the first time in days, Marc fondled Sebastian's silken ears, delighting in the feel of the cocker spaniel's soft fur against his fingers, while trying to ignore the inadvertent jabs of the ecstatic pooch's sharp little paws into his thighs.

Finally, Tim got up, intending to remove his wriggling dog from the other man's lap.

"No, he's fine," Marc assured his friend, waving him off. "He'll settle down. Besides, it's nice to have someone be this glad to see me."

While he tried to come across as sounding lighthearted, Val and Tim exchanged a sorrowful glance, having heard the underlying distress in Marc's voice.

(11:15 a.m., May 10 – Wednesday)

As soon as he opened the door and the bell overhead jingled, Marc was beset by the aroma of lilies and chrysanthemums. He walked to the display case and took note of the available blooms. Then he approached the cheerful young woman behind the counter.

"Good morning. Let me guess: You're here for Mother's Day flowers."

Marc feigned astonishment. "My goodness, you're amazing! That's *exactly* why I'm here. How ever did you figure that out?"

"It's our busiest week of the year. Even busier than Valentine's Day." When she thought he wasn't paying attention, she gave him a fleeting once over; his left ring finger was obscured from her view. "What can I help you with? Flowers for your mom? Your wife?"

He shook his head. "For my children's mom."

She beamed in approval. "Aren't you sweet! Did you have anything in particular in mind? Or would you like me to suggest something appropriate?"

"A dozen purple irises," he replied. "Her favorite. With two yellow roses – one for each of the kids. And ferns. Plus anything else you think would look nice. Preferably in a tall clear-glass vase."

"You've done this before," she commented, nodding appreciatively.

He shrugged. "Once or twice."

As she wrote up the order, the florist indicated a rotating display rack on the counter, filled with cards to include with the floral arrangement. "Our Mother's Day cards are here, in this section." She turned it so the indicated cards faced him.

Marc selected a card with kittens on it. One of the kittens looked exactly like Oscar. On it he printed, *Happy Mother's Day, Mommy! Love, Edward and Isabella.*

He handed the woman a slip of paper on which he'd written the address. "Could you have it delivered here, please? Tomorrow or Friday will be fine." Then, almost as if as an afterthought, he said, "I may as well get an arrangement to send to my mom."

He picked out stargazer lilies, pink roses, white roses and magenta peonies. On the card he printed, *Feliz Dia das Mães, Avó Fernanda!*

(8:27 a.m., May 14 – Sunday)
Marc slipped into a rear pew, way over on the left side of the church. Marie and the children sat in their customary pew, partway up on the right side. From where he sat, he could see them, but he was fairly confident they wouldn't notice him.

The church was packed today. All around him families sat together. The priest even offered a special blessing for mothers at the beginning of Mass.

Every time he caught sight of Marie, Marc's heart ached; he was sure he wouldn't make it through Mass.

As the priest reverenced the altar at the end of Mass, Marc uttered a silent apology to God for skipping out early. His hasty departure yielded a bevy of disapproving glares from several people in back. But he couldn't stick around. To see his wife and kids up close and not be able to go home with them would destroy him.

Once outside, Marc hurried to the Jeep and sped away up Washington Avenue.

Just after noon, he drove to his parents' house with a card and a box of dark-chocolate truffles for his mom.

He breathed a sigh of relief when he didn't see his dad's car in the driveway. That meant they were out somewhere. Probably out to lunch. Or, more likely, at Emily and Clive's place, cooing over Grace, their newest granddaughter. At least he wouldn't have to explain why he had come alone. Grateful it wasn't too warm out, he left the chocolates and the card on the front porch, then headed back to his apartment.

***

"Mommy, why doesn't Daddy live with us anymore?" Edward asked as Marie slid aside the vase of flowers and set a casserole dish on the trivet in the center of the table. The six-year-old knew enough to keep his little fingers away from the just-out-of-the-oven pan. He inhaled deeply. Mom's homemade baked macaroni and cheese smelled delicious.

"Did he find another family he liked better than us?" Fern put in, momentarily distracted from conducting an imaginary orchestra with her fork.

Marie quashed her daughter's suggestion a little too harshly. "Of course not. Now put your fork down before you stab somebody." She ignored Edward's question as she spooned up steaming bowls of the golden, breadcrumb-topped deliciousness for the three of them. "Both of you, turn around, sit up straight and eat your lunch."

"Those flowers are pretty, Mommy," Fern observed. "Where did they come from?"

"They were from you and your brother... for Mother's Day." The flowers had unexpectedly shown up at her office Thursday afternoon. Marie handed her daughter the card Marc had printed.

"They are?" Fern said, studying it carefully.

At the same time, Edward piped up with, "Well, aren't we thoughtful?"

Marie's smile felt sad. It sounded just like the kind of thing his daddy would have said. She wondered what Marc was doing today... and what kind of terrible things he was telling his family about her.

"That looks like Daddy's writing," Fern observed, her tone matter of fact.

"Yes, it does," Marie replied. She reclaimed the card and tucked it back amid the blooms.

Chapter 36

(7:03 a.m., Tuesday, May 16)

Marie was making the kids' lunches when a key slid into the lock; a moment later, the old deadbolt clunked back. Her heart pounded. Prepared to defend herself and the children against a potential intruder, she grabbed the large chef's knife from the wooden block on the counter.

The doorknob turned.

She let out a gasp. "What are you doing here?" she demanded in a hiss. Feeling foolish, she hastily slid the knife back into its block.

"It's nice to see you, too."

Marie recognized the hurt in Marc's tone. *Good.* "What are you doing here?" she repeated.

"I've come to see the kids."

"They're getting dressed for school. Then they've got to have breakfast and brush their teeth before they go out to catch their bus."

He nodded slowly. "I'm aware of their schedule. If you recall, I used to help them adhere to it. Back when I lived here." The pain in his voice was unmistakable. "I came here to talk to them."

"About what?"

"About us, Marie. About why we're living apart. Unless you've already talked to them about that."

"Of course not," she snapped back at him, indignant. "And you can't just waltz in here and demand to see them whenever you want."

"Actually, I can. My name's on the lease. So I belong here every bit as much as you do. And don't forget: They're my kids, too." He continued in a conciliatory tone. "Look, *querida*, I don't want things to get contentious or ugly between us. I just want a chance to talk to the kids an—"

"And tell them what?" Marie folded her arms across her chest. "That Mommy's so horrible she made you leave? So you can turn them against me?"

Marc felt his throat constrict. He kept his tone even. "Of course not. I'm not here to assign blame or point fingers, Marie. All I want is to talk to our kids and let them know that, no matter what happens between us, no matter how it en— how it *turns out…* we both still love them. And that's not going to change."

Marie looked away and let out a soft sigh. She nodded. "Okay. But don't make them late for their bus."

"I won't."

Marie went to the back bedrooms. "Kids, hurry up. Breakfast is almost ready." She returned to the kitchen. "Do you want to stay for breakfast?"

A faint smile graced his lips. He nodded. "I'd like that. Thank you."

Marie went to the refrigerator to get two more eggs and two more slices of bread for toast.

Edward emerged from his bedroom first. When he saw his father, he let out a yelp and ran to greet him. "Daddy! You came home!"

Marc crouched to hug him. "Hi, sweet boy. I'm so glad to see you." Emotion choked his voice as he held his son close.

"Are you home for good?"

He shook his head. "No. I came here to talk to you and Fern."

The little boy's expression turned worried. "Why aren't you coming home?"

"Let's wait 'til Fern gets out here and then we'll talk, okay?" Standing, Marc cast a glance at his estranged wife, who wore an annoyed expression as she cracked the eggs into a mixing bowl and whisked them with milk.

Marie heated butter in a pan. "Fern!" she called.

"Coming, Mommy," the little girl called from the other room.

Footsteps thumped down the hall. She was barefoot. That kid was always barefoot.

"Daddy!" she shrieked, hurling herself at him. "Oh, Daddy – I missed you so much! Are you staying now?"

Fighting back tears, Marc bent down and wrapped his arms around his little daughter. "I'm staying for breakfast, baby. But I'm going after you guys get on the bus."

"Why, Daddy?" she asked, not quite pouting yet.

"That's what I came here to talk to you about." He herded the twins to the table to sit down. He crouched between them and looked from one of them to the other. "I wanted to talk with the both of you about why I'm not living here with you and Mommy right now."

"Why, Daddy?" Edward asked, his eyes wide and serious.

"Mommy and I… we're having a little trouble getting along at the moment. And we needed some time to be apart from each other."

"Are we getting a divorce?" Fern looked worried. "My friend Tina's mommy and daddy got a divorce and she said it's awful." Her face crumpled and tears filled her eyes. "She only gets to see her daddy once a week. I don't want you to go away again, Daddy. I want you to come back home and live with us."

Stroking his daughter's hair, Marc stole a glance at Marie. "It's nothing like that, sweetheart," he reassured the little girl. "But you know how sometimes you and your brother have a cranky kind of day and you just need to get away from him? Or when you fight and Mommy and I tell you to go to separate rooms?"

Both children nodded.

"Well, grownups have days like that, too, sometimes. And Mommy and I have been having some cranky days lately. And we just needed some time in separate rooms to work things out. But we both want you to know that no matter what happens with us, we love you more than anything – and we always will."

"Are you and Mommy going to get a divorce?" Edward fretted.

"I hope not, honey," Marc told him. He gave another look at his wife; her expression was grim. "We're just going through a little bit of a rough patch, that's all. We still love each other, and we love both of you kids. More than anything. And I promise, we're going to do our best to work on what's wrong and try to get it all straightened out."

"So what's wrong?" Edward asked, his little brow furrowing in concern.

Damned if I know! Marc shook his head. "It's grown-up stuff, honey. And it's complicated."

"And then when you get it all straightened out, you can come home?" Fern asked, her eyes bright. She gave a hopeful nod.

Marc smiled. "I hope so, sweetheart." He looked back at Marie again. "I really hope so."

"Where are you living now?"

He didn't want to get into this – and he didn't want Marie to know where he was staying. "I… found a place here in town so I could be nearby."

"Can we come and live with you?"

Marc ventured another glance at Marie. *How do I address this?* "No, honey. Mommy would be so sad if you and Edward left. You stay here with her and keep her company, okay? And take care of Oscar."

"But what about you? Aren't you sad? And Mommy – aren't you sad that Daddy left?"

Tears stung at Marc's eyes. He blinked them away. "Sweetie, don't worry about Mommy and me," he replied hastily, stroking his daughter's silken hair. "Yes, we're both sad. But we're grownups and this is something grownups have to do sometimes."

Chapter 37

(9:15 a.m., Monday, May 22, 2000)

"C'mon, kids," Marie prompted, her heels clicking against the hardwood floor. "We don't want to be late."

Edward emerged from his room in a dark-blue suit with a white shirt and red clip-on tie.

"You look so handsome," she told the little boy, smiling as she bent to tuck in his shirt tails.

Fern ran from her room in her black patent-leather shoes. "How about me, Mommy? Do I look handsome, too?" Reaching the living room, she twirled in her favorite dress, the blue flowered one with the fluttery cap sleeves and flowing skirt.

As Marie watched her daughter, she recalled her own favorite blue flowered dress – the one she'd worn the day she and Marc were summoned to the presidential palace in Lisbon seven years earlier. She felt an unexpected, involuntary swell of love for her husband when she thought back on that day. After saving a planeload of passengers from a would-be hijacker, he was knighted by the president of Portugal. Marie recalled Marc's genuine humility in repudiating the notion that what he'd done was the least bit heroic. She smiled at her little girl and blinked away a mist of tears. "You look beautiful, sweetheart."

Now she herded the pair toward the door. "C'mon, doodlebugs, we don't want to be late for Daddy's graduation."

"Mommy, what's gravitation?"

Marie ushered the kids ahead of her. "Hold on to the railing."

When they reached the outside door, she answered her son's question. "It's grad*u*ation, honey. That's a ceremony where Daddy will get his college diploma, and then he'll be able to start designing buildings."

"Is it going to be a long ceremony?" Edward wanted to know.

"It might get a little long," she replied, "but we're all going to be patient and pay attention as best we can, because this is an important day for Daddy. Okay?"

The little boy dug his hands into the pockets of his suit jacket. "I brought some of my cars with me. Is it okay if I play with them if it gets too long?"

Marie smiled as she buckled the twins into their car seats. "Of course, sweetheart. As long as you promise not to make any noise while you play. People around us will be wanting to hear what's going on. That means no 'vroom-vroom' sounds, okay?"

Edward nodded in understanding. "Okay, Mommy."

Fern reached into the little purse she clutched in her long-fingered hands. "I brought my box of crayons. Those are quiet, huh?"

Marie nodded. "Mm-hmm. Those are quiet, sweetheart. That was a good choice. Did you remember to bring paper to color on?"

The little girl shook her head, her expression quickly turning sad.

"That's okay, honey," Marie told her, climbing into the front seat and pulling her door shut. "I've got a pad of paper in the glove compartment you can use. Remind me to get it out for you when we get there."

"Daddy! Daddy!" Fern ran up to Marc after the 10 a.m. ceremony, her arms and legs flailing in her excitement. Marie held Edward's hand as they approached at a more dignified walk.

He bent to pick up the little girl, then straightened up.

Grinning, she kissed him, tilting his mortarboard askew. She clutched at the violet-blue tassel on his cap – indicative of the college of architecture – delighting in the silken feel of its strands in her fingers. "You look nice in your hat and dress, Daddy."

He caught his wife's eye as she smiled.

"It's called a cap and gown, sweetheart," Marie corrected gently.

The little girl turned toward the sound of her mother's voice. "Oh," she replied, then turned back to her father. "I mean, cap and gown," she corrected herself seriously.

Marc snuggled her. "That's okay, baby. You can call it a hat and dress if you want to. And thank you." It felt good to smile – really smile – again, he realized.

"Can I have this dangly thing?" she asked, enthralled with its rich color and sleek texture.

"Not right now," he replied, delicately removing it from her grasp. "Maybe later."

"Did you do it? Are you all gravitated now?" Edward asked, tugging at the grey suit jacket beneath his dad's partially unzipped black robe.

"Graduated? Yes, I've graduated, honey," he replied, stooping to meet the boy at eye level, but still holding his daughter in one arm. "But I haven't gotten my diploma yet. I've got to get over to the art gallery now for the ceremony there."

"*Another* ceremony?" the little boy asked, sounding weary. "Is this one gonna be as long as the first one?"

Marc smiled at his little dark-haired son. "No, Edward. This one won't be nearly as long, and there's going to be lunch afterward."

The child's demeanor brightened a bit. "Okay," he agreed with a dramatic sigh. "I guess I can survive another ceremony. As long as there's lunch. Will there be hamburgers?"

Marc smiled. "I don't know. If not, and you're still hungry, on the way home we'll stop and get you one. Okay?"

"How about me, Daddy? Do I get one, too?"

"If you wish, Princess Fern," he replied planting a kiss on the girl's forehead. He set her on her feet again and stood. "Now, c'mon, we've got to get going. Shall we all ride over together?"

"Yeah!" the twins exclaimed, hopping up and down. Fern clapped her hands in excitement.

"You can drive my Jeep, Daddy," Edward told him seriously.

Marc smiled solicitously at the little boy, then directed a playful wink at Marie. "Well, thank you, Edward," he said, sounding equally earnest. "I was just about to ask you if we could take it."

When they piled out of the Jeep at the art gallery, just before Marc hurried to meet up with the rest of his class, Marie looked him over.

"Fix your mortarboard."

As he straightened it, their young son asked, "Why's Daddy got to fix his motorboat?"

Marc and Marie stifled mirth at the child's misheard wording. But as soon as their eyes met, their spontaneous smiles decayed, and his gaze darted uneasily away from hers.

"Daddy's got a broken motorboat?" Fern exclaimed, her eyes widening. She whipped around to look at her father. "When you fix it, can we go for a ride?"

"No, sweetheart," Marie told the little girl, bending to speak to her and quell her excitement. "Not motorboat. Mortarboard. That's what they call that square cap Daddy's wearing."

Her enthusiastic expression withered. "Oh. Well, that's no fun."

Marc repressed a smile at his daughter's disillusionment. "Sorry, honey. That's just what it's called." He bent to give her a kiss on the nose. "But if I did have a broken motorboat, I'd let you help me fix it."

That night, Marc seemed uncharacteristically quiet when he arrived at work. He avoided making eye contact with anyone and spoke in as few syllables as he could get away with. If anyone asked, he said he wasn't feeling particularly well – not sick enough to stay home, but not exactly on top of his game.

Gary attributed it to the emotional crash after Marc's graduation ceremony today – all that stress and anxiety during finals and the buoyancy and excitement leading up to today, and then suddenly everything was all over and he was left with a gaping hole in his routine.

Marc felt disinclined to set him straight. "Yeah, that's probably it," he replied, hoping ready concurrence would end the discussion.

But Gary wanted to talk about how soon he'd have to take his boards, how much time he would get to study for them – and how many sections of the licensure exam he'd have to sit for.

"Six. But I can't take 'em 'til after my apprenticeship ends."

"How long is that?"

"Three years. I start end of next month. With luck, I'll be an architect before the end of '03." He forced a smile in his brother-in-law's direction, then retreated to the DJ prep area. Fortunately, just about everyone on the FM side had already cleared out of the building, leaving no one else with whom he'd need to avoid engaging in small talk.

About quarter to seven, coming out of his last commercial break, Gary read the evening's updated weather. He wrapped it up with, "Sixty degrees right now outside our Middlebury studios, and here's a cheery little number from Styx. Who remembers this, from their monster album, *Kilroy Was Here*? For that matter, remember *albums* – those big round flat vinyl things that used to be all the rage? Ah, but I digress. Seventeen years later, this song still sounds amazing. Here's Dennis DeYoung singing lead on 'Don't Let It End.' Z97-3."

Flipping the microphone off, Gary headed down the hall toward his office. On his way there, he glanced into the DJ prep room. The audio monitor overhead was on and he noticed Marc hunched forward in his chair, his keyboard shoved to one side and his head resting against the front of his desk. It looked to Gary like he was shivering.

He stepped inside and shut the door. "Marc? You okay?"

Startled at the sound of the other man's voice, Marc looked up. Huddled into a nearly fetal position, his face was streaked with tears.

Ignoring the still-tender incision line from his surgery sixteen weeks earlier, Gary crouched beside his brother-in-law and rested a hand on his shoulder. "Hey… do you want to talk?"

Marc shook his head. When he tried to speak, all that came out was a wrenching sob.

"You don't have to go on at seven if you don't feel up to it. I'll call Rob and stay on the air 'til he gets here. You want me to do that?"

Marc shrugged but offered Gary no answer.

Meanwhile, the singer crooned about being filled with loneliness at missing his love.

Figuring the song had triggered Marc's implosion, and understanding he certainly didn't need to hear more of it, Gary stood. Without thinking, he reached up for the monitor's volume knob. He winced at the sudden tug. "Ooh," he exclaimed quietly, putting a hand to his side to quell the pain. *That wasn't bright!*

Gary helped Marc to his feet. "C'mon, you don't need to be hearing this drivel."

He hugged his best friend, then walked him unsteadily down the hall to the music office, forgetting he'd left the monitor on in there, too.

They arrived just in time to hear Dennis DeYoung's plaintive plea for his loved one not to leave.

Cursing under his breath, Gary switched off the monitor as Marc slumped into a chair by his brother-in-law's desk.

Gary lifted the phone receiver. "Am I calling Rob?"

After a moment's hesitation, Marc nodded, not looking up.

Swiftly, he punched in the fill-in guy's number and waited while the call connected. "Hey, Rob, it's Gary. Sorry for the short notice. Any chance you can fill in for Marc tonight? He's… not feeling real well."

He listened as the other man spoke.

Gary smiled. "Great. Take your time. I'll hold down the fort 'til you get here. Thanks, Rob. I really appreciate it."

Replacing the receiver in its cradle, he rested a hand on Marc's shoulder and addressed him again. "You hang out here, okay? I'll be back soon as Rob gets settled in." Not waiting for a reply, he darted back to the on-air studio.

"Hey," Rob Tyler greeted Gary as he hurried into the studio half an hour later. "I thought you said Marc wasn't here" – he thumbed over his shoulder – "Isn't that his Jeep parked outside?"

"I didn't say he wasn't here," Gary countered. "I said he's not feeling well."

"Is it serious? Does he have to go to the hospital or something?"

"Nah. Nothing like that. Just… not up to doing a five-hour show."

Rob uncoiled the cord from around his headphones. "Hope he's okay."

"Me too." He donned his headphones. "It's twenty past seven, Z97-3. And that'll do it for me. I'm Gary Sheldon. Thanks for stickin' around with me a few bonus minutes this evening. Marc Lindsay's feeling a little under the weather tonight, so all the other jocks were fighting over who got to hang out with you 'til midnight. Oh, you shoulda seen it – it was mayhem out there! The rest of 'em are lying in a bloody heap in the corridor, and a victorious Rob Tyler's up next. I'd better get on out there and mop up the blood before the big guy sees it and blows a gasket. I'll leave you with Giorgio Moroder and Philip Oakey, 'Together in Electric Dreams.' I'll see you in *your* electric dreams, and I'll see you back here tomorrow at three, right after Pete Donovan. Make it a good night now. Bye."

Chapter 38

(May 25 – Thursday)

When Gary arrived at work, Pete called to him from down the hall.

"What's up, chief?" he asked, appearing in the doorway to the program director's office.

"Just wanted to give you a heads up. Rob's filling in for Marc tonight. He just called me to let me know."

Gary nodded. "Okay." He thought for a moment. "Wait – Rob called you? Why didn't Marc call?"

Pete shrugged. "I dunno. Didn't Rob cover for him a few nights ago, too?"

He nodded again.

"Did he say anything to you? Marc, that is. What's goin' on with him lately?"

Gary shrugged. "I dunno. You'll have to ask him. We haven't really talked a whole lot lately. I'm as in the dark as you are."

It wasn't really a lie, he reasoned. All he really had to go on was speculation based on his grandfather's statements while he lay dead on the operating table. And he still wasn't even a hundred percent certain that conversation had happened.

Five minutes later, Pete leaned in the door of the break room, where Gary had stowed his lunch in the fridge and was brewing a new pot of coffee. "Can I talk to you for a second?"

He turned, wondering why he didn't say whatever it was while he had him in his office a few minutes earlier. "Sure. What's up?"

The program director came in and shut the door. "What the hell is going on with Marc?"

Perplexed at the question, Gary eyed his boss with caution. He knew Marc had been going through some tough times with Marie lately, but it wasn't his place to reveal that – or anything – to their boss. He worded his response with care. "Didn't we just have this conversation? And what do you mean, what's going on with him?"

Grim faced, Pete threw his hands in the air. "I *mean*, he just called a minute ago and quit."

He continued speaking, but Gary couldn't focus on anything beyond the word 'quit,' which echoed in his head. The next thing he heard his boss say was, "I doubt Rob's gonna want the slot on a permanent basis. Reach out to your network, would ya? See if anyone's looking to make a move."

Still reeling from Pete's surprise news about Marc, Gary almost stepped on a small envelope with his name on it that had been slid beneath his office door.

Recognizing the writing, he set the steaming mug on his desk and stooped to pick up the envelope. He didn't even wait 'til he got to his chair to open it. Inside was a folded sheet of paper with a few lines of Marc's careful handwriting. The envelope contained something else – a tiny packet wrapped in another sheet of paper.

Curious, Gary unfolded the note first.

> Gary,
> I figured you should have this back. It wouldn't be fair to you for me to keep it, given how things have turned out. It belongs in your family and you should pass it down to one of your kids.
> It was great while it lasted.
> Thanks.

Gary stumbled backward. His breath caught in his throat.

Throughout the day, Gary tried several times to contact Marc. Each time, the call went unanswered. He left message after message, imploring Marc to return his call.

Sometime after 4:30, Marc left a terse reply message on Gary's office line.

"Hey, it's Marc. Please stop calling me, huh? I know you're concerned, but I'm not ready to talk. And your leaving half a dozen messages in the space of four hours won't make me want to talk to you any sooner. I'll be in touch when I'm ready."

Arriving home that evening, anxious and unsettled, Gary searched the first floor and couldn't find Michaela. Bounding up the stairs, he found her in the nursery, laying the twins in their cribs, settling them in for the night. As she moved back and forth between the cribs, she sang softly to the babies.

When she straightened and headed for the door, she let out a little "Ohh!" of surprise "You startled me," she said, moving toward Gary, who stood in the doorway.

He backed into the hall so she could pull the door almost shut.

She studied his face. He looked stricken, his eyes sadder than she'd seen them in years. "Are you okay?"

In response, he wrapped his arms around her.

She felt his chest heave as he took in a shuddering breath.

"Gary?" His name was a question. "What's the matter, honey?"

He didn't respond for a long time, just held her close, trembling.

At last, Micki pulled away from him. His eyes swam with unshed tears. Worried, she touched his cheek. "What's wrong, Gary?"

He pulled Marc's note from his pocket and handed it to her. "I found this in my office when I got to work this morning."

Michaela unfolded the note and read it. Her brow furrowed in perplexity.

"This was with it."

She gazed at his grandfather's gold wedding band in the hollow of her hand, then stared at her husband, open mouthed. She felt as if she were carved from wax and someone had just cranked the thermostat up to 150 degrees. Her features drooped; hot tears sprang to her eyes. Her lower lip trembled.

"Poor Marc," she whispered, reaching for the comfort of Gary's arms.

They hugged one another and wept.

Late Sunday afternoon, the phone rang.

Expecting it to be one of her friends, Erin lunged to answer it. "Hello?"

"Hey, sweetie."

"Uncle Marc! It's so good to talk to you!" she gushed. "I miss you. How are you?"

Marc swallowed hard. He forced himself to smile, knowing it would come through in his voice. "I'm fine, honey. It's nice to hear your voice, too." He paused. "Hey, is your dad home?"

"Yeah, I'll get him. Hang on a sec." She hesitated. "Uncle Marc, we haven't seen you guys in ages. Can't you please fix things between Daddy and Auntie Marie?"

"I wish I could, honey. Sometimes, though, it's not that easy."

Erin sighed. "I miss you so much…"

"I know, sweetie. I miss you, too. But right now, I really need to talk to your dad. Can you get him for me, please?"

Gary's hand trembled as he picked up the phone in his study. He'd spent the last three days trying to reach Marc, but now he had him on the other end of the line, he couldn't think what to say. Not a single thing. "Hey…"

"Tell me you're not just gonna try to talk me out of leaving," Marc said, forestalling anything else Gary could say.

Gary didn't acknowledge his directive. "How are you?"

"My wife kicked me out, I only get to see my kids at church on Sunday – and I have no idea why! – and I just quit a job I've had half my life. I'm fucking wonderful." Before Gary could respond,

Marc added, "I'm sorry, Gar'. You didn't deserve that. I'm… having a hard time."

"I figured. You wanna talk?"

"That's kind of why I called," he admitted. "It was either this or head to the nearest bar."

"Don't do that, Marc. Why don't I meet you somewhere?"

"Where?"

"You name it, I'll be there."

"How 'bout your office?"

It was familiar and they could talk in private. "That works." Gary checked his watch. 4:30. "I can be there in twenty minutes."

When Gary ran upstairs for his keys and wallet, he found Micki in the rocking chair in the nursery, reading Josephine a story. "Hey, honey. Going out for a bit. I'm meeting Marc. We'll be at the station. I'm sorry, Mick, but I probably won't be home in time for dinner."

Family dinner on Sundays was sacrosanct.

Michaela laid the storybook aside and tipped her head up to meet his kiss. "Don't even think about apologizing. This is way more important. Take all the time you need. And give him a hug for me."

When Gary arrived, Marc was already there. Gary parked beside the red Jeep.

Marc got out. He looked more dejected than his best friend could ever remember seeing him.

"Sorry I'm late. Hope you weren't waiting long." Gary gave him a warm hug.

Marc pulled away. "Nah," he muttered. He wouldn't make eye contact – barely looked up at all, just trailed morosely behind Gary to the building. "I got nowhere else to be, anyway."

After his brother-in-law unlocked the door, Marc followed him to his office.

Even though there was still plenty of afternoon sunlight in the room, Gary flipped on the light switch. Rather than sitting at his desk, he settled into one of the two seats in front of his desk. Marc sank into the other one.

Gary sat forward, elbows on the arms of his chair. He didn't waste any time on small talk. "Talk to me, Marc. What's goin' on?"

The other man heaved a sigh and wiped both hands down his face. "It's all falling apart," he admitted from behind his hands.

"What is?"

"Everything. My whole life."

He nodded. That sounded strangely like what he'd told his therapist a few years earlier, back when Michaela had him committed before the start of his trial. Dr. Benson had picked through the examples Gary gave and helped him piece his life back together.

Gary's eyes automatically sought out the St. Joseph statue on the bookcase behind his desk. He silently prayed for guidance now to help Marc navigate the relational icebergs in his life.

"You're having a really rough time right now," he said. "I know it must seem like everything's piling up on you. Why don't we focus on one thing at a time and see if we can't sort through it all."

Marc looked up and offered a head bob and a slight smile. "You sound like my shrink."

Gary returned the smile. "Actually, I was hoping I'd sounded more like *mine*. He made some pretty good sense."

Marc's gaze darted away; his smile decayed. "Well, whoever you sound like, thanks."

"What would you like to talk about first?"

Just as they began talking, they heard voices. The six-to-midnight weekend kid had seen the music director's car in the lot and knocked at his door.

"It's open," Gary called.

Chris Stephens opened the door and poked his head in. "Hi, Gary. Oh, hey, Marc. I'm sorry, I didn't mean to interrupt. I just wanted to say hi and see if there was anything I should know about, music wise, this week."

Gary thought for a moment, then shook his head. "Nothing out of the ordinary, Chris. I expect we'll have some concert tickets to give away for next week, but – as usual – probably nothing for the overnight or weekend shifts."

"Isn't that always the way." Chris flashed a grin. "Us weekend slobs never get to take part in any of the fun. Well, thanks for the info. I'll leave you alone now." Giving the men a wave, he shut the door.

As Chris left, Gary worried that during the disruption Marc might have reconsidered wanting to talk.

But while reticent, Marc opened up at last and shared his concerns about the crumbling of his marriage.

Gary listened with compassion, but he refrained from offering suggestions unless Marc asked for input.

Several times during their talk, Marc bordered on tears as he described the various ways in which Marie had put distance between them over the prior eight months, eventually asking him to leave altogether several weeks earlier.

Some time later, beset by the onset of hunger pangs, Gary glanced at his watch and was surprised to find it was already 6:30. "You hungry?"

Marc pulled a tissue from the box on Gary's desk and wiped at his eyes. "Yeah. I haven't really eaten today," he admitted.

"That's not good. You want to come back to the house? Micki and the kids would love to see you. Not to mention you'd get to overload on your quota of hugs."

Marc tried to force a smile. He shook his head. "Thanks, but I don't think I'm up for seeing anyone I know." His head drooped. "I just feel like such a failure."

Gary grasped his hand. "You're not a failure, Marc. You're just going through a really rough time right now. I don't know what's up with Marie, but I'm so glad you reached out. You need to surround yourself with people who love you. That's why I suggested coming home with me."

Marc shook his head. "I don't think so."

"Want me to get something delivered? We can stay here and talk, long as you want."

He shrugged. "I dunno. What's open at seven on a Sunday?"

"There's a diner up on Route 6. Or we can drive in to Waterbury. There's bound to be something still open up that way."

"I don't care. Whatever you want to do." His lackluster tone didn't convey disinterest as much as despondency.

"I hate to see you like this."

Marc gave a wry smirk. "How do you think *I* feel about it?"

Gary stood and reached for his keys, which lay on his desk. "C'mon, let's get you fed. I'll drive."

"You just don't trust me not to run off the road."

"You've found me out," Gary deadpanned, slipping an arm around Marc's shoulder.

They ended up at *Abundância*, a Portuguese restaurant in nearby Naugatuck that stayed open 'til ten.

Soothed by the cozy surroundings and enticed by the heady aromas of familiar fare, Marc's demeanor brightened. Over the next hour and a half, the two friends talked and savored delicacies from his grandmother's homeland.

When Gary tried to broach the subject of Marie, Marc shook his head.

"*Não, não quero falar sobre isso.*" The foreign words slipped out, unintended. At Gary's look of perplexity, he translated, "No. I don't want to talk about that."

"Fair enough." Then he added, "I didn't realize you were fluent in Portuguese."

"I used to be. Not so much anymore. A lot of it came back while we were over there, but I've pretty much lost it again."

"That's too bad. Have you taught the kids?"

At the mention of his children, Marc's expression grew somber again. He glanced down at his plate. "Not much," he murmured. "Although while they're still little is probably the best time for them to learn."

The sun had long since set by the time they left the restaurant.

When they pulled in to the parking lot, Gary let Marc out by the Jeep.

"Thanks again," Marc said, bending to peer in the Camaro's open door. "For dinner, and the talk. I really needed that."

Gary nodded. "Glad I could be here for you. See you tomorrow night then, huh?"

Marc nodded. "Yeah." Shutting the door, he gave it two parting thumps with the flat of his hand. He got into the Jeep and drove away with a small wave.

As Marc's tail lights disappeared into the night, Gary returned inside. He headed to his office to write an email he'd meant to send the other evening.

Before he left, Gary jotted a note and slid it beneath Pete's door.

Talked Marc into staying on 'til June 16. He'll be in to do his shift Monday night.

Chapter 39

(1:07 p.m., May 27 – Saturday)

It was a perfect spring afternoon. Sunny skies, mild temps. After Gary finished mowing the lawn, he showered and changed, then meandered into the kitchen, car keys in hand. He leaned to kiss Micki. "Taking the kids to the park."

She gave him a questioning look. "We've got swings and slides here."

He shrugged. "Yeah, but this way they get to play with other kids if they want."

"Okay. Have fun. When do you think you'll be home?"

"Sometime before winter, I expect."

Grinning, Micki playfully swatted his butt. "Get outta here."

Once released from their car seats, the kids scrambled out of the car and raced ahead of Gary to the playground area.

Beneath the shade of a tall oak, Amanda stopped and pivoted toward her father. "C'mon, Daddy," she prompted, hands poised on her hips.

"Right behind ya, sweetie," he assured the little girl. "Michael, slow down, buddy."

The little boy stopped and turned around. His shoulders drooped as he saw how far behind his dad was. "Hurry *up*," he urged.

Obligingly, Gary broke into a jog and caught up with his son in no time. He scooped the five-year-old into his arms and twirled him around; his still-tender midsection protested with a little twinge. Then he slung the giggling boy over his shoulder and hustled over to Mandy.

"Where to first?"

"The swings!" the pair answered in excited unison as Gary set Michael on his feet again.

"Okay – let's go." He raced them there.

Gary held the seat steady as the little boy clambered up into his swing. He always chose the blue one. It was his "most favorite-est" color.

Taller and more independent than her little brother, Amanda climbed up into the red-plastic seat of her swing all by herself. Her long hair fluttered behind her in the breeze she created as she swung.

Gary smiled as he watched the little girl.

"Push me, Daddy?" Michael asked, rattling the thick chains that secured the brightly colored swing to the pole overhead. Then, without being prompted, he added, "Please?"

"Hang on tight." Holding both ends of the blue-plastic seat as the five-year-old complied, Gary stepped carefully backward until child and swing were just over his head.

He released the swing. Michael careened forward and then swung back. The motion elicited gleeful giggles from the little boy.

After spending a few minutes pushing his son's swing, Gary exhorted him to keep going on his own, then went to sit on a nearby bench.

A woman seated at one end of the bench studied Gary as he watched his laughing children.

"I wasn't sure you'd come," she ventured after a time.

Still keeping an eye on his kids, Gary turned his head slightly toward the sound of her voice. "I said I'd be here."

"I wouldn't blame you if you didn't."

Ignoring her statement, he eyed her with reservation. He almost didn't recognize her. She looked gaunt, her eyes sunken. What remained of her blonde hair, once neatly coiffed, now appeared drab and limp. Despite the warmth of the afternoon, she clutched a woolen shawl about her shoulders. "How are you?" Gary tried to keep a tone of alarm out of his voice.

The woman shook her head. "The prognosis isn't good."

Now his tone sobered. "I'm really sorry to hear that."

"Michael's been taking good care of me." The fingers of her right hand discreetly touched the gold band on her left ring finger. She inclined her head toward the swings. "They're adorable. How old are they?"

"Amanda's eight and Michael's five."

She gave a vague nod of acknowledgment. "They look like the two of you."

"That's a good thing."

The woman's bleak expression brightened for a moment, almost resembling a smile. She remained silent for at least a dozen back-and-forths of the kids' swings.

"How long has it been?"

Gary sat in silence, his head tipped slightly upward, trying to recall their last interaction. Was it Valentine's Day, when he proposed to Micki? That must have been it. "Too long," he admitted at last. "At least a decade."

"I'm sorry about that," she said with a rueful headshake, "about all the time we lost."

He bit back a harsh comment about its being her choice to ignore their wedding invitation. What good would it do now to dredge up the past and its hurts?

Amanda dragged the toes of her sneakers in the dusty, tromped-down rut of dirt beneath her. When her swing remained only a few feet in the air, she leapt off, landing in the grass. Running over, she climbed up into Dad's lap for a snuggle.

"Hi, baby. All done swinging?"

"Uh huh. For now. Can I go play on the slide?"

"Okay, but stay where I can see you. And what's the rule?"

"Never go with anyone – even if they say they got puppies. And if someone gets too close, come back here right away."

"And?" he prompted. "What else?"

"If anyone touches me or tries to make me go with them," she intoned seriously, "scream bloody murder."

Gary gave her a kiss on the forehead. "Good girl."

Susan watched their interaction. Gary spoke to his daughter in a gentle tone, but one that conveyed authority and expected obedience.

As a condition of this meetup, Gary had insisted Susan not attempt to engage the children in conversation. She realized if she wanted any kind of relationship with her grandchildren in whatever remaining time she had, she'd best comply with Gary's wishes.

As Amanda sped away and navigated the ladder stairs to the slide, Susan nodded in approval.

"You've taught them well," she observed as the little girl giggled on her way down the slide.

"It's a team effort," he replied evenly, acknowledging Michaela's influence in their children's upbringing. "Parenting is the most challenging thing I've ever done. But it's also the most fulfilling."

Chapter 40

(May 30 – Tuesday)

Elisa looked up. "Oh! Hi, Marc. Haven't seen you around these parts in a while."

Marc smiled at the warm greeting. "Well, between studying for my finals and interviewing for an apprenticeship, I've kept pretty busy."

"That's right. Hey, congratulations on your graduation. Marie's pretty darn proud of you. I swear she can't stop braggin' on you."

He shrugged. "I dunno why. Hundreds of thousands of people graduated from college this year. And most of 'em were half my age."

"Yeah, but how many graduated seventh in their class? While working full time *and* raising a family? Not to mention dealing with a handful of a wife like her?" She flashed a teasing grin.

Marc rolled his eyes heavenward. "It's an enigma," he replied with a sigh. Then he changed the subject. "Speaking of my handful of a wife… Is my beloved in?"

"Yeah, just a second." Elisa pressed the intercom. "Dr. Lindemeyr, Mr. Midnight Coffee is here to see you."

A flicker of a smile lit Marc's face at her use of the nickname she'd given him back when he and Marie first started dating back in '92.

After several seconds of silence, during which Marc feared she would ask her assistant to tell him to get lost, the door opened.

Marie's smiling face appeared.

"Thanks, Elisa. Well, this is a nice surprise. Get in here, you," she greeted him, draping an arm around his neck.

Marc's heart stuttered; he could scarcely recall the last time she'd voluntarily touched him – even in a way as innocuous as this.

When the door shut behind them, her smile evaporated. She pulled her arm away from him as fast as she could. "What are you doing here?"

Marc's insides tightened at her curt tone. "*Querida*, please." He reached for her hand.

She drew it away, then went to sit behind her desk. "Don't '*querida*' me, Marc. What are you doing here?" she repeated. She looked away, rather than acknowledge the mist of tears glistening in his eyes.

"I needed to see you. Please, Marie." He sank into one of the chairs opposite her desk.

Her eyes darted upward, to the wall clock. 2:53. She heaved an exaggerated sigh. "I can give you five minutes. But then you have to leave. I've got a three-o'clock session down the hall and I can't be late."

Marc swallowed hard. "Can we talk?"

Her tone was frostier than he'd ever heard it. "I just told you, I've got a session."

"I didn't mean now. I meant, can we schedule some time to talk?"

She folded her arms. "We have nothing to talk about, Marc."

We have everything to talk about! Feeling his insides crumble, he shook his head. "That's not how I see it, *queri*— Marie. There's plenty to talk about. Our *marriage* – our *family* – is at stake. I know there are issues we need to discuss. And I can't go on like this without you. Please don't shut me out. Not now. I need you. And the kids." A tear that had wobbled for several seconds along the lower edge of his right eye escaped and slid down his cheek.

With an audible exhale, Marie flipped to the next page in her appointment book, as if she were scheduling a session for a client.

Her tone remained terse. "I can see you on Thursday at three. For precisely half an hour. Where shall I meet you?"

He looked stricken. "What's wrong with here?"

She shook her head and stood abruptly, crossing her arms in front of her. "No. Work is off limits." Before he could respond, she added, "I've got to get to my session."

Marie reached for the white coat hanging on the back of her chair. Sliding her arms into its sleeves, she eyed him with growing disdain. Her mouth twisted into a sneer. "Pull yourself together, Marc, and get out of here. I don't want you coming around here anymore. Do you understand?"

His heart lurched as his gaze fell upon the name, *Dr. Marie C. Lindemeyr*, embroidered in blue script across the left front of her coat. He expected she would most likely go back to wearing her *Dr. Marie C. Sheldon* coats. He couldn't bear the thought of her divorcing him. His mouth felt dry. "Then where shall I meet you on Thursday?" He hated that he sounded so needy, so desperate.

"Not here," she replied in a hasty staccato. "Figure something out and text me."

Marie opened the door and pasted on a smile as she stepped into the main office. "I'll see you later, honey. I'm so glad you stopped in," she called out pleasantly. Then, solely for Elisa's benefit, she leaned in, caressed her husband's cheek and gave him a sultry kiss on the mouth.

Late the next afternoon, Marie texted Marc. CAN'T MEET YOU TOMORROW. NEXT TUESDAY INSTEAD.

No apology. No excuse. Just seven words that broke his heart.

Chapter 41

(10:45 a.m., June 3 – Saturday)

The last religious-ed class for the year was over. To celebrate, Gary took Amanda and Michael out for lunch and then to the park.

When they arrived, the lady on the bench was there.

"Hi, lady!" the kids shouted, running over to greet her with hugs.

"Hi, darlings," she cooed, wrapping her too-thin arms around them. Even in the warmth of the day, and although she was bundled in a coat, she shivered a little.

"Aren't you hot?" Michael asked her.

"No," she replied softly. "I get cold very easily – even when it's warm outside."

"Are you sick?"

"Michael," Gary corrected gently, "that's not a polite thing to ask someone."

The park-bench lady smiled up at the children's father. "That's okay. It's a normal sort of question to ask." She met the child's gaze seriously. "Yes, Michael. I'm sick. But it's not a kind of sickness you can catch from me," she added as he backed away from her. "The kind of sick I am is inside, and it makes me weak... and tired. And I feel cold all the time."

"Can we pray for you?" Amanda asked.

The lady's smile lit up her pallid face. "I'd like that," she said with a nod. "I'd like that very much."

"Now?"

"I think that would be nice," Dad told his daughter.

The four of them joined hands. Amanda said, "God, I'd like you to help this nice lady who's sick inside. Help her feel better so she can play on the swings with us and not have to just sit here on the bench and be cold and tired all the time."

Gary added to the prayer. "We ask You, Father, to bless Susan and heal her," he said. "We ask You to keep her in Your care and to heal all the wounds we cannot see, the wounds she may carry inside… even the deepest wounds of many years. We ask You for healing and wholeness in all areas of her life. And we ask all this through Christ our Lord."

The children responded, "Amen."

Susan smiled at Gary. "Thank you," she mouthed, because she couldn't trust her voice.

"Who's Susan?" Michael asked.

The lady held up a hand. "I am."

"How do you know her name, Daddy?"

Gary tweaked his son's nose. "How do you think? We talk every week while you and your sister are playing."

"Oh." The little boy fell silent for a moment. Then he spoke up again. "Is it okay if we go play now?"

"Not until I get another one of your special hugs," Susan told him. "You too, Amanda."

Both children climbed up onto the bench beside Susan and hugged her tight.

Chapter 42

(3:47 p.m.)

While he was at the grocery store, Marc's phone vibrated. When he pulled it out of his pocket, he saw he'd received a text. His heartrate quickened. Only one person ever texted him.

CALL YOUR PARENTS.

His heart sank. He hadn't been able to shake the memory of Marie's smoldering kiss four days earlier. She hadn't kissed him like that in months. He'd hoped she was texting to say she missed him and wanted him to come back home… or she didn't want to wait 'til Tuesday to see him… or even simply that she was thinking of him.

Marc jammed the phone back into his pocket and returned his attention to his pathetically minuscule shopping list: eggs, cereal, milk, toothpaste.

When he'd collected the four items on his list, he decided he probably should check in with his folks. Maybe it was important. He doubted it, but there was always that chance.

He pulled the phone from his pocket again. Shoving aside a swell of emotion, Marc poked in the digits for his parents' home phone and waited as the call connected.

"Hello."

"Hi, Dad. What's up?"

"You're a hard guy to get ahold of." Hearing the jovial tone in his dad's voice, Marc envisioned the older man's broad, welcoming smile. "I've been trying to reach you for days."

"Well, ya got me," he replied, forcing a smile as he tried to sound upbeat. Years of working in radio had taught him a smile – even a forced one – lent warmth to his voice. "What's up?"

"We were sort of wondering the same thing. Your mother and I haven't seen you, Marie and the kids in ages."

Marc let out a pained sigh. There was no sense putting off telling him, no reason to hide the ugly truth any longer. "Yeah, well, that kinda makes three of us."

"What's that supposed to mean?"

"It means Marie asked for a separation," he admitted quietly. "And the only time I get to see her and the kids is if I happen to run into them at Mass."

"That's absurd! She can't do that to you. Can't you get visitation rights?"

He really didn't want to have this discussion – especially not in the middle of the toothpaste aisle. "It's a separation, Dad. Not a divorce. Yet," he added in a mumble. "And there's really nothing preventing her from keeping me from the kids. I don't think I have a legal leg to stand on."

"That's not true. You should get yourself a lawyer and take that lousy bit—"

"Hey!" Marc interrupted, his tone suddenly sharp. "That's my wife you're talking about. You watch what you say about her."

Glancing around, he saw other shoppers approaching. "Look, I gotta go, Dad. I'll call you later, okay?"

"Wait – before you go…"

Marc sighed. "Yeh?"

"I'm sorry," Willem Lindemeyr told his son. "What I said about Marie. Why don't you come for dinner tonight, son? Let's talk."

He heard himself mumble an acceptance of his dad's offer, and immediately regretted it. But he'd had already said goodbye and hung up.

"Fuck," he whispered, shoving the phone back into his pocket. Casting his gaze upward and blinking rapidly, he willed away the tears he felt building. Avoiding the other shoppers' half-curious looks, Marc darted up the aisle and hastened toward the checkout area.

He noticed Laura, his favorite cashier, at register six, so he made a beeline for the furthest open register from her. He couldn't bear to attempt making small talk with her today – she was too perky for him right now. At least on the air, when the tears caught him by surprise, he could delude listeners with the lame excuse he sounded congested because of allergies or a summer cold. But here, out in public, he couldn't hide behind the anonymity of a microphone.

Mercifully, the sullen, acne-riddled teenage cashier on register 14 couldn't be bothered to chat. He barely even took the time to ask Marc for his store loyalty card. Marc paid cash for his purchases and left with his meager items in a single grocery bag.

The steady drizzle that rendered him uncomfortably damp by the time he reached the Jeep at the end of the parking lot did nothing to help his spirits. Tugging the door shut, Marc sat for a long time, trying to collect himself, before sliding the key into the ignition. Staring out at the rain coursing down his windshield, he ached for a drink. It'd be so easy to run in to the package store a little further along the plaza and grab a six-pack of beer. Or a fifth of vodka. Or gin. Anything. It didn't really matter what.

A sudden sharp pain in his hand jolted Marc out of his haze of longing. He'd been gripping his keys so tightly, the edge of his house key dug into his palm, nearly piercing the skin. Shaking off the discomfort, he plucked up the key to the Jeep and slid it into the ignition.

When he got back to his apartment, he put away his groceries and changed into a dry shirt before heading over to his parents' home in Danbury.

Fernanda Lindemeyr answered the door. "Marc!" She wrapped him in a firm hug. "I'm so glad to see you, *meu filho precioso*. How are you?"

Marc shuddered. "Hi Mom," he mumbled from within her embrace. Dad must have told her about him and Marie. He knew if he tried to offer anything more than a simple greeting, he wouldn't get more than a couple words out before his composure fled.

She drew back from him and, stroking his cheek, looked up into his face. "Are you okay?"

He moved her hand away, avoiding her gaze. "I'm fine. Really," he lied.

"Sweetheart, what happened?" she asked her eldest, tugging him into the living room to sit on the couch. She sat beside him, her dark eyes filled with concern.

His head drooping, Marc gave a slow headshake. He wiped a hand across his eyes. "We're separated."

"But how is this possible? Why? What happened?"

He simply shook his head and shrugged. Just then his father ambled into the room. Marc knew the timing of his arrival had to have been carefully orchestrated beforehand.

When it became clear her son wouldn't divulge any further information, his mother retreated to the kitchen, leaving the men to retire to her husband's cozy study.

Willem Lindemeyr poured two brandies and returned to his son. As he extended one glass, Marc slapped it out of his father's hand, sending the amber liquid cascading across the room. The crystal snifter smashed against the fireplace.

"You sick bastard! What are you trying to do to me?" Marc's eyes flashed with fury. "Do you have any idea how hard it's been for me to stay sober right now? How badly I want that drink? Every moment of every day… and you do *this* to me?" Clenching and unclenching his fists at his sides, he turned away, fuming, trying to hold his emotions in check in front of his staid Norwegian father.

"I wasn't taunting you, son. That was a test. I did it to let you prove to yourself how strong you are."

When Marc didn't respond, his dad laid a comforting hand on his son's shoulder. "Even if you *had* reached for it, I wouldn't have let you drink it, Marc. I know how much of a struggle it is for you, and how hard you've worked to get where you are today." He set the other snifter on the table and drew his son into a hug.

Dinner was the most awkward hour Marc could remember spending with his parents since he'd been a teenager. When he answered their questions, he responded in as few syllables as he could get away with. Some questions he dodged altogether. To others, he simply replied, "I really don't want to talk about that right now." And once he even responded, "Hey, how 'bout those Mets, huh?"

Chapter 43

(8:15 a.m., June 6 – Tuesday)

"Gary – good to see you!" Laying her paperback on the chairside table, Diane rushed down the porch steps. She wrapped her son in a hug on the front walk. "You look wonderful, sweetheart. How are you feeling?"

"I feel pretty good. I hope this isn't a bad time…"

"Of course not. I was just enjoying a good mystery. What's going on?" she asked as they climbed the stairs to the wide, welcoming front porch.

"I wanted to talk to you about something."

"Everything okay?"

Gary nodded as she motioned him toward an inviting cluster of white wicker chairs with blue floral cushions. "Sure. I just need some advice, and I know you're good at that kind of thing."

Diane smiled. "You flatter me, Gary. Will this talk require ice cream?"

"Oh, it's nothing *that* serious." As a teen, Gary often engaged in late-night discussions with Mom, often about his relationship with Ellen, and usually over dishes of chocolate or rocky road. He settled into a chair. "Besides, it's kind of early for ice cream."

"Then how about some iced tea?"

"Sounds great. Thanks."

Diane retreated inside and emerged carrying a tray with two glasses of iced tea with sprigs of fresh mint. She shoved her book aside and set the tray on the glass-topped table.

The tray also held a plate of fragrant cinnamon-walnut cookies. Gary's favorite. Still warm.

"Just finished baking those. I'll package some up for you to bring home, too."

"Cookies for breakfast? You're too good to me."

"Yeah, but don't let that get around. I've got a reputation to uphold."

Mother and son exchanged conspiratorial grins as she settled into the chair beside him.

Diane reached for a cookie and nibbled at it. Gary did likewise, but his was gone in three bites.

"What did you want to talk about?"

"You don't beat around the bush, do you?"

She raised an eyebrow. "This your first rodeo, kid? Do I ever dance around a subject?"

Gary shook his head. "No, ma'am, you don't. You do tend to get right to a point."

She leaned forward. "So, spill it. What did you want to talk about?"

"I got a call… at work. A couple months back. Out of the blue. Micki's mom. She hasn't spoken to either of us since before we got married."

"She called you at work?"

"We're not listed. It was the only way she knew how to contact me."

"What did she want?"

"Apparently, she's got less than a year to live. And she wanted to meet her grandkids." He reached for his glass of tea.

Diane gave a considered nod. "What did you tell her?"

He gave a helpless shrug. "What could I tell her? No? So for the past month and a half, I've been taking the kids to the playground and letting her interact with them there. But I stipulated she's not to say anything about being related to them. As far as they know, she's just a nice old lady who sits on the same bench as Daddy while they play on the swings. They say hello and make polite conversation — you know how chatty Amanda and Michael are — but that's it. She's just the nice lady at the park."

"And you feel guilty about keeping this from Michaela."

Gary looked away. "Yeah."

Diane exhaled softly. "Sweetheart, I think it's admirable, your wanting to let her get to know her grandkids, even from a distance, and under false pretenses… but I wonder whether it's good for your relationship with Michaela. Secrets in a marriage are seldom a good idea — even if they're for a noble reason."

He nodded. "I figured you'd say something like that. So what should I do?"

"Does Michaela know her mother's dying?"

"I don't know. I mean, Michael might have told her, but she hasn't said anything to me about it."

"That could be your starting point, then. If they've been on the outs for so long, you're not doing her any favors, keeping her mother's prognosis from her. I'm sure they've got conversations they'll want to have while there's still time."

"I never thought about that. But when you put it that way, it makes sense."

"Of course it does," Diane said, taking a sip of her tea. "You don't get to be as old as me without picking up some wisdom along the way."

A comfortable silence settled between them.

Gary drummed his fingers along the arm of the chair. "I like this chair — it's comfortable. Is the set new? I don't remember seeing it before."

"James got it for me as a thank you for letting him stay here while he recuperated."

"That was nice of him."

"He's a nice guy. I'm so glad he ended up with a good family… and I'm thrilled you two have finally connected! It's too bad Marie can't see past her hostility and give him a chance. She and I talked ages ago, about how we knew this day would eventually come." She shook her head. "Even after all this time, she's still so bitter."

Gary looked confused. "How long has she known about him?"

"Years."

"How'd she find out?"

Her lips tightened into a slim line. "I told her."

"*You?*" Alarm widened Gary's eyes. "How long have you known?"

Diane paused for a long time before answering. When she spoke, her voice sounded pained. "Since before you were born."

He stared at her in astonishment. "So you knew? All this time? You knew about him?"

She gave a slow, silent nod.

"And you never did anything about it?"

"Other than cut Laura out of my life…" She shrugged.

Confusion clouded Gary's countenance. "Who's Laura?"

Diane gave a deep sigh. "Ohh, Gary. Maybe this'll require ice cream after all…"

Gary paled as his mother revealed the heart-wrenching details of his father's long-ago betrayal, the one affair that cut deepest and left their marriage in shambles.

Gary trembled with rage. "Why didn't you *do* something?"

Diane shrugged. "What could I do? I was completely dependent on him. It was 1963. I had a three-year-old and another one on the way. Where was I going to go?"

"Wouldn't Grandpa have helped you?"

"I'm sure he would have. If I'd asked. I didn't."

"So you're saying my entire childhood – the whole happy family thing – was all faked?"

Diane gave a grim nod. "Every bit of it."

"But you seemed so content, even joyful at times…"

"I did what I had to do. I had kids to protect. And you kids brought me immense joy – every day. But after I found out, I never again willingly slept with your father."

Gary took this in silently. Perplexity darkened his grey eyes. "But… Joey?"

Diane sighed. "I never again *willingly* slept with your father," she repeated, her words slow, measured.

Realization slackened his jaw. He recalled the look of vacant pain in Michaela's eyes for so long after she was raped during her senior year in high school. Tears sprang to his eyes. "I'm so sorry," he murmured, his voice thick with emotion. His hand closed firmly around his mother's. "I can't even imagine how awful that must have been for you."

"It was no picnic. But he was my baby. I loved him. I loved all you kids. I wasn't going to let who – and what – your father was taint my love for my children. 'Sins of the father' and all."

"Did Grandpa know?"

"I think so. I never told him outright, but you know how he always sort of knew things." Her brow furrowed. "I'm sure he must have known."

That night, as they put the twins down for the night, Gary touched Michaela on the arm.

"Can we talk?"

She looked up. His expression seemed serious. "Everything okay?"

He gave an indifferent shrug but said nothing.

They retreated down the hall to their room. Micki perched on the bed. "What's going on?"

Gary paced, uncertain how to start. When he reached the far end of the room, he turned and came back, stopping just in front of her. "What's the worst thing I could do?"

"Excuse me?" Michaela's eyebrows shot up. She looked at him strangely.

Gary repeated the question.

"That's an odd way to start a conversation. Are you looking for… suggestions?"

He shook his head. "In your eyes, what would be the worst possible thing I could do?"

Her nose wrinkled as she considered her husband's question. Her mouth tightened into a slim line. "Murder or child porn," she decided at last.

"Okay," he told her with a relieved sigh. He shook his head. "It's neither of those."

"*What's* neither of those? Gary, what did you do?" Michaela asked, suspicion rising in her voice.

He sat beside her on the bed and took her hand. "I haven't been entirely honest with you, Mick. W-well," he added when her eyes narrowed, "at least, not exactly forthright."

She crossed one leg over the other and bobbed her foot up and down. "I see. About what?"

He looked uneasy. "Taking the kids to the park all these weeks."

The foot bobbing stopped. "I'm sorry. You've lied to me about taking the kids to the park? Where have you been taking them? R-rated movies? Smoking cigarettes behind the barn?"

"Oh, we've gone to the park. It's just... well, it's *who* they've been seeing while we're there that I haven't exactly been upfront about."

"Okay." The corners of Micki's mouth turned downward. She folded her hands in her lap. "I have a feeling I'm not going to like where this is going, but why don't you go ahead and explain."

"A few months back, your mom called me at work."

At her husband's mention of her estranged mother, Michaela's gaze hardened. Her back stiffened and she squared her shoulders in anticipation of what Gary was about to tell her.

"She didn't know how else to reach us. She asked to meet me. I did, and we talked. She's, um... sick. Mick, it's cancer."

The word made a lump rise in Michaela's throat. "How bad is it?" She couldn't feel her lips move as she spoke.

He looked away momentarily. "Pretty bad. The doctor gave her... months."

She nodded, taking this in. Tears misted her eyes.

"Mick, I wanted her to meet the kids," he admitted, his words coming out in a guilt-ridden rush. "I arranged to meet her at the park when I brought Amanda and Michael. I never told them who she was – in fact, the first few times I didn't let her talk to them at all; she just watched them from a bench near the swings. It's only been the last couple of weeks I've even let them interact with her at all."

Michaela remained silent.

"I'm so sorry I went behind your back like this, sweetheart… but I couldn't let her die without getting to know at least some of her grandkids."

Still she said nothing.

"Will you say something?" he urged, feeling the weight of his guilt pressing on him.

A slow grin crept across Michaela's face. "Would you like me to get you a shovel so you can dig yourself in a little deeper?"

Gary looked at her, perplexed. He opened his mouth to speak but didn't know what to say.

"Not bad. Seven weeks," she intoned with a nod. "I wondered how long it'd take you to say something. I figured you'd crack two, three weeks ago."

"You mean you knew?"

Her face relaxed into a full-on smile. "Of course I knew. I mean, not right off the bat, but the first time I brought the twins to see her last month, she mentioned how much they looked like Amanda and Michael. And when she came by last week, they wanted to know how I knew 'the lady from the park.'"

"Wait… you mean we've both been sneaking around with your mom? Is that what you're telling me?"

Her expression sobered briefly. "I'm afraid so."

Gary shook his head. "The kids didn't act like they knew who she was – I mean, when we got to the park on Saturday. They didn't behave any dif…" his voice trailed off.

She shrugged. "It was an act. I told them not to let on to you they knew who she was."

"Well, you'll be happy to know they played their parts really well. Those little sneaks!"

"Yeah, I think they get it from their father," she deadpanned.

Gary's left eyebrow arched. "Or maybe their mother."

They hugged, laughing now.

"Do they know she's their grandmother?" Gary asked when he pulled back from her.

Michaela shook her head. "I didn't want to overwhelm them. I think it's best they get to know her as a nice lady who cares about them. I mean, it would just be cruel to let the kids know they've got another grandmother and then maybe in a few months have to tell them she died. I think it's enough that she knows about them."

Gary nodded. "That makes sense."

After a brief silence, Michaela asked, "Out of curiosity, what made you come clean?"

"It just felt wrong, deceiving you the way I did. I had a long talk with my mom this morning and she said it wasn't fair to you to keep your mom's condition from you."

Micki smiled. "I love your mom. She's like your own personal Jiminy Cricket."

A slow smile lit his face at the mental image of his mom dressed as the fabled cartoon insect with the blue top hat, natty vest, tails and red umbrella. "That she is. Have you and your mom had a chance to talk?"

"Yeah. We've been talking a lot lately. We're going to lunch next week. I'm glad we got to reconnect after all this time. It feels strange, being on an even footing with her. It's almost like we can relate as friends, now that she's not trying to exert control over me." She paused. "I didn't even realize how much I'd missed having my mom in my life."

Gary gave a pensive nod. "I know what you mean."

Micki squeezed his hand. "I know you do." She thought back to their early years together, before he and Diane had reconciled. No matter how happy he was, there'd always been a lingering melancholy about Gary; but that evaporated once his mom was back in the picture. It was almost eerie, how their situations paralleled one another: They'd been on the outs with their respective mothers — for a decade each. And now both enjoyed satisfying relationships with them. Except hers was about to come to a permanent end. She tried to banish that sad notion.

Michaela snuggled into her husband's arms. "I'm glad you finally came to talk to me about this. And despite your overwhelming sense of guilt, there's really nothing to forgive." She grinned. "You're off the hook… this time."

Chapter 44

(June 4 – Sunday)

Marc joined his family for 8:30 Mass. Because it was a neutral space, Marie couldn't legitimately object to his presence. From the moment they entered the church, the twins squabbled bitterly over who got to sit beside Daddy.

He offered to sit between the two of them; but, not wanting to have him that near, Marie insisted that arrangement was out of the question and said he either sat at the end of the pew or he couldn't sit with them at all.

In the end, Edward sat next to him, but not until Daddy promised Fern she could sit beside him next time.

Edward delighted in having his father sit with him at Mass. He held tight to Daddy's hand and snuggled close to him during the sitting times. And he pulled Daddy's arm around his shoulder whenever they stood or knelt.

Positioned at opposite sides of the children, Marc and Marie faced straight ahead during the whole Mass, a pair of stoic bookends. They scarcely acknowledged one another's presence. When it came time for Communion, Marc exited the pew and stood back to usher the kids and Marie ahead of him. Returning afterward, Marie stopped the twins before they re-entered the pew and slipped in ahead of them, to avoid having to sit next to her husband.

Outside, after Mass, before Marie walked the children home, Edward hugged his father goodbye.

"Don't you want to live with us anymore, Daddy?" the little boy asked, painful longing in his voice.

Marc swallowed a lump in his throat and held his son close. "Of course I do, Edward."

The child drew backward and touched his father's face. "Then why don't you come home?"

"That's up to Mommy, honey." His voice wavered. "We have some things we need to talk about."

"So come home and talk about them. I miss you, Daddy. Please come home," he pleaded.

Marie pulled the child from his father's arms and set him down on the sidewalk. "Come on, Edward, it's time to go home. And Daddy has to leave now. Say goodbye and come with me. You too, Fern." She grasped her son's hand and tried to lead him and his twin sister along the sidewalk.

Dragging his feet, Edward turned and gazed longingly back at his father. "But I don't *want* to say goodbye, Mommy. I want Daddy." Tears filled the child's eyes. He stopped walking and tugged his hand away from Mom's. Folding his arms in defiance, the little boy pouted fiercely.

Her voice was firm, unyielding. "Edward, come along."

"No! I want Daddy to come home with us."

Fern, who had been silent thus far, piped up. "I want Daddy to come home, too, Mommy. I miss him." Tugging at Mommy's hand in protest, she thrust out her lower lip in a pout that matched her twin's. When Fern turned her big brown eyes toward her father, he noticed they were filled with tears.

"No, kids," Marie insisted, leading them away. "Daddy has to leave now. But maybe we'll see him at church next week." She gripped their hands more firmly and tugged them along the sidewalk.

Marc watched them go, doing everything in his power to keep from running after them and begging Marie to let him come home. He forced back the tears that welled in his eyes. By her taking the children away, he felt as though Marie had torn his heart from his chest and ground it beneath her heel.

By the time they reached their apartment, three houses up, both children were in tears.

"I want Daddy," Fern wailed.

"Me too, Mommy," Edward cried, rubbing at his eyes with his fists. He turned back toward the church to see Daddy still standing on the sidewalk, staring after them. "I want Daddy to come home, Mommy. Why won't you let him come home?"

"Stop it, both of you," Marie scolded sternly. "Daddy had to go. He's probably not coming home – and I don't want to hear another word about it!"

"But he's still there, Mommy," Fern wailed, pointing at him. "He's right there! I want Daddy to come home, Mommy. Why can't he come home?"

Not answering her daughter, Marie hurried the twins inside, aware they were creating a scene on the sidewalk.

That afternoon, Marc texted Marie: TUESDAY AT 3 – MIDWAY DINER?

Late that night she texted back: BETTER MAKE IT 3:15.

Chapter 45

(6:35 p.m., June 5 – Monday)

When Marc arrived at work, Pete was still in his office. He called to the nighttime announcer.

"What's up?" Marc leaned in the open doorway and tried his best to act nonchalant.

"Come on in," the program director invited. He nodded toward the open door. "Shut the door?"

Now on guard, Marc pushed the door. It clicked shut. He slumped into a seat opposite the boss' desk.

"What's goin' on, Marc? You haven't seemed at all like yourself on the air lately. Everything okay?"

Marc shot a hand through his hair. His head bobbed mechanically. "Yeah. Just kinda anxious about starting my apprenticeship later this month" – he rubbed at his eyes and sniffled – "and these damn allergies."

"Allergies, huh? They really suck," Pete commiserated. He nodded, although Marc suspected he didn't believe him. "Pollen?"

He shrugged, sniffed again. "I dunno."

Pete eyed the nighttime jock for several long, uncomfortable seconds.

Just when Marc was going to exhort him to say something, he did.

"Allergies notwithstanding, I hope you know you can come to me – anytime – if there's anything bothering you. My door's always open."

Marc glanced backward. "I see a closed door here that would beg to differ."

In spite of himself, Pete grinned. "You know what I meant, Marc."

Looking down, elbows on his knees, he nodded, willing away the tears that were always close at hand these days.

"Is there something you want to talk about?"

Still not looking up, Marc shook his head. "Not particularly." He stood, gestured toward the door. "Look, I got production work to finish up before my shift." He wouldn't meet his boss' gaze.

Pete nodded. "Okay. Go ahead. I just wanted to touch base with you, make sure everything's alright."

Marc felt like one of those bobble-head dolls. "Yeah. Thanks, Pete." As quickly as he could, he ducked out of the office and down the hall, before the program director could engage him in any more chatter.

At the end of his shift, Marc crashed on the couch in the DJ prep area. Around 3, he drove back to his apartment. When he awoke, he shaved, showered and dressed. As he brushed his teeth, Marc offered a silent prayer Marie would be receptive to talking and wouldn't shut him down. He didn't think he could stand a repeat of this past Sunday.

Chapter 46

(3:27 p.m., June 6 – Tuesday)

Marc had already ordered coffees for the two of them; he'd even stirred cream into hers. Marie slid into the booth facing him, a hint of a smile playing about her lips.

"Wow, this brings back memories, huh? Sorry I'm late. Thank you for getting coffee. That was considerate of you."

I love you. "I thought it'd save us some time. I know you've only got half an hour."

Marie wouldn't meet his gaze. She picked up her coffee cup, holding it poised at her lips while she spoke. "How are you doing?"

I'm dying inside. "Today" – Marc exhaled tremulously – "I guess I'm feeling okay. Better. Sunday was brutal," he admitted, "having to say goodbye to the kids."

Marie set her cup down and looked away. "I'm so sorry about that, Marc. I'm afraid I didn't handle it very well," she admitted. She hesitated. "I'm just not ready for you to come home, that's all."

Fear rose within him. He reached a hand toward her across the table. "And *I* don't want you to start feeling like you and the kids are better off without me." His voice got that fearful little warble to it – that one he loathed. He despised his weakness.

Marie laid a hand atop his. "Of course not, sweetheart" – the endearment slipped from her lips unexpectedly. "I – I just need some time to figure a few things out."

"Like *what?* What are the 'few things'? Figure out what? And once I know what they are, can't we figure them out together?"

Marc hated that he sounded so needy. But there really was no other word for it. Without Marie in his world, he *was* needy.

He thought back to when they'd sought couples counseling after they first got engaged. He turned his hand palm-upward in a gesture of warmth, openness. He met his wife's gaze and held it. "Let's start with this: What's the single biggest issue you have with me right now?"

Marie's hand rested comfortably in his; the slightest hint of a smile brightened her countenance. "I see you were paying attention all those years ago."

He wasn't sure how to take that… but she was smiling, so he counted it as a point in his favor. "It was important to me then," he admitted, his fingers closing gently around her hand. "It's even more important now."

She gave a considered nod. Then, raising her coffee cup to her lips again, she took a slow sip before setting it back in its saucer. She leaned back against the red leather-upholstered booth, letting her hand slip free from his and into her lap. "The biggest thing?"

Nodding, Marc raised an eyebrow. "Please."

"I'd have to say your refusal to support me about James."

He'd expected as much. He wouldn't argue. He nodded again, folding his hands on the table before him. "Okay. Tell me how you feel about that."

Her gaze grew a bit harsher. "It makes me feel like I can't trust you with my heart anymore." She fidgeted, then swiped at a sudden tear. "If we're so far apart on this one issue, Marc, is there any hope for us with the rest?"

Alarm bells sounded in his head. She'd already broken physical contact. He couldn't let her disconnect from him emotionally, too — not now, not when they'd just opened a dialogue. "Don't get ahead of yourself," he cautioned tenderly. "Let's stick with that one thing. What I hear you saying is you feel emotionally abandoned — that *I've* emotionally abandoned you — regarding James. Is that about right?"

Marie nodded.

He met her gaze and held it. "I want to be supportive of you, Marie. Tell me what you need from me."

"I need you to see things my way – from *my* perspective. At least about this."

Marc hesitated. "May I ask you a question?"

Her gaze flickered away for an instant. "What's that?"

"We have differing opinions on a number of things. What makes *this* one such a hot-button issue?" He reached a hand toward his wife in supplication. "Please understand. I'm not trying to be contentious here, Marie. I'm asking a genuine question. Why this issue? What is it that's so… *visceral* for you?"

Tears swam in her eyes. As she shook her head, they dislodged and slid down her face. "I remember my Aunt Laura. My mom's youngest sister. She and Mom were always so close. They did everything together. I remember her coming over to the house to play with me all the time, at least three or four times a week. And she spent acres of time with us. Then, right about the time Mom was pregnant with Gary, Aunt Laura stopped coming around… and then Mom seemed so sad and weepy all the time." Sniffling, she wiped at her tears with trembling hands. "I remember I used to ask her when Aunt Laura was going to come back to play with me again, and she'd just get angry. She'd shut me down and tell me not to ask about her ever again, that she wasn't part of our lives anymore. That made me feel like I'd done something to upset her and made her want to go away. I never understood. Not then. I was *four*, Marc. It wasn't 'til years later Mom told me what happened to her kid sister."

She wiped away more tears as they filled her eyes. "If it had been anyone else – just another one of Dad's women that he'd managed to knock up – that wouldn't've been such a big deal for me. But Aunt Laura? The way she betrayed her own sister? Obviously, I never understood it at the time. But now? Now I know what a heartless bitch she was – what a conniving, awful bitch." Marie's face grew hard, cold at the memory. "I don't know whether Gary knows the truth about James' mom… who she was – or if he'd already formed the basis of a relationship with him before he found out… so I don't know if I can legitimately hold that against him. But I certainly would've expected he'd have more consideration for our mother than to flaunt their relationship in the open like that."

Marc sat in shocked silence, unsure what to say. He recalled wondering how Gary and James could look so much alike – so eerily similar – with only one parent in common. But this explained everything. And it felt so wrong! In a sudden flash of realization, he understood his wife's side of the dispute, understood why she'd felt so betrayed by his alignment with Gary about their half-brother. He reached across the table and wiped a torrent of tears from Marie's wide blue eyes. A few stubborn tears clung to her eyelashes and quivered there, then let go and spilled down her cheeks.

"I'm so sorry, honey," he murmured. "I had no idea." Getting up, Marc went to the other side of the booth to sit beside her. He slid an arm around his estranged wife and drew her close. It surprised him when she didn't pull back or make any move to shove him away.

"And now he's gone and given him a *body part*, for crying out loud!" she wailed. "That's gonna tie them together even more strongly. Forever!" Marie tried to stifle a sob, but it slipped out. She leaned in to the comfort of Marc's embrace, and the tenderness of his touch, and wept.

Her hair felt like silk beneath his fingers. "I had no idea," he repeated, stroking her auburn tresses comfortingly. "Now I can understand why you were so upset, and so bothered by my having sided with Gary on this. Does he know? I mean, are you *sure* he knows?"

Marie shrugged and tried to speak amid hiccupping sobs. "I… I… I don't know." She wiped at her streaming eyes. "I mean, he never knew our aunt. Mom got rid of all the pictures of her – and there were a lot of those. She either folded or tore Aunt Laura out of a ton of family photos…" Her words trailed off as the tears overwhelmed her again.

Despite his wife's obvious distress, Marc couldn't help savoring having Marie so near to him: the scent of her hair, the smoothness of her skin where his hand rested against her arm. "Shh," he murmured. "I'm glad you told me this, *querida*. I had no idea. This obviously changes things."

She looked up at him. Sniffled. Her body trembled at Marc's nearness. "You mean that?"

He nodded. "It really does. Now I understand why you felt so betrayed. I'm so sorry, honey. But have you talked to your mom about this? Do you know how she actually feels toward James? I mean, she's always been so welcoming – I remember how readily she accepted me, once Gary and I became friends – almost like I was another son. And James *is* her nephew, after all. Besides, it's not like she can blame any of this on him; it's not his fault who his parents were. Do you know for certain how she feels toward him?"

Marc didn't mention yet Diane had welcomed James into her home during his recuperation from kidney-transplant surgery. He wondered whether he was being deceitful or prudent in that regard. On one hand, he didn't want Marie to accuse him of withholding information; but he also didn't want to set her off again.

Sniffling loudly, Marie swiped a hand across her drippy nose. Marc plucked a napkin from the chrome tabletop dispenser and handed it to her. She accepted it gratefully and blew her nose.

"I don't know," she admitted meekly.

Marc leaned in and kissed his weeping wife on the forehead. He brushed away her tears with his thumb and offered her a loving smile. "I think that might be a good first step. No sense trying to guess what she's thinking, huh?"

She gave a hesitant shrug. "I suppose."

"Want me to go with you to talk to her?"

Marie looked up, her eyes still streaming with tears. She nodded. "Would you?"

When she gazed at him with such earnestness, she reminded Marc of Fern. His voice was as tender as his embrace. "Of course."

"You'd do that? For me?"

He kissed the end of her nose. "For *us*. And yes. I'd be happy to go with you."

Marie was quiet for a long time. When at last she stopped crying, she dried her eyes, looked up at Marc and met his gaze. Her voice was thin, hesitant. "Can I ask you something?"

He gave a slow nod. "Of course."

New tears formed in her eyes. "Can you name one thing you like about me?" That was one of the questions they'd been taught to ask one another in their couples-counseling sessions to help foster communication. He heard fear in her voice as she continued. "*Is there anything you still like about me?*"

Marc gave her a compassionate smile. He caressed her still-damp cheek. "*Querida*, I can name a dozen things I love about you."

Marie sniffled. At her husband's affectionate words, her tears spilled over again. She gazed up at him through her tears with a hesitant smile. "Just one will be fine."

He drew her closer and stroked her hair. "Hmm… just one, huh? Can I have a few minutes? It's gonna take some time to narrow 'em down."

His warm, conversational tone made her smile. She nodded. "Okay," she said agreeably. She snuggled closer to her husband and he felt her body relax.

After a brief silence – during which he held her close and she managed to get her new rush of tears under control – he spoke again. "One thing I particularly like about you, Marie, is you're not afraid to be seen as vulnerable. You talked about some really difficult things here this afternoon and you didn't shy away from them. You've exposed your soft white underbelly and left yourself at risk of a potential attack. But that didn't stop you. I admire your strength in that regard." *I also really love that soft white underbelly.* He paused, wondering about the propriety of what he was about to say. He didn't want to scare her off or antagonize her. Marc nuzzled the side of her throat and added gently, "But what I like best about you right now is that you're here in my arms, and we're not fighting."

After a long, comfortable silence, Marc asked the expected followup question. "What's one thing you like about me?"

Marie cuddled closer, but didn't immediately look up into his eyes. "I like that you listened. I like that you didn't judge me. You listened and understood where I was coming from." She paused. "And I really like having your arms around me again. I like how safe it makes me feel."

Amid another long silence, he glanced at his watch. "Not that I'm trying to get rid of you or anything," he said, "but it's almost four."

Marie snuggled more closely in his arms. "That's okay."

"I thought you said you could only stay half an hour. Don't you have to get back?"

She didn't respond immediately. "No," she admitted at last. "That was so, if it didn't go well, I'd have an excuse to leave."

"I see. So, I guess it went well?"

Marie nodded. "You could say that." She gathered her courage. "In fact, it went well enough for me to want to ask if you'd like to spend the night."

Marc drew in his breath audibly. Part of him — most of him, really — ached to say yes, to go home with her now and spend the rest of the afternoon and into the evening making love with her.

"As much as I'd love that, *querida*," he began, "I really don't think it's such a good idea — not yet, at least. Let's give it some more time."

She twined her fingers with his. "That's probably a good idea," she agreed, longing in her voice. "But I want you to… and soon."

"So do I," he whispered, still feeling terribly vulnerable. He kissed her cheek. "So do I."

Chapter 47

(6:43 p.m., June 9 – Friday)

"How are things going with you and Marie?" Gary asked when Marc arrived for his shift.

He bobbed his head. "Pretty good, actually. We talked the other day. *Really* talked."

"That sounds promising."

"It is. It felt good to have a real conversation that didn't end in accusations or yelling. It's been months since we've done that."

"That's good… isn't it?"

Marc nodded. "Yeah, of course. It went so well she actually suggested I spend the night."

Gary's eyebrows rose a smidgen. "Really? That's progress." His song was ending; he held up a finger and put on his headphones. "Hold that thought a second."

He turned on the mic. "Sixteen minutes 'til seven, Z97-3. Glad you could join me this evening. I'm Gary Sheldon along with you for another little while, then I'll scoot on out of here and make way for my pal Marc Lindsay. He'll be hangin' out with you 'til midnight. He's got your Seventies at Seven, Late-night Love Songs and I'm guessing he's probably got all kinds of fun stuff to talk with you about, too. Up next we'll take a look at your weather for the overnight, and then we've got R.E.M., Crowded House and a classic from David Bowie. Stick around."

He started the first of four commercials, tapped the button to shut off the microphone, then tugged his headphones off. He jotted run times in the program log and signed the bottom of the page. "And?"

Marc shook his head. "I wasn't ready. I mean, I – I want to. *Man,* do I want to! But I didn't want to complicate things by throwing sex back into the mix. It's just too soon. And as much as I miss—" He stopped, shook his head again.

"What?"

"I can't talk to you about my sex life – or lack of one," he said, uneasy. "This is your *sister* we're talking about."

"No, Marc, it's your *wife* we're talking about," Gary reminded him gently. He honestly didn't want to hear about his sister's sex life, but he felt he owed it to his best friend to ask. "How long has it been?"

Marc shrugged. "I dunno. Too long," he mumbled, looking away. "Five months, maybe? No. Longer. Before Thanksgiving. And then, only reluctantly."

Gary gave a pensive nod. "I can understand that. Feels kinda like crawling through a desert. I'm sorry to hear that."

"Being unwanted by your own wife has got to be the worst feeling in the world," Marc said, sounding helpless. "Things used to be great between us… but now? She hasn't wanted anything to do with me in ages… It's like I'm repulsive to her."

Gary didn't know what to say.

"But frankly, I think I miss the conversation – and the sense of connectedness – more than the sex," Marc admitted.

"Okay." Then, not sure how else to respond, Gary forced a grin for his brother-in-law's sake and said, "You realize this is my sister you're talking about."

Marc managed a weak return smile. He parried back, "I know. But, like you said, she's also my wife. Look, I know you don't exactly feel comfortable talking about this… and I do appreciate your willingness to discuss it at all. But I" – he shook his head – "I just… can't talk about it right now." With a resigned sigh, he slunk away to finish his show prep.

Gary recalled a few years earlier when things had grown so strained between Micki and him. Falsely accused of sexual assault and mired in a deep depression, he'd gone at least four and a half months without so much as touching his wife, let alone making love with her. But he'd been the one who had withdrawn, while Michaela remained supportive, encouraging him to talk with her about the issues that had crushed his drive. Eventually, after he opened up to her and they made love again that first time, it felt remarkable. Granted, he'd still had underlying issues to resolve, but that lovemaking had rekindled a spark between them. And even now things were still almost how they'd been when they were newlyweds. But this was different: Marie had put deliberate physical distance – in addition to the emotional chasm – between herself and her husband.

Gary shook his head, thinking about how despondent, how morose, Marc had seemed. It really *was* kind of like crawling through a desert. Sudden guilt assailed him. *Is that what I did to Micki? Good Lord, is <u>this</u> how I made her feel all those months?* He couldn't imagine how he would have reacted if things had been reversed and Michaela had been the one to shut him out.

Once they swapped places at the control board and Marc launched his nightly Seventies at Seven feature, Gary attempted to resurrect their conversation. "Marie's behavior is really odd lately. I've been thinking: Have you had her evaluated for a brain tumor?"

Marc's sullen expression immediately turned stormy. "That's not even funny, Gary," he rebuked him.

"I wasn't trying to be funny," he said, shaking his head. "I'm dead serious. When Michaela and I started having babies, my mom told us she was a carrier for a condition that can lead to brain tumors. It's a recessive gene carried along Mediterranean bloodlines. I've been tested and I don't have it… All I'm saying is maybe Marie ought to get herself tested. It could be why she's been acting so… wonky."

Marc's shoulders drooped. "That would explain a few things," he mumbled. He sighed heavily and gave a reluctant nod. "It sure would explain some things."

Chapter 48

(8:23 a.m., June 11 – Sunday)
The twins sat on either side of their parents at Mass. As promised from the week before, Fern got to sit next to Daddy. Marc and Marie held hands through much of the Mass, and even exchanged a whispered "Peace be with you" and a fond kiss during the sign of peace.

After Mass, Marie asked Marc to come back to the apartment to join them for breakfast.

They enjoyed a lovely meal out on the front porch, and Marc spent some time playing with the kids before he had to leave under guise of needing to catch up on some production work.

He gave the kids hugs and kisses, and even kissed Marie good-bye at the back door.

The next morning, Marc sat facing Dr. Merino. "I don't know what to do," he admitted, slumping forward in his usual chair. "Things have been going better. But we're still living apart. It's been like five weeks. And that kills me."

The therapist swung a curtain of dark hair back over her right shoulder. "Okay. Let's talk about that, Marc. What are your options?"

He considered the question. "I can let her go… or I can fight for our marriage."

With a pensive nod, she replied, "I think I know what your answer will be, but which do you want to do?"

"Fight for the marriage," he replied almost too quietly for her to hear. "This past week or so has been better. A lot better. We talked last Tuesday – a *real* talk. With actual communication. And zero fighting. We sat together at Mass yesterday – and even held hands. That doesn't sound like a big deal, but it was huge! Then she invited me back to the apartment afterward, for breakfast with her and the kids. It felt so good to be there with them, to share a meal and… and to feel like a family again." He blinked away tears.

"That does sound nice."

His head bobbed. "It felt almost normal."

After a long awkward silence, Marc spoke again. "Gary made an interesting observation – or, rather, a suggestion – the other day."

She tilted her head to one side, her pen poised above her ever-present notepad. "What's that?"

"He said his mom had a recessive gene for something that can cause brain tumors. He told me he thinks it's more prevalent in women than guys, and recommended Marie get tested."

Dr. Merino nodded slowly; she jotted a note. "What do you think about that?"

He shrugged. "It's not a bad idea. And while I hope it's *not*, part of me almost hopes *that's* what's making her act so…" Marc's voice trailed away and he shook his head as he struggled for the right word.

"Off kilter?"

He nodded gravely. "Yeah. But the thing is, I don't know how I can bring up the subject without her blowing up and accusing me of calling her crazy or unbalanced." When he looked up again, unwelcome tears glistened in his eyes. "I don't want to lose her, Doc… not when we're just starting to make some real progress. We're actually starting to see eye to eye again. These past eight months have been…" He shook his head and sniffled as his words trailed off to silence.

The therapist reached out and took his hand. "I know these months have been difficult for you, Marc. And I realize this is unconventional – maybe even bordering on *unethical* – but I'll be having lunch with Marie on Friday. If I can find a way to bring it up in conversation, would you like me to talk to her? As a friend, and a colleague? I might be able to get her to consider an underlying medical reason for her recent behavior."

"Would you?" Marc looked equal parts relieved and hopeful for the first time in a long time. He wanted to hug her. "You think she'd actually listen to you?"

"It's worth a shot," she replied. "The worst she can do is say no… right?"

His head drooped and he sighed. "She's done a lot worse. But yeah, it's worth a try. Thanks, Doc."

That afternoon, Marc's cell phone rang.

"Hi, sweetheart," Marie greeted him. "It's me."

He could hear the smile in her voice.

"Hey," he replied, his voice part purr. "What's up?"

"I was wondering if you might want to come over tonight after work…"

"At midnight?"

"Yeah… and you know… stay the night?"

Marc could envision her twirling a lock of her hair around and around her index finger. She was probably chewing at her lower lip. His heart rate quickened at the thought of being with her again. A hesitant smile played about his lips. "Are you sure about this?"

He heard her trembly sigh through the phone. "Yeah, I am. I think it's time… if you want," she added, sounding hesitant.

He couldn't think of anything he wanted more. He smiled. "I think that'd be nice. Yeah."

Chapter 49

Just after 12:30, Marc fumbled with the key. He let himself in and carefully set two parcels on the kitchen counter. Shouldering a small satchel containing his clothes and toiletries, he crept into the bedroom he hadn't set foot in for weeks.

As he clicked the door shut, Marc sensed motion from the bed. The bedside lamp went on.

"Hi honey," Marie greeted him sleepily.

Leaning down over the bed, he kissed her. "Sorry, *querida*, I didn't mean to wake you."

"You didn't. I was listening for you." She reached upward and slid her arms around him. She kissed his mouth. "I missed you."

Marc's arms went around his wife and drew her close. "I've missed you, too, *querida*."

"Mmm… make love to me, Marc," she urged, craving his touch, her breath hot against his throat.

His lips curved upward in a tantalizing smile. "You have to let go so I can get undressed first," he replied, his eyes warm with affection.

"Oh, alright." Reluctantly, Marie released him.

Stepping back, Marc hastily stripped off his clothes, then slid under the covers beside her.

(6:47 a.m., June 13 – Tuesday)

Marc's side of the bed was empty. Marie stretched, then sat up, calling to mind their delicious, albeit hesitant, lovemaking earlier that morning. Hugging her arms around her knees, she wondered when he had left and realized she hadn't even felt him go. A small part of her seemed relieved, but the greater part of her felt horribly empty at his absence. She'd wanted to ask him to stay, but she wasn't sure he'd be receptive – and she was terrified he'd turn her down. She didn't think she could stand his rejection – not now, not when they'd just begun rebuilding their relationship.

Just then she heard what sounded like activity in the kitchen. She strained to listen. It didn't sound like Oscar. Then again, she realized, the little tuxedo cat was asleep in a ball on Marc's still-warm side of the bed. *He must have just left.* Pulling on her robe, Marie stuck her feet into her slippers and headed out there to see what sort of mischief the twins were getting into.

When she reached the kitchen, she found it wasn't the kids at all. The coffee was on and Marc stood at the counter, untying the red-and-white string from a white cardboard bakery box. Once it was undone, he coiled the string and set it to one side. Raising the lid on the box and deeply inhaling the rich aroma, he withdrew half a dozen *pastéis de nata* – the exquisite, mouthwatering egg-custard tarts like the ones they'd savored during their honeymoon in Lisbon. He arranged the delicacies on a plate and set them beside the only other item on the counter: a lush green basil plant in a bright, hand-painted pot. A showy yellow tissue-paper flower poked from amid its fragrant greenery.

Now he looked up and noticed her watching him. A smile lit his face as their eyes met.

"Happy Saint Anthony's Day," he greeted his wife, coming over to kiss her. He slipped his arms around her waist and pulled her close.

Tears filled Marie's eyes and she trembled in his arms. Seven years ago Marc had surprised her with a similar gift, explaining it was a tradition in Portugal. He'd explained that on June 13, a single man would present a potted basil plant to the woman he hoped to marry.

Overwhelmed by this romantic gesture, she pulled away from Marc's tender embrace and wept. She put her slender fingers up to her face to wipe away her tears.

Marc caught her hands in his and drew them together. He raised her fingers to his lips and kissed them. Then he took her right hand in his and gently slid the engagement and wedding rings off her ring finger.

"It's time for these to be back where they belong," he murmured, placing them on her left hand.

When she stopped crying, she kissed him. "It's time for you to be back where you belong, too," she murmured when she could form words. Her voice wavered. "Will you come home?"

As much as Marc ached to say yes, Marie's recent behavior had been so inconsistent he couldn't be certain she wouldn't change her mind and throw him out again. Perhaps this was the opening he needed, to ask her about getting evaluated for a brain tumor.

"Let's give it a couple more days," he said instead. "I want to move back home, Marie – I want that more than anything. But we need to be sure it's for good. It'd be confusing for the kids for me to be here and then maybe gone again." He hesitated. Dare he say it? "And *I* need to know you want me back here."

She put her hands up to the sides of his face. "I *do*," she assured Marc, then kissed him. "I *do* want you here, sweetheart. Please come home." Her voice held a needy, desperate-sounding warble.

"Let's give it another few days," he said again, taking her hands in his. "I'd like for us to talk again – like we did last week. If we can make more headway, I'll move back home this weekend. But, as a condition of my coming home, I think we need to see a couples therapist again. Would that be acceptable to you?"

Marie nodded. "Yes," she squeaked. "Of course. I want you to come home, sweetheart."

Chapter 50

(June 16 – Friday)

"So, how are things?" Paola asked as Marie settled into her seat.

"Stressful," Marie replied, raking a hand through her loose curls. "But starting to get better."

"How so?"

She let out a pained sigh. "I'm sure Marc's told you we've separated."

Paola frowned. "Marie, you know I can't discuss anything he may have said in our sessions," she replied evenly. Then she added, "Or even whether he's seen me."

"Oh, come on, Paola. We both know you've been treating my husband for a dozen years."

"And in all that time, have I ever divulged to you anything he's shared during a session – or told him anything you and I have talked about?"

Marie gave a reticent head shake.

"Exactly. And I'm not about to start now." Paola drew her lips into a skinny line. "And for you to suggest otherwise really concerns me, Marie. You're a mental-health professional. You know better than that."

Marie shrugged. "I know… I just – I'm sorry. I don't know what came over me."

Paola's eyes narrowed slightly. Her gaze intensified. Maybe this was her chance. She leaned forward a bit. "Are you okay, Marie? I mean… physically. Mentally. Both."

Marie's hand shook as she reached for her water glass. "I don't know," she admitted, looking frightened. Glancing around her, she took a sip. Her hand trembled as she set the glass on the table again. "These past several months, I've noticed… well, I just haven't been myself."

Paola placed a hand atop hers. "What's the matter?"

"I wasn't going to say anything, but I've been having these little memory lapses… and brief blackouts."

Her eyes seemed to darken with concern. "That's not good."

Marie gestured awkwardly. "And this whole mess with Marc…"

"The separation?"

"You said you wouldn't divulge anything you and he discussed," Marie challenged.

"You just mentioned the separation a few minutes ago," Paola reminded her evenly.

She looked perplexed. "I did?"

Now Paola met and held the other woman's gaze. "Marie, what is going on with you?"

She drew in her breath sharply. Her fingers fidgeted with the napkin in her lap. "I've made an appointment… with a neurologist. Would you be willing to come with me?"

Paola's hand closed around Marie's. "Of course," she responded immediately, noting the fear in her friend's voice. "When?"

"Next Thursday. One forty-five."

"Where?"

"Here in Danbury. At the medical-arts building."

Paola nodded and met her friend's gaze. "I'll pick you up at one. Unless you want to have lunch first – in which case, I'll pick you up at eleven thirty."

Marie wiped away the tears that sprang to her eyes. "I'd like that," she said softly. It felt good to have someone to confide in. She looked down for a moment at her hands twisting the napkin in her lap, then her gaze met her friend's again. "I'm frightened, Paola."

"Of course you are. But you're doing the right thing, Marie, getting checked out."

When Marie returned to her office, she asked Elisa to cancel her afternoon appointments. "I'm not feeling very well," she told her assistant. "I think I'm going to go home."

"Are you sure you're okay to drive?"

Marie hesitated, momentarily dizzy. She put a hand on Elisa's desk to steady herself. Then she nodded, giving a forced smile. "I'm fine. I just feel a little weak, that's all."

Nearly twenty minutes later, Marie drove along Route 188. She often took this way home, but today she felt disoriented and couldn't recall where she was, let alone how to get home. Having trouble seeing the road, she rubbed at her eyes when her vision blurred. Less than a minute later, her Volvo veered off the road, where it careened into a lightly wooded area. The vehicle slowed as it plowed through a stand of birch and maple saplings, then came to rest with a dull thump against a large pine tree.

Chapter 51

Marie came to when she heard a persistent banging at her window. And yelling.

"Are you okay?" someone shouted. "Lady, are you okay?"

It took several seconds for her to remember how to roll down her window. As she pressed the button to lower the window, she gazed out at the worried face of the man who'd been banging at the glass.

"Are you okay?" he asked again.

"Wh-what happened?"

"You must have run off the road and into the trees," the man responded. "Are you hurt?"

"I uh… I don't think so," she said. "Where am I?"

"You're on Route 188 in Seymour. In my front yard."

She rubbed her forehead and felt a lump. Despite the deployed airbag, she must have hit her head against the side window. "Oh."

"Are you okay?"

"I uh – I don't know."

"Stay right there. Don't try to move. I called 911 when I heard the crash," the man said. He looked to be in his mid 60s. "They said they're sending an ambulance. It should be here any minute. Is there someone you want me to call?"

Marie looked up at him. Suddenly, she couldn't make out what he was saying. His words sounded jumbled and they weren't making any sense to her. Her brow furrowed deeply. She shook her head. "I'm sorry, what?"

"Is there someone you'd like me to call for you? Husband? Friend? Anyone?"

"I don't know," she mumbled, laying her head back against the headrest. "I just feel so… so sleepy."

A moment later, approaching sirens wailed. An ambulance pulled up and disgorged EMTs. They hurried over to assess Marie's condition.

"I asked the lady if she was okay," the man told them as they approached, "but she didn't really seem to be coherent. I think she must have hit her head."

As the police arrived, the EMTs helped Marie out of the car and tried to evaluate her. Her responses seemed vague and unhelpful. Minutes later, the ambulance sped toward nearby Griffin Hospital.

Upon arrival at the hospital, a bewildered and frightened Marie was hurried inside on a wheeled gurney. Based upon what the emergency-room nurses conveyed to him of what the EMTs reported about her condition, the doctor ordered a series of neurological tests and a cranial CT scan for a suspected concussion.

Chapter 52

Marc didn't recognize the number. "Hello?"

"Mr. Lindemeyr?"

"Yes… Who is this, please?"

"I'm calling from Griffin Hospital, sir. The emergency room. Your wife's been brought in. She's okay, but—"

Fear constricted his throat. "What happened?" came out in a strangled squeak.

"She had an episode and crashed her car."

"What kind of episode?"

"She blacked out. We're running tests right now – we thought you'd want to know."

"Of course. Thank you. I'll be there" – he checked his watch – "in half an hour."

Twenty-two minutes later, Marc raced into the main entrance of the emergency room. He stopped at the front desk, panicked. "My wife was brought in a little while ago – Marie Lindemeyr. Can I see her, please?"

"Right this way, sir." The receptionist escorted Marc back into the treatment area, where she checked the patient-status board. "She's in number three, right over here."

Thanking the woman, Marc entered the curtained area, his heart clattering anxiously. "Honey?"

Marie's head jolted up, toward the sound of his voice. Her eyes looked frightened. So frightened she didn't even attempt to look annoyed. "Marc." His name escaped her lips as a sigh of relief.

He rushed to her side. "Are you okay, *querida?*"

Her hand trembled in his. "I… I think so."

"What happened?" Marc smoothed wayward curls back from his wife's face, then reached for her other hand.

Marie gave a vague headshake. "I don't know. I wasn't feeling well, so I left work. I guess I must have blacked out while I was driving." She sounded apologetic. "I crashed my car."

Marc tried not to panic. Gary's recent question – *Have you had her evaluated for a brain tumor?* – returned to him now. He touched the bulge at the left side of her forehead. She flinched.

"Looks like you got quite a lump there."

She nodded. "I guess… yeah."

"What tests have they run?"

Marie shrugged. "I don't know."

Don't know?! He tried to keep his voice calm. "What did the doctors say?"

Another shrug. "I can't remember," she admitted, shaking her head.

Marc's insides clenched. For the second time in as many weeks, alarm bells went off in his head. But he maintained his serene façade, so as not to worry her. Resorting to a familiar gesture in the midst of uncertainty, he stroked her hair. "That's okay, *querida*. We'll talk to the doctor when he comes back, and we'll figure it out. Don't worry, sweetheart." His last statement was as much for his benefit as hers.

Marie looked at him with question in her eyes. "Why are you being so good to me?"

I hope she hasn't forgotten she wants me to come home. "Because I love you."

Marie reached for his hand. "Thank you," she told him softly. "For being here."

Where else would I be? Just as he pressed her hand to his lips, the curtain opened.

The doctor came in. "Mrs. Lindemeyr, we— Oh!" he exclaimed, noticing Marc beside her.

Marc turned to face the doctor. He extended his hand. "Hi, Doctor. I'm Marc Lindemeyr. I'm Marie's husband."

The doctor shook his hand. "Your wife's a lucky woman, Mr. Lindemeyr. If it hadn't been for that crash, we might not have run these tests so soon. A lot of times these things go undetected and undiagnosed for years… often until it's too late."

Confusion clouded Marc's face. "What things?"

"She didn't tell you?"

Marc cast an anxious glance in his wife's direction before he looked at the doctor again. "Tell me what?"

"Have you noticed any unusual behavior from her lately?"

You mean like demanding a separation? Like turning the charm on and off in front of her coworkers and ripping me to shreds at every opportunity? "What are you saying, Doctor? Tell me *what?*" Then he blurted out, "Is it a brain tumor?"

"So she *did* tell you…"

Marc felt a strange buzzing in his ears. Numb, he shook his head. His mouth formed words but no sound would come out. Finally he managed to say, "N-no. No. She couldn't remember what you'd said. *That* was something her brother had mentioned – some kind of hereditary condition on their mother's side – some Mediterranean thing…"

The doctor wore a grim expression. "Well, that may be, but it's not what caused this one."

A lump rose in his throat. "How serious is it?"

"It's pretty serious, Mr. Lindemeyr. We don't know whether it started in her brain or spread there from her lymph nodes. But if it's capable of causing blackouts, short-term memory loss and significant behavioral changes, it's not something we can ignore."

"What kind of treatment options are we looking at?"

"There are a few options we can consider. Most of them involve surgery. One of the most promising new management options we're trying these days involves surgery and an experimental infusion of donor cells."

Marc nodded, processing this information. "Okay." Now he peppered the doctor with questions. "What kind of success rates are we looking at? Twenty percent? Fifty? Eighty? Marie's a psychiatrist. How will this affect her ability to treat her patients?"

"It's too soon to tell," the doctor admitted. "It's a complicated situation. Brain tumors are always serious stuff – and every case is different. Not to mention the lymphoma."

Marie looked from one man's face to the other. Instinctively, she grasped at her husband's hand, her trembling fingers closing around his.

Marc moved closer to his wife and stroked her hair again. His eyes remained fixed on the doctor. "How soon will we need to decide on a course of action?"

"Obviously, the sooner we start treatment, the better. There's no telling how long the tumor has been there, or how fast it's growing. I'd say you won't want to wait more than a week at the outside to make a decision." The physician pulled his prescription pad from the pocket of his white coat. A moment later, he tore off two sheets and handed them to Marc. "In the meantime, we'll get her started on steroids and anti-seizure medication."

Marc nodded his understanding. He did his best to quell the icy fear that seized him around the midsection. He couldn't let Marie think he was anything close to rattled by the doctor's words. Judging from her vise-like grip on his fingers, she was depending on him to be the rock here. Once again he smoothed back her auburn hair, unnerved by the panic in her pretty blue eyes, along with the tears that shimmered there. He bent to kiss her forehead and patted the trembling hand that still clutched his. "It'll be okay, sweetheart," he reassured her. "We're going to get through this. Together."

Chapter 53

(5:12 p.m.)

"Don't you have to leave for work soon?"

Marc stared at his wife. "Are you kidding? You just got home from the emergency room – after a brain-tumor diagnosis! And they want someone here with you around the clock for the next twenty-four hours to monitor your condition. I'm not leaving you here alone." *Ever.*

Marie laid a gentle hand on his arm. "I'm hardly alone. Val and Tim are just downstairs if I should need anything."

He shook his head. "Someone's got to be *right here* with you."

She sighed. "If it'll make you feel better, I'll ask Val to come up and sit with me 'til you get home. Anyway, isn't tonight your big announcement? You've only been talking about it for days."

'Til you get home. For the first time since Marc answered the call from the hospital this afternoon, his mind strayed from Marie's medical condition. *'Til you get home.* Plenty to think about in those four words. For that matter, lots more to think about in that whole exchange. He hadn't realized she'd been listening to his show. Plus, she presumed he was coming home afterward. *'Til you get home.* And then there was that warm, inviting touch… unless he was reading too much into it.

He shrugged. "I guess, yeah."

"So, what is it? Your big announcement?"

A playful glint lighted Marc's deep-brown eyes and a teasing smile replaced his pensive look. "Ahh, if I told you, then you'd have no reason to listen to the show, now would you?" He leaned and kissed the tip of her nose.

(6:15 p.m.)

"You look drained. Everything okay?"

Marc's shoulders slumped. He shook his head. "You were right."

Gary grinned. "That's often the case." He tilted his head. "What was I right about this time?"

"Brain tumor."

Gary's smile fled. "Tell me you're joking."

Marc shook his head. "She passed out this afternoon while driving. Ran into some trees and crashed her car. Hit her head. They ran a bunch of tests at the hospital and that's when they found the tumor."

"Oh, Marc! I'm so sorry. Is she gonna be okay?"

He gave a helpless shrug. "Too soon to tell… but it's not just the brain tumor. They also found lymphoma."

"Oh no!" Gary paled. "So what are you doing here? Why aren't you at home with your wife?"

Another shrug. "I wanted to be – but she insisted. Said she's fine. Val and Tim are with her. So at least she's in good hands. Your mom's got the kids overnight. And besides, she wanted to hear what my big announcement was going to be." He gave a labored sigh. "Like I even care anymore. I should be home with her. Not here playing radio."

Gary rested a hand on his brother-in-law's shoulder and drew him in to a hug. "It'll be fine. Sounds like she's in good hands. The kids are probably running my mom ragged – and she's loving every second of it. So all you need to focus on these next five hours is your final show." He paused, drew back from Marc and motioned backward with one thumb. "That and the party going on down in the conference room."

Marc's eyes registered concern. "Party?"

"You didn't think we'd let you sneak out of here without some kind of raucous celebration in your honor, did you? Didn't you get suspicious when you saw all the cars in the lot?"

Marc shook his head. "Didn't even notice 'em."

"Well, they're all waiting for you in the conference room"

"I hate being fussed over," he fretted, wincing.

Gary nodded. "I know. But it's as much for the rest of us as it is for you. Probably more so. It's really to give us a chance to express how much we love you – and how much this place won't be the same without you. And, hey, any excuse for chocolate cake and Snickers bars, right?"

Now Marc smiled. "I suppose. Since you put it that way. And anyway, you didn't tell me there'd be Snickers bars! Why didn't you say that in the first place?"

Grinning, Gary draped an arm around his brother-in-law's shoulder. "C'mon, let's go get you pumped full of junk food."

Chapter 54

(10:27 a.m., June 20 – Tuesday)

Marc held tight to Marie's trembling hand as they waited to be called in for her appointment.

She leaned against him. "I'm scared," she admitted in a tiny voice.

He slid his other arm around his wife's shoulder and pressed a tender kiss against her temple. "Of course you're scared." He did his best to keep his tone soothing. "But you're in the exact right place. Doctor Fleming's the best neuro-oncologist in the state, and you heard what the ER doctor said – they caught it early, so there's a far greater chance of recovery. We'll get through this, *querida*."

"But what if it's already too late? What if the tumor's too badly entwined and they can't get it all out? And what if it's spread even further?"

He put a finger to her lips. "Shh," he soothed. "Don't talk like that, honey. They said there's an excellent chance they can get it all. And you heard what they said: The recovery rate is high."

Dr. Stuart Fleming welcomed the anxious couple into his office. "Mr. and Dr. Lindemeyr, please, sit down." He indicated a pair of comfortable-looking wingback chairs alongside his desk.

As Marc ushered his wife ahead of him, Marie assessed the oncologist's choice of seating accommodations. *You want patients and their family members to be as relaxed as possible when you deliver bad news.* She stiffened slightly as she lowered herself into a chair. As Marc settled into the seat beside her, she instinctively reached for his hand.

Once they were seated, the doctor looked from one of them to the other. "I won't sugarcoat this. I've examined the MRI and PET scans. We're going to have to operate. I've also consulted with Dr. Kaufman, who recommends we try an experimental stem-cell therapy to treat the lymphoma. But I have to caution you: Because this treatment is experimental, I'm not sure whether your insurance will cover the cost of the procedure."

Marc and Marie shook their heads. "That's not even an issue," Marc replied solemnly, reaching for his wife's trembling hand. "Money's not a concern. We'll pay cash if we have to. I just want you to save her life."

As Dr. Fleming described the various procedures, and the risks associated with each, Marie gripped Marc's hand more tightly. A lump formed in her throat as she listened.

"Could I be a stem-cell donor?" Marc asked.

"Possibly. You'd have to be a close enough match in the HLA test." When Marc looked baffled at his words, Dr. Fleming patiently explained. "A series of various markers has to be compatible. You need at least six to be considered a match."

Shaking his head, Marc frowned. "We're different blood types."

"Blood type isn't actually one of the criteria. All things being equal, a sibling donor would be preferable to a non-related donor."

Marc looked at his wife.

Certain she knew what he was going to suggest, Marie shook her head and looked away from him. "Forget it. He'd never go for it… not after the way I treated him," she mumbled, sniffling. "I wouldn't blame him, either."

Marc gave her hand a reassuring pat. "Let me ask him."

***

A little before 2, Marc pulled in to the radio station parking lot.

"Just couldn't stay away, could you?" Brenda greeted him with a smile.

He grinned, but only halfway. "Something like that. Gary in?"

"Yeah… but it's Tuesday," she cautioned.

Marc knew that meant he was up to his eyebrows in new music releases, not to mention prepping for his show. "I won't keep him long."

Brenda nodded toward Gary's office. "Go on in."

Gary looked up when he heard the tap at his open door.

On seeing Marc, he grinned. "What are you doing knocking?" he chided. "Get in here."

He did, then sat in one of the seats opposite the music director's desk.

Gary pushed away his keyboard in anticipation of a friendly chat. "To what do I owe the pleasure? Couldn't stand being away from the place? Or was it just force of habit?"

Marc pasted on a smile. "Something like that, yeah." He rested his elbows on the arms of his chair. "Actually, it's about Marie."

He waited for an eye roll or a snarky response from his brother-in-law. When none came, he continued.

"We saw the neuro-oncologist this morning. She needs surgery. And to treat the lymphoma, they've decided against surgery; they'll continue to monitor its growth and, in the meantime, they want to try an experimental stem-cell therapy."

One of Gary's eyebrows arched. "Experimental? How do you feel about that?"

"They said it shows real promise. It could even become the standard for treatment in years to come."

"Okay, so the professionals are optimistic. But how do *you* feel about it? Gut level, Marc. Do you think it's safe?"

He shrugged. "I don't know what to think. I just want her to be well."

"When will they do the surgery?"

"Maybe a week or so. They'll do it at Yale. They have to let her know once it's scheduled."

"What about the stem-cell therapy? Would they do that at the same time?"

Marc shrugged. "Dunno. They said they want to do it as soon as they identify a compatible donor. I've been tested. We'll know in a week or so if I'm a close enough match."

"What about me? Isn't a sibling likely to be a close match?"

He shook his head. "I can't ask you to do that."

"I'm offering. And anyway, why wouldn't you ask me? She's my sister."

Marc looked uncomfortable. "You have to ask why?"

"You think I'd jeopardize my sister's life over a ridiculous spat — especially one probably brought on by that stupid brain tumor?"

"I didn't know what to think."

"I'm not that petty, Marc. How do I get tested?"

Marc pulled a card from his pocket and handed it to Gary. "Just go here. They're open from seven 'til six. It'll only take a minute to do the test — it's just a cheek swab."

"Oh! It's the HLA test. I had that done for the kidney donation. They should still have my results on file. Let me give them a call."

Over lunch on Thursday, Gary related Marie's situation to James. "They're looking for donor candidates for stem-cell therapy."

"Would stem cells from a relative help?"

"Yeah. They've already got my test results from December."

James shook his head. "Not you, ya big lunk. I meant me. I've still got frozen stem cells left over from when autologous therapy didn't work for me. She's welcome to 'em."

Chapter 55

(June 26 – Monday)

The twins' summer vacation had just begun and they were still asleep. After an unhurried breakfast, Marc and Marie lingered over coffee and sporadic talk at the kitchen table. Still getting used to living together again, their conversation often felt stilted. And Marie's recent cancer diagnosis only added to that general sense of awkwardness.

The ringing of the phone shattered the quiet. Marie leapt from her chair to snatch up the receiver on the wall phone. "Hello?"

Marc watched his wife's face in profile. He wondered who – and what – had made her expression turn serious so quickly.

"That's wonderful," he heard her say. The warble in her voice seemed incongruous with her words.

He watched Marie twirl a lock of hair around her finger and wondered what the other end of the conversation was sounding like.

"I see," she said at last. She flipped a page in the large calendar on the refrigerator and jotted something. "And when should I come in for that?" She paused, wrote something in on a different date. "Okay, that sounds good. I'll see you then. Thank you so much."

When she hung up, Marie looked pale.

"Who was that?" Marc already suspected it had something to do with her upcoming surgery.

"Dr. Fleming's office. They've identified a stem-cell donor."

"That's great! Did they say who?"

Returning to her seat, she shook her head. "Just that they got a compatible donor, and my surgery's next Monday. I go in for registration and pre-surgical testing on Wednesday."

Marc tried to sound upbeat. "That's good news."

Her nod looked like it felt painful. "Yeah. It is," she agreed through lips that barely moved.

He reached for his wife's hand and gave it a reassuring squeeze. "You're going to be fine."

The trembling of her lower lip reminded Marc of their usually indomitable daughter on the first day of school last year.

"I'm scared," Marie admitted.

"I'm sure that's normal, *querida*." Marc offered an encouraging smile. "And frankly, I'd be worried if you weren't."

Chapter 56

(3:20 p.m., July 3 – Monday)

When Marie regained consciousness in recovery, the first face she saw was Marc's. She'd expected as much; he promised he would be there. She reached toward him as a weak smile bloomed across her lips.

When he took her hand, she felt the familiar comforting warmth as his fingers closed around hers. "Hi," he greeted her in a voice that was part murmur, part purr.

Her head felt as unwieldy as a bowling ball balanced on a celery stick. She didn't have the strength to raise it from the pillow. "Hi," she replied, her drowsy eyes expressing the question her mouth couldn't yet articulate.

Marc smiled and gave her hand a gentle squeeze. "You did great. The surgeon's confident they got it all; we just need to wait for the pathology report to come back. That'll take a few days." He leaned to kiss her cheek. "In the meantime, you just rest and get your strength back."

"The kids," she managed to whisper. "Who's got the kids?"

"They're staying with Gary and Michaela." Marc watched for signs of argumentativeness or dispute in her eyes at the mention of her brother. He saw none.

Rather, Marie's mouth relaxed into a smile. "Oh, good," she breathed on a weary exhale. She fell limp against the pillow and shut her eyes.

(2:23 p.m., July 4 – Tuesday)

When Marie awakened from her nap, she looked up into Marc's anxious brown eyes. "Hi," she greeted him sleepily.

"Hi." He smiled. "How do you feel?"

She let out a soft sigh. "Exhausted."

"I'm not surprised; it's been a rough few days."

When her eyes filled with tears, Marc grew concerned. "What's the matter? Are you in pain?"

Marie shook her head. "Can you ever forgive me?"

Anxiety yielded to perplexity. He reached for her hand. "For what?"

"I was so awful – I threw you out! And wouldn't let you see the kids! How can you forgive me for that?"

Marc curled his fingers around Marie's. "There's nothing to forgive."

She shook her head vehemently. "How can you say that?"

Marc patted his wife's hand. "It wasn't your fault, *querida*. You had a brain tumor."

"But you didn't know that," she protested. "And I was horrible to you…"

He shook his head. "None of that matters," he assured her. "All that matters is the surgery was successful and you're going to be fine."

Tears filled her eyes.

Marc wiped them away. "Hey, now, cut that out." He drew her close. "Don't you be getting all weepy, lady. The kids'll be here any minute. You don't want to frighten them, do you?"

Marie pulled back and looked at him in surprise. "They will?" Sniffling, she wiped at her eyes and asked fretfully, "You don't think the bandages will scare them, do you?"

"Val told them you'll have your head wrapped up, but not to worry. She said she told them it didn't hurt and Mommy was going to be just fine."

Her bottom lip trembled. "But what if I'm not?"

Marc leaned in to kiss her on the forehead. He kept his tone reassuring. "We're not going to worry about that. We're going to focus on you being just fine. *Just fine,*" he reiterated as she balked.

Ten minutes later, the twins dragged Val and Tim along the wide, linoleumed corridor, toward Room 732.

"Mommy!" the kids exclaimed in excited unison, rushing into the room.

Marie's expression brightened into a genuine smile at the sight of them. "Edward! Fern!" she greeted them, her eyes awash with tears. "I'm so glad to see you!"

Marc lifted the little boy onto the bed beside Mommy. Not waiting to be helped, Isabella clambered up on her own and scrambled over to snuggle next to her.

"Why are you crying, Mommy?" Edward asked. "Does it hurt?"

She shook her head and put an arm around her son, drawing him close. "No, sweetheart. I'm just happy to see you and Fern."

"How are you feeling?" Val asked her friend.

With tremendous effort, Marie managed a weary smile. "Tired. But grateful to be alive." She reached for Marc's hand and gazed up at him with love in her eyes. "And *really* grateful for this guy. He's been my rock."

Val nodded. "And quite a rock he is. Everything's great at home. As you can see, the kids are fine. Oscar's been asking for you."

"He wanted to visit, but I didn't think we could smuggle him in," Tim put in. "I tried to get him into one of Fern's baby dresses, so we could wheel him up here in a stroller, but he was having none of it."

His gentle teasing set aside Marie's anxiety.

Within a few minutes, as much as she enjoyed Val, Tim and the kids' company, exhaustion won out. Marie rested her head against the pillow. She stopped struggling to keep her eyes open and drifted off to sleep.

Edward shook her arm. "Mommy? Mommy… wake up."

"Honey, Mommy's tired," Marc told him quietly. "Let her sleep, okay?"

"But we came all this way just to see her."

"I know you did, little man. And she was really excited to see you," Marc whispered to him.

"You know what I think?" Fern piped up. "I think it's just rude of her to be sleeping while we're trying to visit."

Val and Marc exchanged a look of amusement over the little girl's head.

Repressing a grin, Marc stroked his daughter's hair. "Mommy's not being rude, sweetheart. She's just really tired right now and she couldn't stay awake any longer. You know how you like to try to stay up all night? And no matter how hard you fight to stay awake, at some point you get so exhausted you just fall asleep?"

The little girl nodded.

"Well, Mommy was really excited about seeing you and your brother. She's thrilled you're here, but, honey, she was so worn out after her surgery, she couldn't stay awake."

"But you said her surgery was yesterday."

"It was."

"So why's she still sleeping now? That's just rude," the child proclaimed.

Again Marc forced away a smile. "She's not being rude; she's just got to rest so she can get strong enough to come home."

He glanced at Val and Tim, who seemed to infer his intended meaning.

Val spoke up. "I think it's probably best if we leave now."

"I think you're right," Tim concurred. When the kids started to protest, he said, "Hey, didn't I see a soft-serve machine downstairs in the cafeteria?"

The children's eyes widened at the mention of ice cream.

"Ooh! Ice cream! Can we have ice cream, Daddy?" Edward asked, folding his hands in exaggerated supplication.

He nodded. "Of course."

When Marc reached for his wallet, Tim waved him off. "I got this."

Val, Tim and the twins said their hurried goodbyes and tiptoed out of the room.

Marc walked them to the bank of elevators. Fern insisted on pushing the buttons. Giggling, the little girl pushed both the down and up buttons, and delighted in the green up arrow and the red down arrow that lit up, and the little audible dings within seconds of each other as two elevator cars' shiny metal doors slid open. She looked up at her dad. "Which one?"

He pointed toward the one displaying the red arrow. "That one."

"Why not the other one?"

"'Cause then you'd go to the top floor instead of getting ice cream."

"Oh, we wouldn't want to do that," she said seriously, shaking her head. Fern stepped into the car her father indicated. The others followed. She looked up at her dad. "Can I push the buttons?"

Before Marc could suggest she let her brother push the button for the first floor, Fern poked at all of them in order, giggling as a glowing orange circle lit up around each shiny metal button.

With an exhortation for them to behave, Marc waved goodbye to the kids as the doors slid shut, then returned to Marie's room. She was already asleep. Marc settled into a chair to read.

The next time she awakened, Marie looked around her room and let out a little gasp of surprise. Her demeanor brightened. "Hi." She smiled reflexively and reached a weak hand toward her visitor. "I'm so glad you're here!" She hadn't expected to see Gary. Not today. Not ever. Not after the way she'd run him out of her home all those months ago.

Having just finished praying a rosary for healing between them, he slipped his ever-present beads into the pocket of his jeans and stood, eyeing his sister critically. "I suppose you think brain surgery is a suitable excuse for not bringing the potato salad to our Fourth of July party." Unable to maintain his stern facial expression longer than a few seconds, he broke into a broad grin.

Initially concerned at his tone, Marie's face paled. Realizing he was teasing, she relaxed… until a rush of shame filled her as she recalled their contentious last encounter nine months earlier. Her eyes brimmed with tears. Turning away, she wiped at them clumsily.

Unfazed, Gary bent and gave her a hug, careful to avoid the cumbersome bandage around her skull. "Hey, sis. Heard they did a brain scan and couldn't find anything."

Marie couldn't help giggling at her brother's teasing. She clung to him, laughing through her tears, and felt the emotional distance between them evaporate. "I'm sorry," she mumbled into Gary's shoulder. "So sorry…"

"Hey… no one bled, no one died," he reassured her graciously, drawing back from Marie and tweaking her nose. "I'm just glad the surgery went well. Did they say how soon you'll be up and playing the ukulele?"

Now her smile overcame her tears. "Gee, doc, I always wanted to play the ukulele," she joked. Then, turning serious, Marie reached for his hand. "I really am sorry I kicked you out of the house, Gary. Can you forgive me? And will you come back?"

His fingers closed around his sister's and he smiled, knowing his prayers all these months had been answered. "Of course. And, really, sis, no apology necessary."

Uneasy silence descended between them for a moment.

"How are the kids?"

"Good. Erin leaves end of next month."

Marie looked confused. "Where's she going?"

"Off to college. She's going to BU. She wants to study broad-casting."

"Oh, geez, not another Sheldon in radio," Marie moaned. "That's all we need!"

"Well, she could've gone to med school… not like we have an actual doctor in the family," Gary teased.

The siblings exchanged silly grins and burst into laughter.

After a moment, Marie abruptly fell silent. She grew pensive and her expression turned serious again. "You know, they said the stem-cell infusion might well have saved my life. Thank you."

Gary smiled and glanced at his watch. 3:15. *Perfect timing.* "I'm really glad to hear that. But don't thank me."

She looked confused. "They said my brother supplied the stem cells."

"Ah, that. Yeah, it wasn't me. But on that note, there *is* someone waiting to meet you. And he should be here any second."

Marie gave her brother a curious look.

He got up and went to the door, then motioned to someone waiting outside.

In walked a man who could have been Gary's twin – except his hair was shorter, he was dressed in black and wore a Roman collar. Marie looked from her brother to the priest, a look of befuddlement on her face.

Gary gestured toward him. "Marie, I'd like you to meet Father James Griffin, your stem-cell donor. James, this is our sister, Marie."

After making the introductions, Gary slipped quietly out of the room to find Marc, who was taking a much-deserved break in the cafeteria, and to give the pair time to talk alone.

James stepped closer to Marie's bed so they could see each other better. His smile filled her with warmth, and his voice soothed her. "It's such a pleasure to finally meet you, Marie. I've heard so much about you from Gary and Marc."

Marie's cheeks flushed at his kind greeting. "I can only imagine what they've told you," she replied, her voice unsteady. She put a hand to her mouth to stifle a cry. Tears welled in her eyes. "I can't believe you would even want to do this for me, after all the horrible things I said."

Giving a dismissive shrug, James merely shook his head. "That's just words said in anger and misunderstanding."

"But I hated you for… for *years!*" she insisted.

He smiled. "Marie, Christ calls us to forgive. And what kind of representative of Him would I be if I were to harbor ill will toward you?" He paused. "Besides, I understand you kind of had good reason to feel hostile toward me… considering everything."

Hearing those words from him, Marie dissolved into tears. For so many years it had been easy to hate a concept, to despise the gauzy, nebulous image of a whispered-of half-brother, one whose sordid parentage had led to the destruction of her family. But faced with a flesh-and-blood brother – a priest, no less! – standing right in front of her, the reality of her lifelong hatred for this man crumbled away, leaving her with only shame and bitter remorse for her animosity toward him. She covered her face with her hands and turned away from him.

James laid a gentle hand on her shoulder. "I'm sorry you're hurting. What can I do to help?"

In reply, she shook her head.

"Would you like me to go away?"

A sob caught in her throat. She stopped crying for a moment and, just when he thought she was going to tell him to leave, she shook her head.

James poured a cup of ice water from the pitcher on her bedside tray. "Here" – he peeled one of her hands from in front of her face and closed it around the cup – "have some water."

Still looking away, Marie accepted the offered water gratefully. After taking a long drink, she turned toward him and met his gaze. "Thank you," she said barely aloud, handing the cup back.

He set it down on the tray and gestured toward a nearby chair. "May I?"

She nodded.

He pulled the chair over so it faced her and settled into it. "Would you like to talk?"

For a moment it seemed as if Marie hadn't heard. Then, while accordion-folding the thin white blanket that covered her, she nodded again.

The two sat in silence while almost a minute ticked away. During that time, the only sound was Marie's occasional sniffling as she struggled to compose herself.

"Thank you," she said at last, as if testing her voice. It came out hesitant, wobbly. She reached a hand toward James to pat his arm.

Awkward silence settled between them again.

At last James broke it. "I meant what I said before."

She looked at him in question.

"About your having valid reason to be hostile toward me," he clarified as Marie's mouth fell open in surprise.

"I had a long talk with your mom," he continued, filling the uneasy silence. "Several of them, actually. While I was recovering. She asked me to stay with her after my transplant surgery."

Marie stared at him, her blue eyes wide with astonishment.

"She's a remarkable woman, your mother. Of course, I don't need to tell you that. But she welcomed me into her home and cared for me for a little over three months while I convalesced." When Marie looked surprised at that revelation, James simply shrugged. "I didn't expect you'd have known that. In a lot of ways, she reminds me of my adoptive mom. We'd talk a lot in the evenings, your mom and I. She told me stories about my birth mom, back from when they were kids, and then teenagers… and up until— well, until I came along. I could tell it really pained your mother to talk about her, but she did it for my benefit, and I'll always be grateful to her for that. I never really knew much about my birth mom. I mean, I've got a few vague memories from early childhood, and some grainy photos, but she went to prison before I turned five, and she died of an overdose a few years later."

This was all news to Marie. Tears filled her eyes again as she envisioned her fun-loving favorite aunt dying alone in a dank prison cell, a victim of the drugs that clouded her judgment and ultimately ruined her life. The tears spilled over as she thought of James, having been robbed of his mother at such a young, impressionable age. "That's terrible!" She wiped the rush of tears away but they kept coming. "I never knew what became of Aunt Laura. I'm so sorry to hear that. That must have been awful for you."

"Thank you. It was a long time ago and I was so young I never really knew what was going on. Fortunately, the Griffins were a wonderful foster family, and they adopted me a few years later. So I had a mostly normal childhood after that."

Marie nodded. "Still, I can imagine that would have caused quite a few nightmares for you." When James looked amused at her statement, she eyed him curiously. "Did I say something funny?"

"I'm sorry, no. It's just, Gary mentioned you're a pediatric psychiatrist. I appreciate your sensitivity in having picked up on that."

Marie smiled through her lingering tears. But all too soon the tears won out again.

Sensing they weren't just a result of overwhelm at his story, James took her hand. "Is there something you want to talk about?"

It looked as if her face were crumpling in on itself. "I'm so sorry, James. I was so horrible to you! And not only that... I've alienated everyone I love! I'm afraid I destroyed my relationship with my brother by kicking him out of my home... I'm surprised he even bothered to come and see me. And then I went and nearly ruined my marriage!" Marie hunched forward, put her face in her hands and wept.

Moved with pity, James wrapped his arms around his sister to comfort her.

"I'm so, so sorry," she mumbled, clinging to him and sobbing against his shoulder.

When at last he drew away from her, James offered her a compassionate smile. "That's an awful lot of guilt you've been holding on to all this time."

Sniffling, she wiped a hand across her nose and nodded in reply.

What you loose on earth shall be loosed in heaven. Christ's enjoinder echoed in James' heart. He met her gaze. "There's no need for you to stay mired in all that guilt." This wasn't a traditional setting, but he figured God would forgive him for his improvisation. Reaching out his right hand, he traced the sign of the cross on his half-sister's forehead. "Marie, may God give you pardon and peace. I absolve you from your sins, in the name of the Father and of the Son and of the Holy Spirit." Now he leaned and gave her a kiss on the forehead. "Be at peace, sister."

Marie looked up at him in awe. "Just like that?"

James clasped her hand and nodded, smiling broadly. "Just like that."

When Gary and Marc returned, they found James and Marie chatting companionably, and laughing together, as if they'd been lifelong friends.

Standing in the doorway, Marc turned to his brother-in-law, his expression conveying utter disbelief. He grabbed Gary's arm and pulled him backward. "What happened?" He checked the room number. "Are we in the right room?"

"Oh, it's the right room." Gary gave a knowing smile. "And what's happening is the answer to a whole lot of prayers. There's a lot of healing going on in this hospital."

Epilogue

(5:30 p.m., October 8 – Sunday)

Erin was home on the long Columbus Day weekend from Boston University and the family had gathered for her eighteenth birthday. In addition to the kiddie table, Marc needed to set up a six-foot table extending into the living room to accommodate everyone at the dinner Marie orchestrated.

"Hey, big brother," Emily greeted him, baby Grace balanced on her left hip. Elliot toddled along behind his mother, clutching her skirt. "The family's getting awfully big."

"Yeah." Marc grinned broadly as he looked around the tables set for nineteen – and the four high chairs squeezed in amid the seats. They'd be awfully crowded, but he knew no one would mind. "Isn't it great?"

"You're gonna need more chairs."

He put an arm around his sister and drew her close. "And a far bigger table. Good thing I'm designing a house with an enormous space for entertaining."

"In that case, I'd better get to work on painting. Guess what you and Marie are getting for Christmas."

The siblings shared a laugh.

From across the room, Marie smiled as she silently tallied seats and relatives. In addition to her and Marc and the twins, there'd be Gary, Michaela and their brood of five; Emily, Clive and their three kids; Marc's parents, Willem and Fernanda; Micki's folks, Michael and Susan Conwaye; her mom, her youngest brother, Joey, and her newest brother, Father Jim. Soon they'd be gathered around the tables, laughing and eating and sharing in the celebration of not only Erin's birthday, and this week's excellent news of her own favorable prognosis, but her other piece of exciting news: This time next year they'd be needing another high chair.

Also By Rita M. Reali

Other titles in the Sheldon Family Saga:
>*Glimpse of Emerald*
>*Diagnosis: Love*
>*The Unintended Hero*
>*Second Chances*
>*Tender Mercies*

For Young – and Not-so-young – Readers, from *The Purringest Kitty* series (illustrated by Dee Lynk):
>*The Purringest Kitty Finds His Home*
>*The Purringest Kitty Misplaces His Purr*

How to Pray the Rosary

The Rosary is a powerful devotion regularly prayed by millions of Catholics and other Christians the world over. A rosary comprises a loop of beads with five sets of ten beads each separated by a single bead and short strand with a crucifix at one end and a set of beads arranged in a one-three-one configuration. A medal forms the juncture of the strand and the loop of beads. This devotion is prayed while holding one of the various component parts.

To pray the Rosary, while holding the crucifix, begin by making the **Sign of the Cross**: In the name of the Father and of the Son and of the Holy Spirit. Amen.

Still holding the crucifix, recite the **Apostles' Creed**: *I believe in God, the Father almighty, Creator of Heaven and earth. And in Jesus Christ, His only Son, our Lord, Who was conceived by the Holy Spirit, born of the Virgin Mary, suffered under Pontius Pilate; was crucified, died, and was buried. He descended into Hell. The third day He rose again from the dead. He ascended into Heaven, and sits at the right hand of God, the Father almighty. He shall come again to judge the living and the dead. I believe in the Holy Spirit, the holy Catholic Church, the communion of saints, the forgiveness of sins, the resurrection of the body, and life everlasting. Amen.*

On the first bead, recite the **Our Father**: *Our Father, Who art in Heaven, hallowed be Thy Name. Thy kingdom come, Thy will be done on earth as it is in Heaven. Give us this day our daily bread, and forgive us our trespasses, as we forgive those who trespass against us. And lead us not into temptation, but deliver us from evil. Amen.*

On each of the three subsequent beads, recite a **Hail Mary**: *Hail Mary, full of grace, the Lord is with thee. Blessed art thou among women, and blessed is the fruit of thy womb, Jesus. Holy Mary, Mother of God, pray for us sinners, now and at the hour of our death. Amen.*

On the next single bead, recite the **Glory Be**: *Glory be to the Father, and to the Son, and to the Holy Spirit. As it was in the beginning is now, and ever shall be, world without end. Amen.*

Next, recite the various decades of the rosary (Joyful mysteries on Monday and Saturday; Sorrowful mysteries on Tuesday and Friday; Glorious mysteries on Wednesday and Sunday; Luminous mysteries on Thursday):

Announce the first mystery
On the medal, pray an Our Father; on the ten following beads, ten Hail Marys; and on the next single bead, a Glory Be. Conclude the decade with the **Fatima Prayer**: *O my Jesus, forgive us our sins, save us from the fires of Hell and lead all souls to Heaven, especially those in most need of Thy mercy.*

Continue with the second through fifth mysteries in the same way.

After the fifth decade, conclude with the following: *Hail Holy Queen, mother of mercy; our life, our sweetness, and our hope. To thee do we cry, poor banished children of Eve. To thee do we send up our sighs, mourning and weeping in this vale of tears. Turn, then, most gracious advocate, thine eyes of mercy toward us. And after this, our exile, show unto us the blessed fruit of thy womb, Jesus. O clement, O loving, O sweet Virgin Mary. Pray for us, O holy Mother of God, that we may be made worthy of the promises of Christ. Amen.*

Pray for us, O holy Mother of God, that we may be made worthy of the promises of Christ.

O God, whose only-begotten Son by His life, death and resurrection, has purchased for us the rewards of eternal life; grant, we beseech Thee, that by meditating upon these mysteries of the Most Holy Rosary of the Blessed Virgin Mary, we may imitate what they contain and obtain what they promise, through the same Christ our Lord. Amen.

Mysteries of the Rosary

Joyful:
The First Joyful Mystery – **The Annunciation**
The Second Joyful Mystery – **The Visitation**
The Third Joyful Mystery – **The Nativity**
The Fourth Joyful Mystery – **The Presentation**
The Fifth Joyful Mystery – **The Finding of Jesus in the Temple**

Sorrowful:
The First Sorrowful Mystery – **The Agony in the Garden**
The Second Sorrowful Mystery – **The Scourging at the Pillar**
The Third Sorrowful Mystery – **The Crowning with Thorns**
The Fourth Sorrowful Mystery – **The Carrying of the Cross**
The Fifth Sorrowful Mystery – **The Crucifixion**

Glorious:
The First Glorious Mystery – **The Resurrection**
The Second Glorious Mystery – **The Ascension**
The Third Glorious Mystery – **The Descent of the Holy Spirit**
The Fourth Glorious Mystery – **The Assumption**
The Fifth Glorious Mystery – **The Coronation**

Luminous:
The First Luminous Mystery – **The Baptism of the Lord**
The Second Luminous Mystery – **The Wedding at Cana**
The Third Luminous Mystery – **Proclamation of the Kingdom**
The Fourth Luminous Mystery – **The Transfiguration**
The Fifth Luminous Mystery – **The Institution of the Eucharist**

For more information about praying the Holy Rosary, visit https://www.catholiccompany.com/content/how-to-pray-the-rosary or this Wikipedia site: https://en.wikipedia.org/wiki/Rosary